Vixen

Thomas Brant

CHAPTER 1 - The Vixen Takeover
Sunday 7th September 2019

The makeup bag was open and on the desk for the 30-year-old Brummie, her fingers expertly navigating through brushes, palettes, and powders. Dr Nelly Vixen had been through this ritual a thousand times before. The pre-show ritual before presenting Manic's UK40Chart, a Sunday staple on Manic's CHR stations, which, as of the previous Monday, incorporated the Breeze Media stations, the group having merged into Manic Radio following a contentious buyout.

Of course, she knew that the Breeze hosts were a bunch of dinosaurs which hardly networked, hardly acknowledged the existence of the wider group, and clung stubbornly to their "local legends" status. Nelly had already heard horror stories of the Breeze lot—middle-aged blokes named Gary or Dave who refused to deviate from their well-worn routine of cheesy anecdotes and tired jokes about their hometowns.

But today wasn't just about blending Breeze into the Manic way. Today was about making a statement. The UK40Chart wasn't just a show; it was the show. The one every CHR presenter aspired to host at least once in their career. And Nelly wasn't going to let a few grumpy "local legends" tarnish the pristine polish of her production.

She knew she had an hour until she was on air, and that she'd have to record promos for the grumpy lot in Birmingham who was now taking her network feed. Apparently, one of them, Gary Holloway, had already complained about "having to take some Scouse bird's feed" for their Sunday afternoon show. Nelly rolled her eyes as she tapped her eyeliner into place. These so-called legends could moan all they wanted, but it wouldn't change the fact that their regional mediocrity was about to be replaced by a slick, national production.

"Jamie, lets show those cocks how it's done," Nelly said under her breath as she grabbed her headphones and strode confidently out of the makeup room. Jamie, her ever-reliable producer, was already waiting for her in the studio, leaning casually against the mixing desk while fiddling with his phone.

"Do I detect the faint whiff of a motivational speech brewing?" Jamie teased, looking up from his phone with a grin. His London accent always sounded sharper when he was being cheeky.

Nelly smirked. "More like a declaration of war. These Breeze fossils think they're too good for us. I'll make them beg to take my feed by the end of the week."

Jamie chuckled and motioned to the soundboard. "Well, let's make sure you're not giving them any ammo to fire back. I've got the new transitions loaded and the latest Top 40 tracks prepped. We've even cut that extended ad break from last week. Smooth sailing."

Nelly adjusted her headphones and slid into her chair. The glowing buttons and flickering screens of the studio always gave her a rush of adrenaline. She glanced at the clock—45 minutes to go. Time to get the promos sorted.

"Right," she said, clapping her hands. "What have we got for these lot? I want them to sound so good they'll forget I'm not from their dreary little towns."

Jamie rolled his eyes but pulled up the script anyway. "OK, here's one for Birmingham: 'Coming up on Manic UK40Chart, your ultimate Sunday soundtrack with me, Dr Nelly Vixen. You're listening on 87.7 Midlands Manic, now part of the Manic Radio family.'"

Nelly raised an eyebrow, unimpressed. "'Now part of the Manic Radio family'? Seriously? Could we make it sound any more like a corporate memo? Jamie, come on. We're supposed to be Manic. Where's the energy? Where's the attitude?"

Jamie smirked and threw his hands up in mock surrender. "Alright, alright. How about this? 'Midlands, it's your Sunday with the UK40Chart and me, Dr Nelly Vixen! Hit after hit, and I promise—no dodgy hometown jokes. You're on 87.7 Midlands Manic, where it's all about the music, not the moaning.'"

Nelly burst out laughing, nearly knocking her headphones off. "Better. Much better. But you know Gary'll flip when he hears that. Probably call OFCOM to complain about 'insulting local heritage' or something."

"Let him," Jamie shrugged. "I doubt OFCOM has a category for 'hurt feelings of outdated DJs.' Besides, this is our show. If Gary wants to complain, he can ring the same hotline as the other dinosaurs."

Nelly grinned. "Fine. Let's record it. Then I want to tweak the one for Manchester. Can't have the Mancs thinking we're giving Birmingham all the sass."

She slipped the headphones back on, adjusted the microphone, and leaned in, her voice dripping with effortless confidence as she delivered the line. "Midlands, it's your Sunday with the UK40Chart and me, Dr Nelly Vixen! Hit after hit, and I promise—no dodgy hometown jokes. You're on 87.7 Midlands Manic, where it's all about the music, not the moaning, unlike the shit local presenters that are there in Birmingham, yes, I'm talking to you Gary."

She knew that she hated the Breeze lot with a burning passion, but a part of her relished the opportunity to shake up their comfort zones. She knew that the promo feed was on a separate feed to the live broadcast, so she could afford to throw in a few cheeky ad-libs that wouldn't make it to air. Jamie, ever the enabler, burst out laughing as her words hung in the air.

"You're playing with fire, you know," he said, wiping a tear from his eye. "But damn, it's entertaining."

Nelly smirked and leaned back in her chair. "What's life without a bit of fire, Jamie? Let's see if Gary has the guts to call me out on it. He can't hold a candle to me on air, and he knows it. And that Pete Smith bloke... I can't wait for the boot camp to tell that old fart to finally hang up his headphones and let the real talent take over."

Jamie chuckled, shaking his head as he saved the recording. "You know you're going to make a few enemies with this takeover, right? Not that you care, but just a heads-up."

"Enemies? Please." Nelly waved her hand dismissively. "These people need a reality check. Radio's changed, Jamie. Listeners don't want some bloke droning on about their first pint in some Midlands pub or cracking jokes about roundabouts. They want energy. They want passion. They want me. Anyway, which twats do I have to grace with my presence next?"

Jamie glanced at his clipboard, barely suppressing a grin. "Well, next up are the fine folks of Fermanagh FM."

Nelly rolled her eyes so hard it was a wonder they didn't fall out. "Fermanagh FM? You're joking, right? What kind of backwards little outfit are we dealing with here? Are they even running digital yet, or is it still all AM and tin cans?"

Jamie smirked, shaking his head. "Oh, they're digital, barely. But I've heard their breakfast show still does shoutouts for lost sheep."

Nelly let out a dramatic groan. "Lost sheep? Bloody hell. Right, let's give the fine people of Fermanagh a little taste of what real radio sounds like. Hit me with the script."

Jamie handed her the clipboard, watching as her eyes scanned the pre-prepared line. She immediately let out a derisive snort. "'Get ready, Fermanagh—Dr Nelly Vixen is here with the UK40Chart! Your Sunday soundtrack is bigger and better than ever. Welcome to the Manic family.' Jamie, this sounds like it was written by a headmaster trying to be cool. Do we have to keep shoving 'welcome to the family' down their throats? It's starting to sound like a mafia threat."

Jamie laughed. "I think that's the point. We're assimilating them, Borg-style. Resistance is futile."

Nelly tapped the clipboard with a manicured nail, her brain already reworking the line. "OK, here's what we're doing. Scrap the 'welcome to the family' crap. Let's try this: 'Hello, shit local presenters who are worse than me, it's time to wake up and join the big leagues. I'm Dr Nelly Vixen, and this is your UK40Chart. Hit after hit, no excuses. Let's turn it up and make some noise!'"

She held her finger on the button which sent it to the RCS computers in Dudley, which would allocate it to the Ulster based feed within minutes. She knew that, while the Manic stations like Bee Manic in Manchester, G-Vibes in Glasgow, the nearby Chester & The Wirral Vibes that was co-located with her own station, Manic Radio Liverpool, and other stations such as Wool City Echo in Bradford and Cardiff Vibes down in Cardiff were accustomed to her sharp-tongued style, Fermanagh FM would be in for a shock. The small-town station, still clinging to its quaint charm, would soon realise that the Dr Nelly Vixen show was not for the faint-hearted. She could already imagine the bewildered expressions of their presenters as her promo aired.

Jamie looked at her with a mix of admiration and trepidation. "You're really out to make an impression, aren't you? I'd kill to see their faces when that airs. I bet Gary's already sharpening his pen for an angry email."

Nelly smirked, spinning her chair to face the clock on the studio wall. "Let him. I thrive on complaints. Besides, if they're moaning about me, they're not moaning about anything else. That's what this job is all about—owning the narrative. And let's be real, Jamie: if they're not talking about you, you're not doing it right."

Jamie raised an eyebrow. "Bold words for someone about to drop an ad-lib about lost sheep on a provincial station. Anyway, next up is East London Hits."

Nelly groaned, as she already had Manic's North London Vibes, London Vibes and South London Vibes on her network feed, but the addition of a Breeze station in the mix made things more convoluted. "East London Hits? Bloody hell, how many bloody stations does London need? I've already got three London stations taking my feed, and now I have to cater to this Breeze relic too? I swear, Jamie, I'm one promo away from snapping."

Jamie chuckled as he loaded up the next set of scripts. "Hey, look at it this way. At least East London Hits has a more modern format. No lost sheep shoutouts, no Garys moaning about their first pint, and definitely no roundabout anecdotes. You might actually enjoy this one."

Nelly raised an eyebrow, clearly unconvinced. "We'll see. Let me guess, their morning presenter is another 'local legend' who thinks the UK40Chart is ruining their precious airtime?"

Jamie flipped through his notes, smirking. "Nope, some Paki presenter named Farah Khan. They're based, and you'll love this, at... the Olympic Park."

Nelly's laugh echoed through the studio, sharp and full of disbelief. "The Olympic Park? You mean to tell me that Breeze had their East London lot set up in the Olympic bloody Park, and they still couldn't manage to keep up with the rest of the radio world? That's rich."

Jamie shrugged, biting back a grin. "Apparently, they thought proximity to a major landmark would make them sound more professional. You know, as if listeners care about what postcode the studio's in. Rumour has it they've got this flashy lobby, but their actual tech is about five years behind. Proper style over substance."

"Typical Breeze," Nelly said, shaking her head. "There again we run bloody PlayoutONE and Mixdown Studio. Breeze was probably running something out of the Stone Age like Myriad or even Enco DAD." She shook her head, half-amused, half-disgusted. "It's no wonder they got bought out."

"Erm... they use Zetta and GSelector I believe," Jamie interjected, smirking as he scrolled through some notes on his tablet. "Though, knowing them, they probably haven't updated the software since it was installed. You know I'm a bit of an anorak, right? Well, apparently their original boss, Woody Bones, signed a contract in 2007."

Nelly leaned back in her chair, smirking at Jamie. "Woody Bones? Sounds like a pirate radio reject. Let me guess—he probably thought 'high-tech' meant upgrading from cassettes to CDs. Honestly, Jamie, it's a miracle these Breeze stations managed to broadcast anything at all."

Jamie laughed, nodding as he pulled up more information on his tablet. "Oh, it gets better. Apparently, Woody refused to let them network anything... until 2005. Best thing is half his stations were was running football phone-in until last year. That Pete Smith you mentioned earlier... he's been on Drive on the same station, Midlands Manic, since 2009... and he's over 25 consecutive #1 RAJAR quarters... on Brum CHR drive."

Nelly froze mid-laugh, her smirk slipping just slightly as Jamie dropped that last nugget of information. "Wait. Over 25 consecutive #1 RAJAR quarters? On CHR Drive? From one of those stations? Pete Smith, you said?"

Jamie nodded, clearly enjoying the rare moment of catching Nelly off guard. "Yep. Pete Smith. Midlands Manic Drive. Apparently, he's the golden boy of Brummie radio. Loyal listeners, solid numbers, and, according to the legend, he's impossible to shake. Global and Bauer have all but given up. You'll like this though, Nell... he's got a Business degree... from Wolverhampton Poly."

Nelly burst out laughing, her voice echoing through the studio. "A Business degree from Wolverhampton Poly? Oh, that's rich! The Midlands' golden boy is a polytechnic grad! I bet he still talks about 'the glory days' like they were yesterday. Let me guess—he's probably got a trophy from some local business awards night, sitting on his desk like it's a bloody Oscar."

Jamie smirked, leaning back against the desk. "More like two dozen Sony Awards, won Best Local Radio Show, Best Community Programme, Best Music Presenter – Non breakfast and Individual of the Year at last year's ARIAs. He's got at least three gold Arqiva Awards to his name too. And if that wasn't enough, he's rumoured to have turned down offers from both Capital and Heart because he didn't want to leave his Brummie listeners behind. 'Too loyal for the big leagues,' they say. Honestly, Nelly, he's like the David Beckham of Midlands radio—stuck in his heyday, but no one can deny his stats."

Nelly rolled her eyes so hard Jamie thought they might disappear into her skull. "Oh, please. Two dozen Sony's? ARIAs? That just means he's good at playing it safe and charming OFCOM-approved judges with his same old tired shtick. Bet he still says, 'Let's take a look at the roads and roundabouts,' every time there's a traffic update. He's a dinosaur in a suit, Jamie, and dinosaurs are extinct for a reason."

Jamie raised a knowing eyebrow. "Still, Nelly, you've got to admit—those numbers don't come easy. Listeners clearly love the guy, even if he is clinging to the glory days of 'local radio.' I mean, don't get me wrong, I love watching you take down these so-called legends, but Pete might be tougher to rattle."

Nelly leaned forward, her eyes narrowing in mock determination. "Tougher to rattle? Jamie, I don't care if he's broadcasting directly from the bloody moon with a platinum mic. By the end of the year, Pete Smith will be old news, and Dr Nelly Vixen will be the only name listeners from Birmingham to Belfast care about."

Jamie chuckled, shaking his head as he queued up the next promo script. "Bold words, Nell. Just try not to burn too many bridges on your way up. You know what they say about this industry—it's small, and memories are long."

Nelly waved a dismissive hand, her confidence unshaken. "Let them remember me, Jamie. Every complaint, every moan, every passive-aggressive tweet about how I'm ruining 'their' radio—it's all fuel for the fire. Because when the dust settles, there'll only be one name they can't stop talking about. And that's mine."

Jamie grinned as he handed her the clipboard. "Alright then, superstar. Let's see what you've got for East London Hits. Try not to insult their postcode this time."

Nelly took the clipboard with a wicked smile, her voice dripping with confidence as she prepared to record. "Oh, Jamie. Where's the fun in that?"

****

CHAPTER 2 – Boot Camp Bloodbath
Monday 8th September 2019

Nelly couldn't help but find the irony of the annual Manic Boot Camp being held exactly a week after the borging of Breeze Media and its Manic counterparts. It felt less like a "welcome to the family" event and more like an exercise in asserting dominance. The venue—the M&S Bank Arena in Liverpool, not far from Manic's Network HQ in Speke—meant that all corners of the Manic empire would have to come for what was a one day intensive seminar designed to energise and inspire the newest members of the Manic Radio family.

Nelly, as a 3 year employee of Manic, having been sacked by her previous employer, Worcestershire Beats, a Breeze Media station before it was merged into the Manic empire and brought under the slick Manic umbrella, had mixed feelings about the whole ordeal.

She knew the drill: endless motivational speeches, over-the-top graphics, and an over-caffeinated "Head of Talent Development" rattling on about how Manic was the future of radio. She'd seen it all before. But this time, there was a sharper edge to her presence. She wasn't just a participant; she was a survivor, a success story, and she had every intention of showing the Breeze lot exactly why they were now the lesser cog in the Manic machine.

"Hey, Vixen," Kyler Thompson, a Bee Manic mid-morning host who was playing hooky from his show to attend Boot Camp, called out as he sauntered over to her, coffee cup in hand. His co-host, Emma Lang, Nelly could see, was hooking up with a Colne Valley Vibes producer, a Manic lifer named Mark Burton.

"Hey, Kyler," Nelly said with a grin. "Playing hooky from the show, are we? I didn't think your listeners could survive without your dulcet Manc tones for a whole morning."

Kyler smirked and took a sip of his coffee. "Ah, they'll manage. Got the newbie covering it... right whore she is, y'know."

Nelly raised an eyebrow. "Bit harsh, Kyler. Not every new presenter's out to nick your slot."

Kyler chuckled, the coffee cup pausing mid-air. "Nah, it's not that. She's Cal's ex. Get her on a bit of snow, pile some booze down her throat and she's sucking cocks like lollies. Cassie, her name is... Cassie Longton. Of course, she's calling herself Toni Green on air."

Nelly's eyes widened slightly, more out of amusement than shock. "Toni Green, you say? That's a bit… vibrant for someone you've just described as the station party girl." She smirked, shaking her head. "God, Kyler, you don't hold back, do you?"

Kyler leaned casually against the wall, looking completely unbothered. "Why would I? Truth's truth. Plus, we all know how these things go. She's got the look, a decent enough voice, and management's desperate to make her a thing. They'll shove her in every promo slot going until the next shiny new toy comes along."

Nelly sipped her coffee, glancing around the arena as more presenters, producers, and various radio folk filed in, many looking as if they'd rather be anywhere else. The buzz of conversation and the clatter of heels against the polished floor echoed through the space. It was a bizarre mix of forced camaraderie and quiet resentment—like a dysfunctional family reunion, but with more microphones.

"Sounds like you've already written her off," Nelly said, her tone neutral, but her eyes sharp. "Careful, Kyler. These newbies can surprise you. One minute you're laughing at their demo tapes, the next they're stealing your breakfast slot."

Kyler laughed, a deep, throaty sound. "Oh, come on, Vixen. You think Toni Green's got what it takes to go national? Not with that history. Cal said he got her up the duff when she was 14 and he was 16, and she put the sprog up for adoption."

Nelly chuckled, as, despite being 30, from Selly Oak and married to a Cheshire plastic surgeon, she knew she could hardly talk, as at Manic, there were two things that were common, and that she enjoyed—sex and cocaine—the holy duo of every Manic presenter's life. It was said that by the end of your first week, you were hooked on both, and if you were a lesbian or gay, you'd not just be shagging the gender you were attracted to but probably everyone in between too. It was all part of the chaotic culture Manic Radio had cultivated—a heady mix of high-pressure expectations, relentless networking, and the type of hedonism that made The Wolf of Wall Street look tame.

"Well, Kyler," Nelly said, smirking as she adjusted her blazer, "I wouldn't be so quick to judge. Toni might surprise us all. Or she might burn out faster than a cheap mixer at a student club night. Either way, it'll be entertaining."

Kyler shook his head, a bemused grin on his face. "You're too soft, Vixen. That's why you'll always be Network Royalty but never Management's Darling."

Before Nelly could fire back, the overhead speakers crackled to life. A deep, polished voice—Dr Scott Bennett, the CEO, holder of a PhD in Law, unlike Nelly, who was a PhD in Film and Media—boomed through the arena. Dr Bennett, she knew, was a Ralph Bernard acolyte, being formerly of GWR and GCap Media, meaning that his approach was ruthlessly corporate, with a penchant for buzzwords and efficiency over creativity. He was the type of boss who could turn a room full of colourful radio personalities into a grid of nameless statistics in a PowerPoint presentation.

"Good morning, everyone," Bennett began, his voice dripping with the kind of faux warmth that made Nelly's teeth grind. "Welcome to the 2019 Manic Radio Boot Camp, the first of many under our expanded family. We're thrilled to have you all here, especially those of you joining us from the former Breeze Media network. It's an exciting time for Manic, and together, we're going to shape the future of British radio."

Nelly groaned under her breath. "Here we go. Cue the corporate jargon and the 'we're all in this together' speeches."

Kyler chuckled, nudging her with his elbow. "Don't worry, Vixen. Just imagine him in his boxers or something equally tragic. Makes it more bearable."

"Not unless his boxers are made of spreadsheets," Nelly muttered back, earning a laugh from Kyler.

Bennett droned on, outlining the agenda for the day. There would be breakout sessions, team-building exercises, and, of course, the grand finale: a keynote speech from Bennett himself about "The Manic Vision." Nelly rolled her eyes so hard she thought they might pop out of her skull.

"You see, folks, I'm a bit of an anorak myself—"

The jeering and shouting from the Breeze crew, seated in a clump near the back, cut Bennett off mid-sentence. Nelly couldn't suppress a smirk as the disruption rippled through the arena. The Breeze lot were living up to their reputation: loud, stubborn, and utterly unapologetic.

"Did someone say anorak?" one of them hollered, his thick regional accent cutting through the polite murmurs of the Manic stalwarts. "Oi, Bennett, when was the last time you did a shift behind a mic, eh?!"

The room burst into laughter, even from some of the Manic veterans. Dr Bennett, to his credit, didn't miss a beat. His polished, corporate smile remained plastered to his face, but there was a noticeable tightening around his jaw.

"Well," Bennett began, his tone as smooth as butter but with an edge of steel, "while I can't say I've been behind a mic recently—"

Another round of cheeky interruptions erupted from the Breeze contingent. "Exactly, mate!" someone shouted, "bet you wouldn't know a fader from a kettle lead!"

This time, even Nelly couldn't help but laugh, earning a sharp look from Jamie, who had appeared at her side, clipboard in hand. "You're not helping," he muttered under his breath, though his smirk betrayed him.

Bennett raised a hand, commanding silence, his smile now frozen in place. "As I was saying," he continued, his tone sharper now, "while I might not have been behind the mic recently, I know what it takes to make great radio. And that's why we're here today—to ensure that every corner of the Manic family is delivering the very best to our listeners. Including you lot at the back. Now, I'm sure the presenters from the Manic side of the group know the mantra for when on air, right?"

"Trigger Lead In, Provocative Point, Dazzling Details, Power Out," Nelly, Jamie, Kyler and the Manic crew chimed in almost in unison, their voices blending into a rehearsed chant. It was the classic Manic formula for engaging radio, drilled into every presenter from day one. Nelly could practically recite it in her sleep.

"WHAT'S THE STATION MATE, WHAT'S THE STATION!" some of the bashers, the nickname for the coaches that each presenter had during their initial weeks at Manic, yelled from their spots dotted around the arena, their voices echoing with a mocking enthusiasm.

"Manic Radio!" the Manic crew chanted back, half-heartedly but loud enough to drown out the Breeze hecklers, some of whom were now muttering under their breath or exchanging unimpressed glances.

Nelly felt a surge of pride—maybe even a bit of tribalism—flare up in her chest. Say what you will about Manic's relentless corporate vibe and high-pressure environment, but they did things differently. Efficiently. Sharply. And they weren't afraid to lean into it.

Bennett, clearly pleased by the response, nodded in approval, clasping his hands together like a headteacher who had just regained control of an unruly classroom. "Excellent. That's the energy we need from every single one of you—Manic, Breeze, or otherwise. This is about creating a unified team, delivering groundbreaking content, and making sure we're not just keeping up with the competition, but leaving them in the dust."

Nelly leaned towards Jamie, her voice low but amused. "Leaving them in the dust? We've got Breeze dinosaurs in the room. Pretty sure they've already been left in a tar pit."

Jamie stifled a laugh, but his reply was cut off by the booming sound of Kyler's voice from the row ahead. "Oi, Bennett! When's lunch, mate? Or do us plebs have to forage in the car park?"

"What a cock," the voice of Pete Smith, who Nelly recognised instantly from his smooth Dudley accent. As she was born in Selly Oak and spent the first 20 years of her life, she knew the difference between a Brummie and a Black Country accent like the back of her hand. Pete Smith, the so-called King of Midlands Drive, was clearly unimpressed by Kyler's antics, his comment dripping with disdain as he leaned back in his chair, arms folded.

Nelly turned to Jamie, her voice laced with sarcasm. "Well, well, the legend himself has spoken. I suppose we should all take a bow."

Jamie chuckled, shaking his head. "Careful, Vixen. You don't want to poke the bear."

"Please," Nelly said, waving her hand dismissively. "Pete's not a bear. He's more like… an old lion who thinks he still runs the pride. Majestic, sure, but we all know the hyenas are circling."

Suddenly there was a load of shouting, and the next thing Nelly knew, she was being pushed forward, someone falling into the back of her, and then chants for a fight started to echo through the arena.

"Bloody hell," Jamie muttered, stepping in front of Nelly protectively as the shoving continued behind them. Nelly stumbled slightly but managed to steady herself, turning to see the source of the commotion.

Near the back, a group of Breeze presenters—led by Wessex Soundwave drive time host Jenna Kilmare, a 21 year old graduate fresh out of Exeter Uni—were squaring off against some of the more boisterous Manic lifers. The two factions seemed locked in a battle of egos and sharp tongues, and it didn't take a genius to figure out that Kyler's earlier comment had been the spark that lit this particular fire.

"You lot have already took our normal route of making it to a network gig by buying Breeze, and now you're shagging our newsreaders!" Jenna continued to shout, her voice a mix of fury and frustration. "How's a Wessex girl supposed to climb the ladder when all you lot care about is sex and stats? Before you lot brought us, we'd do our 3 years on the locals, then wait for the call to a Manic, Capital or Bauer network gig, but now we can't get a Capital or Bauer gig as the rep that came from Manic said that TUPE doesn't apply, so we're stuck in this shit ecosystem!"

"Yeah," Pete said, and Nelly looked to see what the dinosaur who she remember hearing on the radio as a teen before going to university and starting her own career in radio, had to say. "The Manic rep even said the Union isn't recognised by them."

"Oh, hark at Scargill over here," Nelly snarked with the venom of someone who knew she could twist the knife and get away with it. "What's next, Pete? A sit-in strike at the M&S Arena until Bennett gives us all fair working conditions? Maybe you can lead the picket line with your 'glory days' stories about when local radio meant something."

Pete turned to face her, his expression calm but his tone razor-sharp. "You can mock all you like, Vixen, but you're just a host who Breeze sacked for fraud."

Nelly froze for a split second, the words hanging in the air like a shard of ice. Her usual arsenal of quick retorts and sharp comebacks faltered, and she could feel Jamie tense beside her. The room had fallen into a hush, the kind of silence that only came when a line had been crossed.

"Fraud?" Nelly repeated, her voice low but biting. "That's rich coming from someone who's been coasting on the same slot for over a decade, Pete. Let's not pretend your #1 RAJAR quarters came without playing it safe. I'd love to see you try and survive a week in Manic without hiding behind your 'local hero' shtick."

Pete smirked, leaning back in his chair with the ease of someone who knew he'd struck a nerve. "I might've been around a while, love, but at least I didn't have to crawl back into the industry with my tail between my legs. What was it again? Oh, yeah, Mark and Lisa told me it was plagiarism on your thesis."

Nelly's jaw clenched as Pete's words cut through the tension like a blade. A flicker of heat rose in her chest, but she quickly stamped it out, refusing to let him see her crack. The room was still on edge, the low murmurs of whispers rippling through the crowd as eyes darted between Nelly and Pete like spectators at a boxing match.

"Oh, and yes, I heard the promo feed yesterday, when your producer called Farah 'some Paki presenter'," Pete shot back, his voice calm but cutting, as though he'd rehearsed this exact line in the mirror a thousand times. The crowd tensed again, waiting for the next blow. Nelly knew she was the kind of personality people either rooted for or rooted against—there was rarely middle ground—but she also knew she could hold her own. "You're just doing a terrible impression of Neil Fox in his Pepsi Chart hosting, GWR hating, wannabe BBC Radio 1 reject who's only here because Manic loves a controversial headline,"

The room fell deathly silent at Pete's final jab, the air thick with tension as every eye turned to Nelly. Jamie shifted uncomfortably beside her, his usually relaxed posture now stiff with unease. Even the Breeze presenters, who had been loudly decrying the Manic regime moments ago, seemed to collectively hold their breath, their animosity towards Nelly momentarily forgotten.

For the first time in her career, Nelly felt the faintest flicker of doubt. Pete's comment wasn't just a barbed insult—it was a calculated strike aimed directly at her credibility. She could see the ripple effect across the room as people absorbed the implications. A misstep like that, especially in a post-2010s world where social accountability reigned supreme, could spiral out of control faster than she could manage.

Nelly took a deep breath, her mind racing through the possible responses. She could deny it outright, but with Pete's reputation and the ripple of murmurs spreading like wildfire, it wouldn't hold. She could deflect, but that would look weak. No, she needed to own this moment, flip it, and walk out the other side with her head held high.

She stepped forward, her heels clicking sharply against the polished floor. The sound cut through the whispers like a blade. "Pete," she said, her tone calm but with an edge that silenced even the most curious whisperers. "If you're trying to paint me as some out-of-control shock jock, you're wasting your breath. But let's set the record straight, shall we?"

She turned to the room, addressing everyone now, her voice steady and commanding. "The promo feed yesterday wasn't perfect, and if something inappropriate was said by my team, I take responsibility for that. It was unprofessional, and it's not the standard I hold myself—or my team—to."

Jamie opened his mouth to speak, probably to jump in with a defence, but Nelly raised a hand to stop him. "But let's not pretend that anyone in this room is squeaky clean. Pete, you've been in this industry long enough to know that radio thrives on personality, on risk, on pushing boundaries. And sometimes? People cross the line. The difference is some of us own up to it. Others—" she gestured subtly to him, "—coast on their safe little bubbles and act holier-than-thou when it suits them."

"Funny you mention holier-than-thou… I've gone up against one presenter on BRMB back in the day who was holier-than-thou, and he and I are still close friends today," Pete interrupted smoothly, leaning forward in his chair like he was holding court. "And yes, its Jezza Kyle, thank you."

The name Jeremy Kyle landed like a grenade in the middle of the tense silence, eliciting gasps, murmurs, and even a few stifled chuckles. Of course, Pete Smith would pull out a name like that—a relic of regional radio-turned-daytime TV controversy, someone equally divisive in his heyday. Nelly's lips curled into a smirk, her eyes narrowing as she leaned slightly forward.

"Jeremy Kyle?" she drawled, her tone laced with incredulity and faint amusement. "Pete, you're really going to name-drop Jezza as your bastion of morality and professionalism? The man who turned family arguments into prime-time entertainment? That's your role model?"

A ripple of laughter spread across the room, but Pete remained unfazed, his expression calm and collected, as though he had expected the jab. He straightened his tie and replied with the practised ease of a man who had seen it all. "Say what you want about Jezza, but he knew how to connect with people. Real people. The kind of audience you, Nelly, wouldn't know how to handle without a pre-recorded soundbite and a script approved by corporate."

Nelly could feel the heat rising in her cheeks, but she refused to let it show. She had to stay sharp, stay in control. Pete was good—she'd give him that—but he wasn't unbeatable. "Oh, I know how to handle people, Pete," she said, her voice icy but steady. "I just don't waste my time on audiences who think phoning in to discuss who nicked their bins is the pinnacle of radio."

A few scattered laughs erupted from the Manic side of the room, while the Breeze contingent bristled. Pete raised an eyebrow, clearly unfazed. "Funny, because you used to be in the trenches, answering calls on your mid-morning show in Worcester from those very same people, didn't you, Vixen? What was it you used to say? 'Let's hear from the real stars of the show: you, the listeners.' Bit of a change in tone now that you've made it big, isn't it?"

The room fell into an uneasy silence again, the tension crackling like static over the airwaves. Nelly clenched her jaw, forcing herself to remain calm. Pete's barbs were precise, his words designed to expose every vulnerable corner of her career. She knew better than to let him win this game, but she also knew that Pete was a different breed. He wasn't Kyler with his crass jokes or the Breeze lot with their loud bluster. Pete was calculated, measured—a veteran who knew how to play the long game.

"Well, Pete," she said after a beat, her tone syrupy-smooth, "if you're so eager to remind everyone of my humble beginnings, let's not forget yours. Hosting early morning breakfast in what... Dudley, wasn't it?"

"Wasn't it Dudley, Pete?" Nelly continued, her tone dripping with faux sweetness as she crossed her arms and leaned casually on one leg. "Back when your big claims to fame were giving out meat raffle tickets and promoting the local car boot sale? A far cry from the gilded halls of Manic, wouldn't you say?"

The crowd chuckled nervously, some of the Manic crew nodding in approval while the Breeze contingent exchanged wary glances. Pete simply leaned back in his chair, a calm smirk playing on his lips. He looked every bit the unbothered elder statesman of radio, the type who'd seen it all and had little left to prove.

"Ah, Dudley," Pete said with a wistful smile, his voice steady and deliberate. "You know, Nelly, those mornings might've been early, and the prizes a little... quaint, but you'd be surprised how much loyalty and trust you can build over a raffle ticket and a well-timed traffic update. Those listeners? They're the backbone of what we do. And last time I checked, it's them, not some exec in a shiny suit, who decide whether you're worth listening to."

The tension in the room thickened as Pete's words settled over the crowd. Nelly's smirk faltered slightly, but she quickly recovered, her eyes narrowing like a cat ready to pounce. "Spoken like someone who knows his audience peaked before the iPhone," she retorted. "Face it, Pete, the industry's moved on. You might've been king of the meat raffle, but this is a different game now. And trust me, I know how to play it."

Pete chuckled softly, shaking his head as though he pitied her. "The industry might've changed, love, but people haven't. You can throw all the slick promos, flashy graphics, and corporate buzzwords you want at them, but at the end of the day, listeners want authenticity. Something you've clearly mistaken for snark and sass. As for the good Doctor who's the CEO, he's just a cheap Ralph Bernard."

Some of the younger Breeze presenters oompahed at the dig at the CEO, Dr Bennett, while the Manic veterans exchanged glances, some stifling laughs, others shaking their heads in exasperation. The room buzzed with a mix of admiration for Pete's sharp wit and disbelief at his audacity to drag the boss into this sparring match.

"Pete, mate," Gary said, and Nelly groaned. "I used to work for Ralph Bernard at GWR as a Swindon host, back in the '80s, and trust me, Bennett is Ralph Bernard in a Poundland suit. The man's all about the bottom line and buzzwords, but he's got none of Ralph's finesse. Ralph knew how to build something real, even if it meant getting his hands dirty. Bennett's just a knock-off, coasting on a legacy he'll never fully understand."

That got the majority of the Manic crew chanting "Poundland suit", and Nelly looked at Dr Bennett, who was walking off the stage looking as if he was about to explode...

And then...

"Couldn't even keep Peter Rowell off people in the Watershed..." Gary said with the venom of someone who had history with Dr Bennett. The room fell into a stunned silence, the weight of Gary's accusation crashing down like a rogue wave. Even the rowdiest of the Breeze contingent looked taken aback, their boisterous grins wiped clean. Amongst the Manic lot, a few sharp intakes of breath could be heard, and whispers began to ripple through the crowd like static interference on a bad signal.

"Ah, Mr Holloway," Dr Bennett said with a tight smile as he turned back towards the stage, his voice clipped but composed. "Always one to dredge up the past in the most undignified manner possible, aren't you? But if you're determined to dig through the dirt, let me remind you that slander is a dangerous game—one you might not be equipped to play."

Gary folded his arms, his expression defiant. "Slander? It's not slander when it's the truth, Bennett. I used to work at Wooton, Swindon and the Watershed, so I know the whole bloody story. What was it you said when I told you my suspicions when you were Deputy Head of Legal? Oh, yeah... 'here's your P45', wasn't it?"

The room was paralysed, the tension crackling like electricity in the air. Gary's words had not just pushed the boundaries; they'd shattered them. The drama of Boot Camp had escalated from playful banter to something far darker, a pointed accusation that no amount of corporate spin could gloss over. Every eye was locked on Dr Bennett, who had frozen momentarily, his polished CEO façade cracking just slightly around the edges.

Nelly, for once, was speechless. She glanced at Jamie, who looked equally dumbfounded, his clipboard forgotten in his hands. Around them, whispers surged through the crowd, a low, rumbling tide of speculation and shock. Even Pete Smith, the unflappable king of Midlands Drive, looked genuinely taken aback.

Dr Bennett adjusted his tie, his professional mask snapping back into place with practised ease. "Mr Holloway," he said, his voice smooth but cold, "this is neither the time nor the place for baseless accusations. If you'd like to discuss matters from over a decade ago, I suggest you do so in private, where they belong, rather than disrupting a professional event."

Gary's laugh was sharp and bitter, cutting through the room like a knife. "Oh, I bet you'd love that, wouldn't you? Keep it all private, just like you did back then. Sweep it under the rug and hope no one remembers. But guess what, Bennett? Some of us do remember. And some of us aren't afraid to call it out."

The Breeze contingent, emboldened by Gary's outburst, began murmuring in agreement, their previously scattered unity coalescing into a shared defiance. Even some of the Manic veterans—those who had been around long enough

to know the whispers and rumours of the industry—
looked uneasy.

Dr Bennett exhaled slowly, his composure faltering just
slightly as he scanned the room. "This event," he began,
his voice clipped, "is about unity. About bringing the
Manic and Breeze teams together to build a stronger, more
innovative radio network. If certain individuals cannot
behave professionally, they are welcome to leave… and,
yes, Gary, you'll have your P45 in the post."

Nelly was stunned when she heard the calm and collected
Scott Bennett lose his temper and actually utter Gary's
name in such a public setting. The room fell into a stunned
silence, the sort of hush that only happens when someone
in authority drops a bombshell. Gary Holloway, for his
part, sat back in his chair with a smug grin, clearly
unbothered. In fact, the man looked as if he'd just won a
lifetime supply of tea and biscuits.

"Well, well," Gary drawled, his thick Swindon accent
cutting through the tension like a knife. "Sacked by the
same bloke twice in my career? If Ralph was here, he'd be
pleased one of his minions has grown up so well. I'll put
that on my CV, Bennett… 'P45 Club, two-time recipient.'
Nice one."

The Breeze contingent erupted in laughter, hooting and
clapping as if Gary had just delivered the punchline of the
year. Even some of the Manic veterans couldn't suppress
their smirks. Nelly, meanwhile, felt a mix of second-hand
embarrassment and admiration for Gary's audacity. Say
what you want about the man, but he didn't go down
quietly.

Dr Bennett's jaw tightened visibly, his usual mask of composure slipping further. "Enjoy the applause while it lasts, Mr Holloway," he said icily. "I doubt it'll carry you far when you're handing out flyers for hospital radio."

The laughter in the room grew louder, this time at Gary's expense. But rather than looking defeated, he leaned back in his chair, crossing his arms with an air of defiance. "Oh, I've already lined a backup job... working for Bauer at Greatest Hits Swindon," Gary shot back, his grin widening as the murmurs in the room turned into gasps. "Funny how word travels fast in this industry, eh? Especially as everyone knows my slot on a Sunday in Brum would have been GWR'd into one of Manic's London or Speke based network shows by the end of the year... just like what happened at Cardiff Vibes last year. Manic is just like GWR... they Borg you, and resistance is futile.

Dr Bennett's face turned an alarming shade of crimson. For someone who prided himself on control, the jab about being a "GWR clone" clearly struck a nerve. Nelly could practically see the steam rising from his collar. The room buzzed with low murmurs, the audience split between those revelling in Gary's defiance and those awaiting Bennett's next move.

"Greatest Hits Swindon, you say?" Bennett finally replied, his voice sharp but quieter now, measured like a blade. "Good luck with that, Gary. I'm sure they'll love your outdated pub anecdotes and rants about the 'good old days.' Just remember, the industry's moved on. Bauer may take you, but they'll use you as a stepping stone for younger, sharper talent. Enjoy being yesterday's news."

Gary laughed, the kind of deep, unbothered chuckle that only someone with nothing left to lose could muster. "Yesterday's news? Maybe. But yesterday's news still has a loyal audience who'd take me over your PowerPoint buzzword nonsense any day of the week. I may be 68, but I still pull in more listeners than half your 'young, sharp talent' who wouldn't know audience engagement if it smacked them in the face. And if I'm 'yesterday's news', at least I'm a headline—unlike you, Bennett, who's just another footnote in a corporate restructure memo."

The room let out a collective "oooh," as if a schoolyard fight had just escalated beyond playful jabs. Nelly almost felt sorry for Dr Bennett—almost. He had walked straight into that one, and Gary, for all his grumpy old-dog tendencies, knew exactly how to twist the knife.

Bennett inhaled sharply, visibly composing himself before speaking again. "Well, since you've already checked out, Mr Holloway, you are free to leave. Security will ensure your swift exit."

That was met with an uproar from the Breeze lot, a mix of protests and jeering. A couple of them even started chanting, "Bollocks! Bollocks!" in true rebellious radio fashion. Meanwhile, a few of the Manic presenters— those who had once worked at Breeze before the merger—shifted uncomfortably, clearly debating whether to back their old colleague or play it safe.

Gary, however, was unbothered. He stood up, stretched, and picked up his jacket with all the casual ease of a man leaving a boring pub quiz early. "Ta-ra, folks," he called out, flashing a wide grin. "See you on the airwaves… assuming Manic hasn't killed all of 'em by then."

With that, he strode down the aisle, head held high, while Dr Bennett rubbed his temples like a man who had aged ten years in the past five minutes.

The room was still buzzing with murmurs when Pete Smith leaned forward in his seat, shaking his head with a smirk. "Well," he said dryly, "that went well."

Nelly let out a short laugh, shaking her head. "That man's got the energy of someone who's been fired so many times, he's developed a resistance to it. He could walk into the job centre, and they'd just have a cuppa ready for him."

Kyler, who had been unusually quiet through the exchange, leaned in. "If Gary's out, that means someone's getting his slot on Midlands Manic. Could be interesting."

"Yeah," Nelly mused. "Breeze lot are gonna kick off about that too."

Before they could continue their discussion, Dr Bennett cleared his throat and forced a smile that did little to mask his irritation. "Right. Now that we've dispensed with the theatrics, let's get back on track. There are still plenty of talented people in this room who are ready to shape the future of radio."

The energy in the room had shifted, though. Nobody was particularly interested in 'shaping the future of radio' when the present had just exploded into chaos.

Bennett pressed on regardless. "Now, as I was saying before we were interrupted, we have a special guest speaker joining us for the afternoon session."

That seemed to pique some curiosity. Even Nelly perked up slightly—who the hell had they managed to rope in for this circus?

Bennett continued, "It is my pleasure to welcome someone who embodies the evolution of radio. Someone who has successfully transitioned through various formats, navigating the changes in our industry with innovation and talent. Please welcome… Jeremy Kyle."

The silence that followed was both stunned and heavy.

Nelly blinked.

Pete Smith sat up straighter, a look of smug satisfaction creeping onto his face.

Kyler let out a disbelieving laugh. "No fucking way."

The Breeze lot looked positively murderous, while a few of the Manic diehards erupted into applause, clearly delighted by the shock jock twist to the proceedings.

Dr Bennett smiled thinly. "Yes, the actual Jeremy Kyle. You may have opinions about him, but he knows how to command an audience, and he knows radio inside out."

As if on cue, the doors at the side of the arena swung open, and in walked the man himself, dressed in a crisp suit, looking every bit like the controversial media figure he was.

Jeremy Kyle.

Nelly exhaled slowly, shaking her head in amused disbelief.

"Well," she murmured to Jamie, who was still holding his clipboard like it might explode, "this just got even more interesting."

Suddenly, Nelly noticed, Pete stood up and walked over to Kyle and hugged the man as if they were old friends reuniting after years apart. The room was still in stunned silence, watching the display unfold like a bizarre crossover episode of reality TV and radio drama.

"Jezza!" Pete exclaimed, clapping Kyle on the back. "It's been too bloody long, mate."

Kyle grinned, the same trademark smirk that had made him infamous on daytime television. "Pete Smith, you old bastard! They still haven't put you out to pasture?"

Pete laughed, shaking his head. "Not for lack of trying, mate. Remember our days with me on Dudley FM, Graham on GWR and you on BRMB?"

"Bloody Late Night Love, my Confessions and your middle of the road rock and pop show—those were the days," Jeremy Kyle finished, shaking his head with nostalgia. "Before everything went to shit and we had to start watching what we said. I was listening to the new network chart show, Pete. Who's that shit Neil Fox impressionist they've got? Neil told me on the phone this morning she's trying to outdo his Pepsi Chart days when he'd dunk on GWR whenever he could."

Nelly was fuming when she heard that last remark. Jeremy Kyle had just waltzed in, greeted Pete Smith like some long-lost war buddy, and immediately taken a swipe at her. The cheek of it. She clenched her jaw, resisting the urge to march over and make a scene, but Jamie, sensing her fury, quickly leaned in.

"Careful, Nell," he murmured, his voice low enough that only she could hear. "You know how this works—let them talk themselves into looking like out-of-touch dinosaurs."

Nelly exhaled sharply through her nose, forcing herself to smirk instead of scowl. "Oh, I love being underestimated," she muttered back. "Especially by relics who peaked when Nokia 3310s were cutting-edge tech."

Meanwhile, Kyle was still reminiscing with Pete, utterly oblivious to the storm brewing behind him. "You know, Jeremy, if you wind Nelly up so much, she goes full Brummie. She did a shift once back at Worcester on loan to the Dudley studios, and she had a caller on the drive she was covering of mine, a Baggies fan, and he'd started talking shit about Villa and she went full Villa on him, live on air. Proper Brummie meltdown, mate. Dropped her posh radio voice, went all, 'Yow wot, mate? Yow ain't got a clue, Baggies are a tinpot club, Villa's the pride of the Midlands,' and I swear, the switchboard lit up like a Christmas tree." Pete chuckled, shaking his head in amusement. "The boss nearly had a coronary, but the listeners? Loved it."

"So says the man who winds up Baggies and Villa fans on his old Midlands footie phone-ins because he's black and gold and proud," Nelly cut in, her voice cool but pointed as she strode over, planting herself firmly in the conversation. "And let's not pretend that's ever changed, Pete. You stir the pot like it's an Olympic sport. What's the over-under on how long it takes before you start another phone-in brawl over Jack Grealish's haircut?"

Laughter rippled through the room, but Pete just smirked, clearly relishing the moment. Jeremy Kyle, meanwhile, had turned to face her properly for the first time, his expression assessing, calculating.

"And you must be Dr Nelly Vixen," Kyle said, his tone laced with something between amusement and condescension. "The one shaking up the network chart show. Foxy said you were feisty. Started out at Worcester, got sacked... fraud, wasn't it? Funny how you started out in Worcester just like Foxy did back in the '80s at Radio Wyvern. Seems fitting, really."

Nelly's fingers curled into fists for a moment before she forced herself to relax, tilting her head with a saccharine smile. "Oh, Jezza, darling," she cooed, voice dripping with manufactured sweetness, "you're still clinging onto Neil Fox's approval like it's 1999 and he's about to give you a Pepsi Chart slot. Bless."

"So says Mrs Robinson... oh, yeah, Vixen isn't your real name, is it? You only adopted it because you wanted to be seen as the next Neil Fox and ended up with a reputation more like the next Howard Stern," Kyle shot back, his smirk widening as the room collectively leaned in, waiting for the next verbal punch. "Now, let's bring on the lie... oh, yeah, I forgot, I'm no longer on ITV, am I?

Shame, that. Reckon if I'd stuck to radio, I wouldn't have had the Daily Mail all up in my business. But hey, what do I know? I'm just an 'out-of-touch dinosaur', right?" Kyle's grin widened, his words laced with thinly veiled menace.

The tension in the room was thick enough to cut with a blunt spoon. Even Pete, who usually revelled in this kind of drama, had the good sense to shift slightly, giving Nelly just enough room to respond. She took her time, folding her arms and leaning into her smirk, deliberately slow, letting the silence linger just long enough to make it uncomfortable.

Then, with a voice as smooth as silk and twice as dangerous, she said, "Oh, Jezza, you're not out of touch—you're irrelevant."

A collective murmur ran through the room, punctuated by a low whistle from Kyler at the back. Pete shifted in his seat, clearly enjoying the show, while Jamie sucked in a sharp breath, ready to intervene if things got messy.

Kyle, for his part, raised an eyebrow, his smirk faltering just slightly. "Is that so?" he mused, feigning amusement, but Nelly caught the flicker of annoyance in his eyes. "Funny, considering I've been at the top of the game longer than you've been in it."

"Yes, and what a legacy it is," Nelly shot back, her voice drenched in mock admiration. "A few years of top-tier radio, followed by a talk show that thrived on publicly humiliating vulnerable people, and then—oh yes—that awkward little cancellation. Remind me, what was it they said? Destroyed a man's life for entertainment? Yeah, that was it, wasn't it?" She tapped her chin, pretending to search for the words. "And now here you are, desperate for a bit of relevancy in an industry that's long since moved on."

Kyle's nostrils flared, but before he could fire back, Pete smoothly intervened. "Alright, alright, settle down, you two." He held up his hands, playing the peacemaker, though his eyes gleamed with amusement. "Let's not turn this into The Jeremy Kyle Show: Radio Edition. Although, Dr Bennett, it does say on the programme that Graham Torrington's also coming for a speech? Might as well bring him in to referee this one."

Right on cue, the side door of the arena swung open again, and Nelly saw Graham bloody Torrington, looking every bit the smooth-talking late-night legend that he was, straight into Pete and Kyle's embrace, as if the Midlands Mafia of the late 1990s and early 2000s had just staged a dramatic reunion in front of the entire Manic and Breeze contingent.

"Bloody hell," Nelly muttered under her breath, crossing her arms. "What is this? A GWR reunion special?"

Jamie, standing beside her, let out a quiet chuckle. "It's like a radio Avengers movie, except all the superheroes are middle-aged men who peaked when CDs were still relevant. Anyway, Pete never did GWR, and Jezza was Capital Group, not GWR. But it doesn't matter, because they all act like they built radio from the ground up."

Nelly smirked. "Yeah, and they all think they're the main characters in some grand radio legacy. Honestly, it's embarrassing."

She glanced over at Pete, Kyle, and now Graham Torrington, who was exchanging handshakes and back-pats like they were a trio of mob bosses at a reunion. The Manic and Breeze presenters watched on, some whispering, others eyeing the spectacle with amusement or outright disdain.

"Graham," Pete said, grinning. "Haven't seen you since the ARIAs last year. Still making people cry on air with those love stories?"

Torrington laughed, his voice as smooth as ever. "Oh, Pete, some things never change. And by the looks of it, neither have you lot. Still bickering like it's the golden age of ILR."

Jeremy Kyle smirked. "And you, mate? Still whispering sweet nothings into the ears of desperate romantics at midnight?"

Torrington waved a hand. "Come on, Jezza, don't be bitter just because I didn't have to spend a decade yelling at people to sit down and shut up." The room erupted into laughter, even some of the Breeze contingent nodding in appreciation.

Nelly, watching the old guard bask in their mutual back-patting, leaned towards Jamie. "It's like watching history unfold, except it's the part of history that should've been left in the archives."

Jamie smirked, but before he could respond, Dr Bennett stepped forward again, trying desperately to regain control of the situation. His face was still tight with irritation from the earlier drama, but he plastered on his best corporate smile.

"Gentlemen," he said smoothly, addressing Pete, Jeremy, and Graham, "while it's wonderful to see such… nostalgia in the room, let's not lose sight of why we're here."

"Oh, of course," Jeremy Kyle said, smirking. "Wouldn't want to derail your 'Manic Vision', Dr Bennett." The sarcasm was so thick it could have been spread on toast.

Bennett ignored him. "Graham, since you're here, perhaps you'd like to share a few words on how radio has evolved and how we, as a unified network, can continue that evolution?"

Graham nodded, stepping up with his usual charisma. "Of course. Look, radio changes constantly, and we all have to adapt. Whether you started in the days of cart machines or are just now learning how to voice-track from an app, the principles remain the same—connect with your audience. The moment you lose that, you lose everything."

Nelly rolled her eyes slightly. It was a nice enough sentiment, but coming from someone who spent decades making lonely insomniacs sob into their pillows, it felt a little rich.

Kyle, never one to be left out of the limelight, chuckled. "Well said, Graham. But let's not pretend the industry hasn't become a corporate meat grinder. These days, it's all about cost-cutting, networking, and pretending local radio still exists. We all know the game."

There were murmurs of agreement across the room, especially from the Breeze presenters. Nelly noticed Jenna Kilmare, the Wessex Soundwave host, nodding along, arms folded tightly.

"And that's why we have to be adaptable," Bennett interjected, his patience clearly wearing thin. "Manic isn't here to destroy local radio. We're here to elevate it."

A snort of disbelief came from the Breeze section, and someone muttered, "By sacking half of us?"

Bennett's eye twitched, but he kept his composure. "We're investing in talent, bringing new opportunities, and ensuring that every presenter in this room has a future in the industry."

Jenna scoffed. "A future? Yeah, right. More like we're stuck in a waiting room, watching you decide which of us gets culled next."

****

CHAPTER 3 – SmackDown on Soundcheck Street

Wednesday 10th September 2019

"You touch my husband again, you fucking slag, and I'll make sure you never work in radio again!"

The words cut through the already tense atmosphere like a knife, and the entire bar fell into stunned silence. It was Wednesday night, and what had started as a casual networking drinks session in a Liverpool city centre bar had rapidly descended into something out of The Jeremy Kyle Show.

The sting from the slap that Jenna Kilmare gave her could be felt across the room. Nelly barely flinched. She'd been in enough industry scraps to know how to take a hit—verbally and physically. But as her cheek burned, she slowly turned back to face Jenna, her smirk only widening.

"Slag?" Nelly drawled, voice smooth as silk but laced with venom. "Sweetheart, if you're throwing around insults like that, I'd at least hope you could land a slap that actually stings."

A few gasps rippled through the room. Jenna, already fuming, stepped forward again, eyes blazing with pure rage. "You think this is funny?" she spat. "You waltz into our industry, treating people like stepping stones, shagging your way through half of Manic like it's some kind of initiation process—"

"Careful, Jenna," Nelly cut in smoothly, brushing her fingers over the barely-there red mark on her cheek. "You don't want to start listing people, because I guarantee my body count isn't half as long as yours. The only difference is, I don't get sloppy about it."

Jenna's nostrils flared, and for a moment, Nelly wondered if she'd just provoked another slap—or maybe even a full-on brawl. But then Jenna took a deep, steadying breath, her jaw clenched so tight it looked like she was about to shatter a molar.

Across the room, Jamie stood frozen with his pint halfway to his lips, eyes wide with a mix of amusement and horror. Kyler, meanwhile, leaned against the bar, smirking like a man watching a football derby about to kick off.

Jenna's voice dropped to a low hiss. "You think you're untouchable, don't you, Vixen?"

Nelly tilted her head slightly, eyes gleaming with barely disguised amusement. She wasn't just enjoying this—she was thriving on it.

"Untouchable?" she echoed, rolling the word over her tongue like a fine wine. "Oh, darling, I know I am."

Jenna let out a bitter laugh, her fists clenched at her sides. "That's where you're wrong. You think because you're Dr Nelly Vixen, the golden girl of Manic, that you can do whatever the fuck you want? That you can step all over people, fuck around, ruin careers, and get away with it?"

Nelly raised an eyebrow. "Well… yes."

Jenna's face twisted in fury. "You're a fucking joke, Vixen. If I ever catch you even breathing near my husband, I'll rip your tits off with a rusty knife. And before you say that I'll never do it, ask the last bitch who crossed me. She's doing time in HMP Bronzefield."

A collective gasp rippled through the room, and for a moment, the entire bar was caught in an eerie stillness. Even the bartender, who had been casually drying a glass a second ago, had stopped mid-motion, eyes darting between Jenna and Nelly as if gauging how quickly he'd have to call security.

Kyler let out a low whistle, shaking his head. "Bloody hell, Kilmare. You always this charming, or just when you're off the clock?"

Jenna ignored him, her entire focus still locked onto Nelly. Her nostrils flared, chest heaving like she was barely restraining herself from lunging forward.

Nelly, however, remained perfectly still. Perfectly composed. She'd spent her career dealing with egos, tempers, and melodramatic outbursts, but this? This was new. And the thing was, she could tell Jenna wasn't bluffing. There was something in her eyes, something unhinged.

"I see," Nelly murmured, swirling the last of her G&T in its glass. "So, let me get this straight. You're threatening me, in public, in front of at least… what, twenty witnesses?" She glanced around the room theatrically. "You realise how stupid that is, right?"

One of the ex-Breeze contingent laughed maniacally and said "Hear what? I didn't hear Jenna say anything apart from that she is going to ensure professionalism in the industry."

"It's like the bloody Mafia," Emma Lang muttered to Nelly, and she had to admit, the former Breeze contingent made the Italian mob look like an amateur pub quiz team when it came to loyalty and omertà, the latter being a code of silence.

Right on cue, the theme to The Godfather began playing from someone's phone speaker, and half the room erupted into nervous laughter, especially as it was the lyricised version from the 1972 UK chart release. The tension in the air cracked slightly as a few people let out relieved chuckles, but Jenna didn't so much as flinch. She was still locked onto Nelly like a predator sizing up its prey.

"Does that make Pete Smith the Don of the Breeze Family, then?" Kyler quipped, taking a swig of his pint. "Because if that's the case, I reckon Jezza Kyle's his underboss, and Graham Torrington is the consigliere, dishing out late-night love advice instead of murder orders."

The sound of more laughter rippled through the room, some of the tension finally breaking, but Jenna's expression remained rigid. She wasn't here for jokes. She was here for blood.

Nelly, however, was in her element. She leaned lazily against the bar, sipping her G&T, unbothered. "You know, Jenna," she mused, "for someone who claims to hate me, you seem awfully obsessed with what I do in my free time. Maybe you should focus on keeping your husband interested instead of worrying about me."

"Well, if you didn't whore yourself to every bloke, you skank, and trap blokes in the loos by making the classic 'oops, wrong door' move, I wouldn't have to worry about keeping my husband interested, would I?" Jenna snapped, her voice thick with venom.

A few of the ex-Breeze lot nodded approvingly, clearly revelling in the hostility, while others looked distinctly uncomfortable. It was one thing to be loyal to their own, but even they had to admit that Jenna was on the verge of tipping into complete chaos.

Nelly simply raised an eyebrow, unfazed. "Oh, darling," she purred, swirling the ice in her glass. "You think I have to trap men in loos to get their attention? Please. That's a you problem, not a me problem."

Jenna lunged.

The next thing Nelly knew, her extensions were being yanked out by the Wessex Soundwave presenter, the 21 year old yanking the elder woman with so much force, Nelly felt herself being slammed against the bar, the cold edge of the counter digging into her back as glasses clattered and toppled around her. The room exploded into chaos—gasps, shouts, and the unmistakable sound of Kyler cackling like a man who had just won a bet he didn't know he'd placed.

"Fucking hell!" Jamie yelped, nearly spilling his pint as he jumped back from the fray. "Security!"

Emma, still holding her drink, blinked in stunned disbelief before muttering, "This is better than Love Island."

Jenna, meanwhile, had Nelly's hair clenched in her fist, her other hand poised mid-air as if debating whether to throw a punch or go full WWE and smash her head into the bar. Nelly, for her part, had just about recovered from the initial shock and was now glaring up at Jenna with pure, unfiltered venom.

And then Nelly picked up Jenna, and without realising it, performed a Tombstone Piledriver on her, slamming the younger woman onto the floor of the bar with the precision of someone who had spent too many late nights watching old WWF matches. The impact sent a shockwave through the room, and for a moment, everything froze—the shouting, the laughter, the sounds of glass clinking.

Then blood.

Lots of blood.

A pool of crimson spread out from beneath Jenna's head, a stark contrast against the polished wooden floor. The laughter and jeering stopped instantly, replaced by stunned silence. The only sound was the muffled bass of the bar's playlist, obliviously thumping away in the background.

"Fucking hell, Nelly," Jamie muttered, eyes wide as he stared at Jenna's unmoving form.

Even Kyler, who had been laughing moments ago, had the good sense to look alarmed. "Mate… I think you might've actually killed her."

For the first time that night, Nelly's heart lurched. She wasn't proud of losing her temper, but she hadn't expected… this. Had she hit her head wrong? Had the alcohol in her system made it worse?

Jenna lay sprawled on the floor, her chest rising and falling in shallow, shaky breaths.

And then, miraculously, she groaned.

"Bloody—" She sucked in a breath, her voice weak but filled with rage. "I'll… fucking kill you, Vixen."

The next thing Nelly knew, Jenna had got her in an armlock, and Nelly knew that both she and Jenna were working on pure adrenaline, the pure, unrelenting instinct of two people who had completely abandoned rationality in favour of settling their score in the most primal way possible.

The bar had erupted into chaos. Some of the ex-Breeze presenters had jumped in, either trying to pull Jenna off Nelly or—more likely—cheering her on. The Manic lot, on the other hand, were caught somewhere between shock, amusement, and making quick calculations about how much PR damage this was going to cause by morning.

Jenna's grip was like iron, her forearm crushing against Nelly's throat, pressing her into the cold, sticky floor. The adrenaline had turned her into something almost feral—

there was no radio politeness, no industry politics, just pure, unfiltered rage.

"You think you can fucking humiliate me?" Jenna snarled, tightening her grip. "Think you can just throw me around and walk away?"

Nelly, struggling against the pressure, managed to choke out a hoarse laugh. "Darling," she wheezed, her fingers clawing at Jenna's arm, "I don't think… I know."

"...and Kilmare has got Vixen in a triangle choke!" Vicky Hennessy, one of the Northern Vibes contingent said with the authority of a wrestling commentator, and Nelly glared at the Stoke and Stone based Breeze presenter who dared to interrupt the madness with actual sports commentary.

Jamie, who had finally snapped out of his stunned stupor, shoved his pint onto the bar and darted forward. "Alright, that's enough!" he barked, grabbing Jenna's shoulders and trying to pry her off. "This isn't bloody SmackDown!"

It was then that Dan Kilmare, Nelly noticed, took a swing at Jamie, resulting in it going from a two women fight to a full-on bar brawl. Dan's punch, Nelly noticed while Jenna was close to cutting off her airway and turning her vision slightly hazy, landed squarely on Jamie's jaw, sending him stumbling backwards into a table of unsuspecting finance lads who'd just been trying to enjoy a midweek pint. Drinks went flying, one bloke let out an indignant yelp, and suddenly, as if on cue, the entire bar descended into absolute anarchy.

Kyler, now fully embracing the carnage, hoisted his pint in the air and roared, "FUCKING GET IN! ROYAL RUMBLE, LADS!"

That was all it took. Chaos. Absolute, unfiltered, Scouse-flavoured chaos.

The ex-Breeze presenters were now piling in, fists flying, beer spilling, and furniture scraping across the floor as tables were shoved aside to make space for the impromptu smackdown. The Manic contingent, after a moment of stunned hesitation, did what they did best—dived headfirst into the mess, some for the thrill, others simply to defend their own.

The fact that most of the Breeze presenters who were over 35 had not bothered to turn up at the event, either due to doing their shows from their hotel rooms, something to do with their RCS systems allowing them to present live and voice-tracked or because they had already resigned themselves to the reality that their jobs were on borrowed time—meant that the ones here were the scrappy younger lot. The ones with something to prove. The ones who weren't going to let Manic steamroll them without a fight.

And fight they did.

The irony that Pete Smith, the most pre-historic of them all, was among the ones who were neatly tucked up in bed with a cup of tea and a copy of RAJAR Figures Through the Years was not lost on Nelly. In fact, the sheer absurdity of the situation almost made her laugh, even as Jenna's forearm pressed down harder on her throat.

She knew that he'd be the first to try and officiate the madness if he were here. Instead, the chaos was left unchecked, spiralling further into a scene that would go down in radio industry folklore.

Jenna still had Nelly in a chokehold, but her grip had loosened slightly in the fray. Nelly seized the moment. With a sharp twist of her body, she shoved Jenna off her, flipping the younger woman onto her back. Jenna let out a frustrated yell as Nelly scrambled to her feet, adjusting her dishevelled dress and yanking her hair out of her face.

"That's enough," Nelly spat, catching her breath as she glared down at Jenna, who was now sprawled on the floor, panting but still full of rage.

But Jenna wasn't done. She shot to her feet like a woman possessed, her blonde hair wild, mascara smudged, and eyes filled with fury. "You're gonna regret this, Vixen," she snarled. "You think you're the queen of Manic? You're nothing but a washed-up slag with a posh accent."

Nelly rolled her shoulders, the adrenaline still pumping through her veins. "And you're a jumped-up little Exeter graduate who thinks being a big fish in the tiny Wessex Soundwave pond makes you important. Newsflash, Jenna—you're in the real world now."

Before Jenna could retort, the brawl around them took a new turn. Dan Kilmare had just landed another punch— this time on Kyler, which was an exceptionally bad idea. Kyler, already a pint or two deep, staggered for a second before roaring with laughter, then launching himself at Dan, sending them both crashing into a table.

"Bloody hell," Jamie groaned, rubbing his jaw. "We're gonna need legal representation by the time this night's over."

Hennessy was still in commentator mode, shouting, "AND KILMARE HAS BEEN SPEARED INTO THE TABLE! KYLER THOMPSON HAS GONE FULL EDGE ON HIS ARSE!"

Suddenly Dan got pulled Kyler's legs from underneath him, the 24 year old going onto the floor like a sack of spuds at Birmingham Flea Market. Nelly barely had time to dodge as a chair went flying past her, narrowly missing her shoulder before clattering onto the floor. A pint glass followed suit, smashing into the wall and sending shards of glass scattering across the bar. The chaos had reached a fever pitch, and at this point, it was impossible to tell who was fighting who—ex-Breeze versus Manic, Wessex Soundwave versus Bee Manic, drunk punters versus anyone in their way.

Jenna lunged again, but this time, Nelly was ready. She sidestepped smoothly, sending Jenna sprawling onto an overturned chair, her designer dress now streaked with beer. The sight would have been hilarious if Nelly wasn't still half expecting a broken bottle to come flying at her head.

And then Jenna dropped to the floor, the blood on the back of her head with some glass that was clearly embedded into her scalp glistening under the dim bar lights. A collective gasp rippled through the room as the sheer insanity of the night finally reached a crescendo.

For a moment, everything seemed to slow down. The yelling, the chaos, the swinging fists—all of it faded into stunned silence as everyone stared at Jenna, crumpled on the sticky floor, her blonde hair now streaked with red.

"Fuck," Jamie muttered under his breath, his hand frozen halfway through trying to stop Kyler from launching himself at Dan Kilmare again.

Nelly stood over Jenna, her own breath coming in short, sharp bursts. She hadn't meant for this to happen. She was up for a fight, sure, but she didn't actually want to cause serious damage.

"She ain't dead, is she?" Kyler asked, looking down at Jenna with something that was almost disappointment. "I mean, if she was, at least it'd be a decent headline. 'Manic Presenter Kills Breeze Rival in Royal Rumble Bar Brawl.' Would probably boost our RAJARs."

Jamie smacked the back of his head. "Not. Helping."

Nelly watched as Dan ran over to Jenna, and, getting on his knees, started crying. It was then that Nelly noticed Jenna wasn't breathing, that she wasn't moving.

The entire bar seemed to hold its breath. The chaos, the fights, the flying pints—all of it faded into a horrifying silence as Dan Kilmare clutched Jenna's lifeless body, his sobs cutting through the tension like a knife.

Nelly's stomach twisted. She'd been in scraps before— some verbal, some physical—but never anything like this. Never something that had actually… gone too far. She stepped back, hands shaking slightly, the adrenaline fading into something colder, heavier.

"She's not breathing," Dan choked out, his voice cracking as he shook Jenna's shoulders. "Oh my God—she's not fucking breathing!"

The words sent a ripple of realisation through the crowd. Someone let out a panicked gasp, another muttered a sharp "Jesus Christ," and suddenly, everyone was stepping back, as if distancing themselves from the scene would somehow erase their involvement.

Jamie was the first to move. He pushed past Kyler, dropping to his knees beside Jenna. "Move, Dan," he ordered, voice steadier than Nelly expected. "We need to check if she's got a pulse."

Dan didn't budge at first, frozen in place as he cradled Jenna's head, the blood seeping into his shirt. But Jamie wasn't waiting. He grabbed Dan's wrist and yanked him aside, pressing two fingers to Jenna's neck.

Silence.

Nelly felt her throat close up. *No. No, no, no, no. This wasn't happening.*

Jamie's fingers stayed pressed against Jenna's throat, his brow furrowed in concentration. The entire bar was frozen, a room full of radio industry professionals—normally so quick with comebacks and cutting remarks—suddenly reduced to stunned, silent bystanders.

Nelly's stomach twisted itself into knots. This had been a joke, a scuffle, just another night in the chaos of Manic Radio's ridiculous, hedonistic culture. But now? Now there was blood on the floor. Now there was a woman— one of their own—motionless, her breath stolen by something that had spiralled completely out of control.

"Jamie," Nelly said, her voice barely above a whisper. "Jamie, say something."

Jamie didn't respond for a second. He just hovered there, his fingers searching, searching—until finally, he exhaled, and the tension in his shoulders loosened.

"She's alive," he said, loud enough for everyone to hear. A collective breath of relief rippled through the room. "Her pulse is weak, but it's there."

Dan let out a choked sob, still kneeling beside Jenna, his hands trembling. "We need an ambulance. Someone— someone call an ambulance!"

Kyler, for all his usual bravado, nodded quickly and pulled out his phone, his fingers fumbling over the screen as he punched in the emergency number. The dial tone rang out, loud in the sudden hush of the bar.

Nelly swallowed hard. Her mind was racing, calculating every possible consequence, every angle. This wasn't some minor bar fight. This was serious. This could be headlines. This could be a career-ending moment. Her career-ending moment.

Her head snapped up, her instincts kicking in. "No one talks to the press about this," she said sharply, scanning the room. "Not one fucking word to anyone. If this gets out—"

"Oh, yeah, because that's the priority right now?" Dan snapped, his voice raw with anger as he glared at her. "Not that my wife's got her head cracked open, but that your reputation stays intact? Fuck you, Nelly."

Nelly clenched her jaw, forcing herself to stay calm. "You think I wanted this to happen?" she shot back, her voice dangerously low. "You think I planned for your wife to come at me like a lunatic? She swung first, Dan. Or did you conveniently forget that part?"

Dan's face twisted with rage, but before he could say another word, Jamie cut in. "Both of you, shut up," he ordered. "We're already knee-deep in shit. Let's not make it worse."

Kyler, still on the phone, looked up. "Ambulance is on the way. They're sending the police too."

Nelly closed her eyes for a brief second. Of course they were.

The next few minutes blurred together—Jamie grabbing bar towels to press against Jenna's head, Dan still half in shock, the ex-Breeze presenters forming a protective huddle, whispering among themselves. Someone handed Jenna's handbag to Dan, who fumbled through it for her phone, his hands shaking too much to unlock the screen.

Nelly watched it all unfold, her mind racing. She needed control. Damage control.

Think, Vixen. Think.

The sirens came quicker than she expected, flashing blue lights flooding the windows of the bar. The paramedics entered first, pushing through the stunned crowd, their faces unreadable as they quickly assessed the situation.

"She fell," Jamie said, answering before anyone else could. His voice was calm, controlled. "She hit her head. We tried to stop the bleeding."

One of the paramedics looked up sharply. "She fell?"

Dan made a noise like he wanted to object, but Nelly shot him a warning look. Stick to the story. Don't make this worse.

Jenna was quickly lifted onto a stretcher, an oxygen mask placed over her face. One of the paramedics spoke into a radio, and the other turned back to the group.

"She's unconscious but stable," he said, his voice brisk. "We need to get her to the hospital. Who's coming with us?"

Dan immediately stepped forward. "I am. I'm her husband and next of kin."

The paramedic nodded, motioning for Dan to follow as they wheeled Jenna towards the exit. The whole bar was silent, a mixture of stunned ex-Breeze presenters and wary Manic staff frozen in place, their earlier bravado now tempered by the cold reality of the situation.

Kyler, ever the opportunist, leaned into Nelly with a smirk. "So, uh… I think it's safe to say you're definitely not getting invited to the next Breeze reunion."

Nelly shot him a glare. "Not the time, Ky."

Jamie, running a hand through his already dishevelled hair, exhaled sharply. "Right, we need to sort this out before the police get here. Because let's be real, they are definitely not going to believe 'she fell' when there's about fifty people here who saw you tombstone-piledrive her into the floor. Although… you know us Manic lot will cover for you."

Nelly rolled her eyes, trying to suppress the flicker of unease creeping into her gut. "It wasn't a bloody piledriver."

"It was," Kyler chimed in. "Textbook stuff, actually. Bit more Undertaker than Kane, but still—solid form."

Emma, who had been uncharacteristically quiet, finally piped up, still nursing her drink. "We all saw Jenna take the first swing. And let's be honest, she was a lunatic before she got knocked out. No one's gonna pin this whole thing on you, Vixen. Anyway, she did say she'd rip your tits off with a rusty knife. Self-defence, innit."

****

CHAPTER 4 – Dead Air
Thursday 11ᵗʰ September 2019

Dead.

Jenna Kilmare was dead.

Not from her injuries. Not from the blood pooling on the floor of that chaotic Liverpool bar. Not from the glass embedded in her scalp.

But from a heart attack.

It turned out that she had had a heart condition, and that the sheer adrenaline, rage, and physical exertion of the fight had sent her into cardiac arrest. She had already been unconscious when the paramedics arrived, but no one realised just how serious it was. The moment she was loaded into the ambulance, her heart had stopped. They'd tried to revive her on the way to the hospital. They'd tried again in A&E. But at 2:47am, Jenna Kilmare was pronounced dead.

And Nelly? She was on police bail.

Affray.

Drunk and disorderly.

Actual bodily harm.

It sounded ridiculous. Ludicrous. Like something out of a badly scripted soap. But up until a few minutes ago, she had been sitting in a stark, windowless interview room at a Liverpool police station, staring at a plastic cup of lukewarm water, the condensation gathering in little droplets like it was mocking her.

"You understand the severity of the situation, Dr Robinson?"

She flinched slightly at the sound of her real name—Nelly Vixen had been the brand, the persona, the radio star. Dr Eleanor Robinson was just a woman in a crumpled dress from the night before, with dried blood on her knuckles and a rapidly deteriorating career.

She licked her lips, her voice coming out hoarse. "I do."

The officer opposite her—a middle-aged Scouser with tired eyes and the distinct air of someone who'd seen it all before—sighed and leaned forward. "Then maybe you'd like to start explaining what the hell happened last night."

Nelly exhaled, pressing her fingertips against her temples as if she could physically push the headache away. "We were at a networking event. It… escalated."

The officer snorted. "Escalated? Ms Kilmare is in the morgue, Dr Robinson. This wasn't a pub scrap over a spilled pint."

She clenched her jaw. "She swung first. She slapped me, pulled my hair, tried to choke me. I defended myself."

"By executing a wrestling move on her?"

"It wasn't a—" Nelly groaned, letting her head fall back against the wall. "Look, I didn't mean to hurt her. It was just adrenaline, instincts. I was just trying to get her off me. And then… then it all just went to shit."

The officer regarded her for a long moment before flicking through his notes. "We've got over twenty witness statements. Some say you were provoked. Some say you lost your temper. The only common thread between the ones that were stating you were provoked are colleagues of yours who had been employed by Manic. The ones who say you lost your temper are former Breeze presenters."

Nelly let out a sharp laugh, devoid of any humour. "Of course they did. Of course, the Breeze lot are blaming me. They hated me before all this. Now they've got an excuse to make me into the villain of the decade."

The officer raised an eyebrow. "So, you think they're lying?"

"Oh, they're not lying," she said, voice dry. "They're just... curating their version of events. Picking and choosing the bits that make me look as bad as possible."

The officer hummed, clearly unimpressed. "There's CCTV footage from the bar. That'll give us a clearer picture."

Nelly tensed. "CCTV?"

"Yes." He nodded, flipping a page in his notebook. "But according to the bar manager, a lot of the cameras in that particular area weren't working. Lucky you, eh?"

Nelly closed her eyes for a moment. Of course. Of course, the universe would give her a shred of mercy just to dangle it over her head.

"Dr Robinson, this is a serious investigation," the officer continued, tone sharpening. "A woman has died. We have to determine whether it was a tragic accident or if there was criminal intent."

Nelly's fingers curled into fists. "You think I wanted this to happen? She hated me. I hated her. We had our issues, but I didn't want her dead. I mean, yes, I shagged her husband in the loos at the M&S Bank Arena yesterday afternoon, but that was radio presenters being radio presenters."

Of course, Nelly's lawyer, paid for because her husband, Dr Nate Robinson, was a plastic surgeon whose main clients were footballers' wives and reality TV stars, had managed to get Nelly out of the interview and the police station before they could press any formal charges. The words "insufficient evidence" and "unclear circumstances" had been thrown around, but Nelly knew the reality—she wasn't out of the woods. Not by a long shot.

As she stepped out into the harsh morning light, the city of Liverpool still buzzing with early commuters, she could feel the weight of what had happened pressing down on her. Jenna Kilmare was dead. And no matter what the police said—or didn't say—there was no coming back from that.

Waiting outside, leaning against a black cab with a cigarette in hand, was Kyler Thompson. He looked surprisingly fresh for someone who had spent half the night being questioned and was now likely front-page news.

"Well, well," he smirked as Nelly approached. "Out on bail already? That posh husband of yours must've written one hell of a cheque. You know Dan Kilmare hasn't come out yet."

Nelly chuckled, as she pulled her coat tighter around her shoulders. "Dan's still inside? Let me guess, he's in full grieving widower mode, making sure everyone knows what a saint Jenna was."

Kyler took a drag of his cigarette, exhaling the smoke slowly. "Oh, he's milking it. Proper sob story. Telling the police that you 'hounded' her for years, ruined her career, humiliated her, shagged her husband—"

"Which I did," Nelly interjected with a shrug. "Even though I never heard of the bitch until last week when Manic and Breeze merged, so it's hardly a 'lifelong vendetta', is it?" Nelly finished, rolling her eyes. "He's rewriting history to make me into some kind of radio supervillain. I mean, I get it. If my missus just dropped dead in front of me, I'd want someone to blame too. But let's not pretend Jenna was some innocent little lamb."

Kyler smirked. "Yeah, well, you know how this works. The dead become saints, the living get crucified."

Nelly sighed, running a hand through her tangled hair. She was exhausted, hungover, and still half-processing the fact that a woman she'd been physically fighting just hours ago was now in a morgue. "Has this hit the press yet?" she asked, glancing around as if expecting to see paps lurking behind lampposts.

Kyler scoffed. "Course it has. The PR guys have spun the death using the heart attack angle, that he was a victim of kebabs and Exeter's nightlife rather than an industry-wide bar brawl. But, mate, this is Manic. We all know the PR lot will spin a flying saucer as some kind of 'innovative new breakfast show stunt'."

Nelly knew from her past year and half at Manic that they would cover anything bar a pervert or a nonce up, and then they'd still try and find a way to spin it. If a presenter got caught drink-driving? "Fatigue from an intense schedule." A messy affair between colleagues? "Passionate industry professionals." A punch-up at a networking event? "Spirited workplace discussion."

But this? This was bigger than the usual mess Manic could sweep under the rug.

Nelly let out a slow breath, rubbing at her temples as they approached the waiting taxi. "So, what's the official party line, then? Jenna Kilmare, tragic young talent taken too soon?"

Kyler grinned around his cigarette. "Oh, you know it. 'Heartbreaking loss to the radio industry. Jenna was a rising star, beloved by listeners, respected by her peers…' and then some sappy shite about how her passion for broadcasting was 'immeasurable.'" He flicked his cigarette into the gutter. "Basically, the exact opposite of what we all know is true."

Nelly snorted. "'Respected by her peers'? Half the Breeze lot didn't even know who she was until this week."

Kyler shrugged. "Exactly. But it's all about optics, isn't it? Jenna's gone, Dan's the grieving widower, and you…" He eyed her up and down. "You, my dear, are the wicked witch of British radio."

She rolled her eyes, yanking the cab door open and climbing inside. "Great. Just what I need. First I'm a GWR reject, now I'm the industry's public enemy number one."

Kyler followed her in, slamming the door shut behind them. "Well, at least you're not boring. No one remembers the safe, dull ones, Vixen. The legends? They always come with a bit of scandal."

The cab pulled away from the station, weaving through the grey morning streets of Liverpool. Nelly slumped back in the seat, exhaustion creeping into her bones. She knew Kyler was right. Manic didn't care about morality, not really. They cared about ratings, about attention, about keeping their name in the industry's mouth. And if that meant making her the villain? They'd do it without a second thought.

Her phone buzzed. She pulled it out, glancing at the screen.

Dr Nate Robinson: *Hey babe, just so you know, I've got a conference that lasts a week and half over in the States, some plastic surgeons bigwig thing in Miami. I'll be flying out tonight. Try not to kill anyone else while I'm gone. Xx*

Nelly let out a dry laugh, shaking her head. Of course, her husband was off to schmooze with Hollywood's finest while she was here, knee-deep in a scandal that could very well ruin her career. She didn't blame him—this wasn't his world. He dealt with Instagram influencers and reality TV stars, people like the Real Housewives of Cheshire, not blood-soaked radio presenters who spent their evenings getting into bar brawls and their mornings dodging police charges.

"Aren't you meant to be on your mid-morning show over in Manc later?" Nelly asked, as she knew that Kyler, as one of the three faces of Manchester's mid-morning show on Bee Manic, the long-time Manic owned station that competed against Hits Radio and Capital, was meant to be back on air after a few days off for "corporate training"—which, in reality, had just been an excuse to drink his way through Liverpool and wind up anyone from Breeze Media who'd give him the time of day.

Kyler smirked, stretching out in the back seat of the cab like he had all the time in the world. "Ah, don't worry about it. Told the boss I needed 'personal time to reflect on the tragic loss of a colleague.' They lapped it up. The slag who Emma and I work with can cope with another day on her own with Cal Ellington. You know she's using a fake name, right, and that Cal knows her... shagged her when she was 14."

Nelly raised an eyebrow, turning to face Kyler fully. "Wait, what? Who the hell is she, then?"

Kyler exhaled slowly, as if savouring the moment. "Toni Green," he said, dragging out the syllables with deliberate smugness. "Real name? Cassie Longton. Local girl from Altrincham. Did some bits at Salford Uni, went off the radar for a bit, and now she's back, rebranded like a failed X Factor contestant trying for a second shot at stardom."

Nelly frowned. The name didn't ring any immediate bells, but Kyler's tone made it clear that it should. "And Cal Ellington—he's got history with her?"

Kyler grinned, lighting another cigarette as he lounged back in the cab seat. "Oh yeah. Big time. Back in the day, when she was a scrawny little teenager, she had a thing with him. He was 16, she was 14. That 'young love' bollocks. Except it wasn't so sweet—she got knocked up, had the baby, and—well, let's just say social services got involved."

Nelly blinked, taking that in. "She put the kid up for adoption?"

Kyler nodded, exhaling a thin stream of smoke out of the slightly cracked window. "Something like that. All very hush-hush. But Cal never forgot. He never let it go. Now he's got her trapped at Bee Manic, low-key blackmailing her to keep her in line. She's a good fuck… doesn't just shag blokes but is a lezza too. You'd like the slut. Ate Emma out like a fucking feral animal in a hotel room after one too many tequilas the other night. Emma told me she couldn't walk straight the next day."

Nelly snorted, shaking her head. "Jesus Christ, Kyler. Do you ever actually think before you open your mouth?"

Kyler just grinned, exhaling another cloud of smoke. "Nah. Where's the fun in that?"

She rolled her eyes, her mind whirring. This Toni Green—or Cassie Longton, whatever her name really was—sounded like someone with a past even messier than hers. The fact that she was on air at Bee Manic, a Manic station, meant she was in their ecosystem now. And from what Kyler was implying, she was in deep with Callum Ellington, who was as much of a snake as they came.

"I bet management don't know about all this," Nelly mused, tapping her nails against the door panel.

"Oh, Buzz knows… he is like the three wise monkeys when it comes to what goes on outside his job as senior producer. He sees nothing, hears nothing, and says nothing," Kyler finished with a smirk. "He's been at Bee Manic long enough to know when to turn a blind eye. But Toni? I'm hoping to manipulate her into being my personal slag."

Nelly arched an eyebrow at Kyler, her patience wearing thin. "You do realise that you're an absolute bastard, right?"

Kyler let out a low chuckle, tossing his cigarette butt out of the cab window. "Yeah, yeah, I've been told. But, come on, Nell, this is radio. It's a bloody cesspit. We all play the game. You just play it better than most."

Nelly sighed, rubbing at her temples. Her headache was worsening, her body aching from the aftermath of the bar brawl, the interrogation, and now this ridiculous conversation. The fact that she was now apparently wrapped up in some twisted web involving a rebranded presenter, an extorting ex, and a dead rival was just the icing on the cake.

"You really think management will let Cal keep hold of this leverage over Toni?" she asked, staring out of the cab window as the city passed by. "If they find out, they'll do what they always do—turn it into some 'gritty redemption' PR story or sack the pair of them before OFCOM gets wind of it."

Kyler shrugged, running a hand through his dark, tousled hair. "Probably. But until then, it's bloody entertaining. And besides, she's got no choice but to keep her mouth shut. She needs this job. Single, no qualifications worth a damn, a past she doesn't want resurfacing… she's ripe for the picking."

Nelly exhaled sharply. "And what's your angle, then? You trying to get your dick wet or something?"

"Well, since the last slut I was nailing decided to throw herself off the roof of the Bee Manic offices, I'm currently in the market for a new one," Kyler said, his voice flippant, but his eyes dark with something unspoken.

Nelly knew that Kyler, the 24 year old chaos monkey, was in a constant state of horniness, and was a walking red flag to every woman with half a brain cell. But despite his usual smirk and bravado, there was something else there—something almost resentful. Like he was playing a game he knew would never end well for him, but he played it anyway, because that's all he knew.

She also knew that the relationship between her and him was one of fuck buddies, friends with benefits, as she was married, and she knew that Kyler preferred the younger ones—the fresh-faced interns, the naive production assistants who hadn't yet learned that a night with Kyler Thompson usually came with a side of regret.

It was an unwritten rule at Manic that affairs, one night stands and hook-ups were just part of the culture—expected, even. It was the kind of place where no one blinked if two colleagues stumbled out of a club together at 3am, or if someone came into work wearing the same clothes as the day before. Manic was chaos. It thrived on it.

But this? This was something else entirely.

Nelly turned her attention back to Kyler, watching him with a careful eye. "You need to be careful with this one," she said, her tone more serious than before. "If she's as vulnerable as you say, then she's got nothing to lose. And people with nothing to lose? They're dangerous."

Kyler snorted, leaning his head back against the seat. "Please. You think I haven't dealt with messy before? She's a pawn, Nell. Just another piece on the board."

Nelly shook her head, watching as the grey streets of Liverpool blurred past. The whole situation stank of something bigger—something messier than Kyler was giving it credit for. And if there was one thing she'd learned in her years in this industry, it was that the pieces you thought were pawns had a nasty habit of turning into queens when you least expected it.

"You know that my home in Knutsford will be free in an hour," Nelly said with a grin, "and its only half past 8, so if you fancy crashing at mine, you can. Nate's off to Miami, so I've got the place to myself."

Kyler smirked, running a hand through his messy, jet-black hair. "Oh, you inviting me round for a sympathy shag, Vixen? Or are we skipping straight to the part where we pretend last night didn't happen?"

Nelly rolled her eyes. "Jesus, Ky, it's not always about your dick. I just don't fancy being alone right now." She exhaled, running a hand over her face. "Not after… all that."

Kyler studied her for a moment, his usual smirk softening just slightly. "Yeah, alright," he said, flicking his cigarette butt out of the window. "But only if you've got something stronger than shite supermarket gin in your cupboard."

"I'll have you know my gin is from Waitrose, not the plonk aisle at Tesco," Nelly shot back, shaking her head as the cab turned onto the motorway, heading south towards Cheshire.

Kyler snorted, stretching out like a man who had all the time in the world. "Alright, posh bird. I'll give you that. But I'm expecting at least a halfway decent whisky to wash down this absolute clusterfuck of a situation."

Nelly rolled her eyes but didn't argue. The truth was, she needed the company. Needed something—someone—to ground her after everything that had just happened. Because no matter how much she played it off, how much she smirked and shrugged and acted like she didn't care, the reality was sinking in.

Jenna Kilmare was dead.

And whether or not it was her fault, she was going to have to live with it.

****

CHAPTER 5 – The Charts, The Chaos, and The Cancellation Countdown
Sunday 15th September 2019

"You're listening to the newest, the freshest, the biggest chart show in the UK… and somehow, I'm still here!"

Dr Nelly Vixen's voice dripped with playful arrogance, her trademark smirk audible through the speakers of thousands of radios across the country. Anyone who had been following the industry gossip—and at this point, that was practically everyone in radio—knew she probably shouldn't be on air at all.

Yet here she was.

The Manic UK40Chart had kicked off as usual, just after 4pm, with the kind of high-energy introduction that was supposed to distract from the fact that its host was currently at the centre of a scandal so messy it was being whispered about in BBC green rooms, Bauer board meetings, and Global's Leicester Square corridors.

Nelly, as ever, refused to let it show.

"Coming up, we've got one of the biggest climbers of the week—some bloke who was probably singing to his mirror six months ago and now has a platinum single. You know how it is."

Jamie Wise, her producer, was sitting across from her in the control room, watching her with barely concealed amusement. He had bet against her even making it to the studio today. After all, she was still officially on police bail. Manic had been scrambling to decide whether to pull her from the airwaves until things died down, but as usual, their appetite for chaos won out.

"Also, a brand-new number one coming your way in about three hours' time—unless I get taken off air before then. Could happen. You never know. Let's get on with it. Now, if you don't know the rules because you live on a rock or are mentally retarded, the Manic charts are simple—we combine the top 40 tracks played across the Manic network with the Spotify Top 40, and weight it as follows—one stream = a hundredth of an airplay, so that way, we get a chart that actually reflects what the UK is listening to, rather than what some exec in London thinks we should be listening to. Revolutionary, I know."

Jamie winced slightly at the mentally retarded remark, his hand hovering over the talkback button, ready to intervene if necessary. It wasn't the worst thing Nelly had ever said on air, but OFCOM had been sniffing around Manic for months now, looking for an excuse to come down on them harder than they had on Kiss back in 2011 when they "accidentally" let a presenter swear during the school run.

"You're playing with fire, Nell," Jamie muttered through the talkback.

Nelly smirked, flicking a switch to kill the talkback in her headphones. "Anyway, kicking us off this week at number 40, Crapital and the BBC would have you believe that it's Burna Boy and his absolute dumpster fire of a track, Location, but because the dinosaurs on half of the Manic network have been pushing Spice Girls' Stop on their 'Throwback Thursday' slots like it's 1998 all over again,

D-Block Europe's Home Pussy sits at number 40 instead. Gotta love a bit of democracy in action, eh?"

Jamie ran a hand down his face. "Nell, I swear to God, you're going to have half the radio industry outside your house with pitchforks at this rate."

Nelly laughed, entirely unbothered, as the opening notes of Home Pussy blasted out across the Manic network. She leaned back in her chair, drumming her fingers against the desk, her mind already racing ahead to what was next.

This wasn't just another Sunday. This was a statement.

The news of Jenna Kilmare's death had sent shockwaves through the industry, but Manic's response had been predictable. They had hedged their bets, waiting to see whether the police would press charges before making any drastic decisions. The statement they'd issued on Friday was so non-committal it could have been written by a lawyer with both eyes on their next corporate gig.

"We are deeply saddened by the tragic passing of Jenna Kilmare, a talented broadcaster who was well-respected by her colleagues and listeners alike. Our thoughts are with her family, friends, and colleagues at this difficult time."

Blah, blah, blah.

There was no mention of Nelly. No direct reference to the fight. Nothing that acknowledged the fact that their very own Dr Vixen had, at best, been involved in a bar brawl that ended with someone dead, and at worst, was still under active police investigation.

And yet, she was still on air.

Looking at the text message screen, Nelly saw that the amount of text messages were double what they normally were by this point in the show. Some of them were the usual chart show fare—requests, shoutouts, people moaning about why their favourite track wasn't higher—but a good chunk of them were about her and her 'now, if you don't know the rules because you live on a rock or are mentally retarded, the Manic charts are simple' remark, half from the outraged, half egging her on.

She half felt sorry for the geeks in the customer services team who were going to have to wade through the complaints on Monday morning. Not that it would matter much—Manic thrived on controversy. The more people moaned, the more people tuned in to see what she'd say next. And if there was one thing Nelly knew how to do, it was keep people listening.

Flicking over to her Twitter screen, she saw that, despite it only being 5 minutes into her show, both her name and Manic were trending UK wide, with the hashtag '#Vixen' trending at number 1 with over 20,000 mentions already. She smirked, knowing full well that half of those were people calling for her head, and the other half were cheering her on.

As the final few lines of D-Block Europe's Home Pussy faded out, and Nelly leaned into the mic, tapping her nails on the desk for dramatic effect.

"Well, that was Home Pussy at number 40, a track I'm sure is making middle-aged Radio 2 execs sweat into their sensible linen shirts. Right, let's get on with it—unless Ofcom want to burst in and drag me off air before we hit number one. I'd give it an hour before they try. Anyway, we've got another wildcard off the top 40, with a new entry," she said, pressing the button which aired the pre-recorded transition jingle, the high-energy voiceover booming,

"This week's highest new entry—straight in at 39!"

The track kicked in—Lana Del Ray– Norman Fucking Rodwell.

A track which the Official Charts Company ranked at number 44, but Manic had, on the overnight shows, been playing in heavy rotation since its release. Nelly leaned back, watching Jamie through the glass as he ran a hand through his already-messy hair.

The irony that it was the execs in the building next door at the Speke complex who arranged the pre-release airplay push for Lana, while also frantically trying to decide whether to suspend her, was not lost on Nelly. The fact that she was trending, that Manic was trending, that every other station in the country would be talking about this show tomorrow morning? That was all that mattered.

She knew that OFCOM would be investigating the show, as usual, and she didn't care, as Manic paid the fines religiously, on time and had a budget thanks to their Russian oligarch backers to ensure that fines were just an operating cost rather than a deterrent. Manic had always played fast and loose with regulations, but today, Nelly was taking things to a whole new level.

By the time Lana Del Rey's track faded out, the text screen had exploded again, the producer's inbox filling up at twice the normal speed. Jamie's expression was somewhere between resigned exasperation and sheer disbelief.

"You really want them to yank you off air, don't you?" he muttered through the talkback.

"Mate, if they were going to, they'd have done it already," Nelly fired back, switching off her mic for a second. "They love the attention. You think Bennett's sitting in his office sweating over this? Nah. He's probably got a bottle of Bollinger open, watching the Twitter numbers climb."

She wasn't wrong. Manic thrived on chaos, and right now, she was giving them exactly what they wanted—headlines, outrage, and most importantly, ratings.

She turned her mic back on, slipping seamlessly back into her on-air persona.

"Now, I know what you're thinking—'Nelly, why the hell are you still on air?' And listen, babes, I ask myself that every single day. But we keep rolling, and so does this chart. Up next, a track that's somehow clinging to life despite being older than my last Waitrose, it's Becky Hill and Sigala, or should I say Shagala, as he's that hot, I'd happily lick whipped cream off his abs in the Ritz in London. But that's for another show. Here's Wish You Well at number 38."

Jamie groaned audibly through the talkback. "Jesus Christ, Vixen, you are single-handedly giving our legal team an aneurysm."

Nelly grinned, adjusting her mic levels as Becky Hill's voice soared through the speakers. She knew she was pushing it. She knew she was toeing the line between ratings gold and outright career suicide. But that was the thrill of it, wasn't it? That was why people tuned in. No one wanted a safe, sanitised presenter reading off a script like they were working in a call centre. They wanted the chaos. They wanted the unpredictability. They wanted *her*.

The Twitter notifications on her screen kept rolling in.

"Nelly Vixen is an absolute menace to society, and I am HERE FOR IT."

"I'm sorry but did she just call Sigala 'Shagala' and imply she wants to shag him at the Ritz? Iconic."

"Ofcom are drafting their statement in real time at this point."

"Manic really said 'laws? We don't know them' when they let her stay on air."

Nelly smirked. The Twitter warriors were having a field day.

Jamie's voice crackled in again. "Oi, enjoy the show while you can, because *someone* from legal is calling a meeting for first thing tomorrow."

"Tell them to book a table at Hawksmoor while they're at it," Nelly shot back, "might as well get a free steak out of the bollocking."

Jamie snorted, but before he could respond, the song was fading out, and Nelly was back in action.

"Alright, that was *Wish You Well* at number 38, and honestly, I think Becky Hill's been in this chart longer than I've been on bail. Speaking of legal nightmares—guess who's climbed to 37? Yep, it's Doja Cat, our favourite TikTok queen who makes bops and questionable life choices in equal measure. Here's *Juicy*."

She hit play and leaned back, exhaling slowly. The show was running itself now—her mouth moved, her mind stayed sharp, but the rest of her was exhausted. The past few days had been a whirlwind of police stations, legal meetings, industry gossip, and enough stress to kill a lesser person.

And yet, she was still here.

Jamie gave her a knowing look through the glass. "You alright, mate?" he asked, his tone uncharacteristically serious.

Nelly's smirk faltered for a brief second before she waved a dismissive hand. "I'm fine. Thriving, even."

Jamie wasn't convinced. "You know, there's a difference between playing up the chaos and actually living in it."

"Yeah, well, chaos pays the bills," Nelly quipped, eyes flicking back to the monitor. "And right now, I'm making Manic a *lot* of money."

Jamie sighed. "Just… don't push it too far."

****

"And now at number 12, me gusta que me llame señorita," Nelly said, as she looked at the clock and knew that, at 6:02pm, she had 12 tracks plus yet another interview with Ed Sheeran, who was number 1 for the sixth consecutive week with his Stormzy collaboration to pre-record for the penultimate minutes of the show. It wasn't as if she hated Ed Sheeran on a personal level, but she hated his and Dua Lipa's monopoly on the top of the charts. It was predictable, it was boring, and it was exactly the kind of thing that made radio execs foam at the mouth while the rest of the country sighed in exasperation.

"Right, Señorita is still hanging around at number 12, which means, yes, we're legally obligated to mention how much TikTok ruined this track for anyone with ears. Also, if you've made it this far into the show without complaining to Ofcom, congratulations—you might actually have a sense of humour. Now, Producer Jamie has reminded me that I need to legally apologise for calling, earlier in the show, those who don't know how the UK40Chart works mentally retarded," Nelly continued, her tone entirely insincere. "So, if you were offended by that, I deeply, truly, with all my heart… couldn't give a toss." She paused for a beat, letting the silence stretch just long enough for Jamie to groan in despair through the talkback. "Nah, I'm kidding. Sort of. In all seriousness, we at Manic strive for inclusivity, and if I upset you, then… I'll try to do better. And by 'try,' I mean I'll last about 15 minutes before I say something else that gets people frothing at the mouth."

As the Shawn Mendes and Camila Cabello collab started playing, Nelly looked on the Twitter feed and noticed that she was now trending worldwide with #Vixen surpassing 50,000 mentions, with reactions split between outrage, amusement, and outright disbelief that she was still on air.

Some of the tweets rolling in were predictable.

"Ofcom must be asleep at the wheel. HOW is Nelly Vixen still on air??"

"Manic Radio are literally just daring the regulator to take them down at this point."

"If she gets fired, I give it three months before LBC offers her a late-night slot."

"This is why the Manic UK40Chart is the only chart that actually matters. Chaotic. Unhinged. Perfect."

Others, however, were starting to get a bit more pointed.

"Can't believe a grown woman who calls herself 'Dr' thinks it's funny to throw around outdated slurs on air. Pathetic."

"Disgusting. Absolutely disgusting. If Manic had any decency, they'd pull her off air mid-show."

"You lot laughing at her don't realise how damaging this is. Someone needs to stop her before she goes full Katie Hopkins."

Nelly rolled her eyes, flicking the screen off. She wasn't stupid—she knew exactly what she was doing. She was walking a fine line between controversy and outright cancellation, but that was where she thrived.

Looking at her emails, she saw one from Dr Bennett which, in a nutshell, was less of a warning and more of a passive acceptance of what was unfolding.

From: *Scott.Bennett@manicradio.group*

To: *Nelly.Vixen@Speke.manicradio.group*

Subject: *Just Keep It Mostly Legal*

Vixen—

I assume you've seen the Twitter numbers. If you haven't, they're currently through the roof, which means our advertisers are happy, our listeners are glued to their radios, and Global's execs are probably screaming into their overpriced flat whites.

However, try not to actively bait Ofcom. I'm already getting calls. We both know they'll fine us—it's just a matter of how much and whether they want to make an example of you. So, do what you do best, but for the love of God, don't say anything that'll have me giving evidence at a tribunal next month.

By the way, if you can get Ed Sheeran to say something scandalous in his interview, that'd be great for next week's press cycle. I hear Stormzy's already teetering on saying something reckless—poke him if you get the chance.

Scott

Nelly snorted, forwarding the email to Jamie with a single-word subject line: *LMAO.*

Jamie, watching from the producer's booth, glanced down at his screen, read the email, and mouthed "of course" before shaking his head.

Nelly knew that she had 5 minutes, as PlayoutONE had already got the sweeper for the next track, it being another new entry as Post Malone's Circles had sneaked into the chart at number 11, and that Jamie was setting up the call to Ed Sheeran for her to pre-record and get the legally required interview in before the number one track aired.

Jamie's voice crackled through the talkback. "Right, Sheeran's on standby. Try not to make him regret this, yeah?"

Nelly smirked, stretching her fingers as if preparing for battle. "No promises."

Jamie rolled his eyes, pressing the button to patch Ed Sheeran through to the studio line. There was a slight crackle before the unmistakable, affable voice of the UK's biggest singer-songwriter filled her headphones.

"Hello? Nelly? Can you hear me?"

Nelly leaned into the mic, her tone dripping with mock awe. "Oh, my God, it's Ron Weasley. Tell me, Ron, how's your mother reacting to you being on Muggle radio?"

Sheeran laughed, clearly used to being compared to a Weasley at this point in his career. "Well, considering I'm still on every radio playlist in the country, I think she's coping just fine."

Nelly smirked, leaning back in her chair. "Yeah, mate, I think that's called world domination. You've been at number one for, what, six weeks now? I swear, you and Dua Lipa are like the Sith Lords of the UK charts. What's the plan—just alternate chart domination until the end of time?"

"Listen," Ed said, his voice full of mock sincerity, "I don't make the rules. People just keep streaming the songs, and I just keep turning up."

Jamie, still hovering in the producer's booth, gave Nelly a warning glance. Keep it light. Keep it clean. She ignored him.

"Alright, Ed, let's get to the real question," she said, lowering her voice conspiratorially. "What's the actual secret to writing a number-one single? Do you have a specific algorithm? Is there a hidden formula in the depths of your little ginger brain?"

Ed chuckled. "Honestly? Three chords, a vaguely emotional hook, and a lyric that sounds deep but is just vague enough for everyone to relate to."

Nelly cackled. "Oh, so it is a formula. Knew it! And here I was, thinking you were just some kind of songwriting wizard."

"Well, I do have a maths GCSE," Ed quipped. "That's basically the same thing."

Jamie made a subtle "wrap it up" gesture from the booth. They had about two minutes before the next link, and Scott Bennett's email still lingered in the back of Nelly's mind. She wanted something—anything—that would get Ed to say something headline-worthy.

Time to poke the bear.

"Alright, Ed, before I let you go, one last thing," she said, a mischievous edge creeping into her voice. "You've collaborated with everyone from Stormzy to Justin Bieber. But be honest—who's the biggest diva you've ever worked with? And don't give me a diplomatic answer, Sheeran, I want tea."

There was a pause. A pause just long enough for Jamie to visibly stiffen in the booth.

Ed hesitated, then exhaled a laugh. "Oh, man. You're setting me up to get in trouble."

"That's the whole point," Nelly said sweetly. "Come on. Who made you roll your eyes in the studio? Who needed their water at exactly 17 degrees or threw a strop over the wrong brand of biscuits?"

Ed sighed dramatically. "Okay, okay. I'll give you a little one. Years ago, I worked with this pop star—won't name names—but they wouldn't record until their dressing room had exactly seven scented candles. No more, no less."

Nelly practically purred. "Oooh, now we're talking. That is some prime diva behaviour. What was the candle scent, though? That's the real detail I need."

Ed laughed. "I think it was… vanilla and something? Honestly, I was too busy trying not to laugh."

"That narrows it down to about a hundred pop stars," Nelly mused. "But don't worry, we'll figure it out. Right, I'll let you go before your PR team throws their phones into the Thames. Ed Sheeran, congratulations on yet another week at number one. I'll try not to resent you too much."

"You say that every time, but I don't believe you," Ed quipped.

"Yeah, yeah. Enjoy your reign, King Edward," Nelly drawled. "I'll see you next month when you inevitably refuse to drop out of the top five."

The call ended just as Post Malone's Circles faded out. Jamie's voice buzzed in through the talkback instantly.

"That was reckless."

Nelly smirked. "Oh, come on. I barely even poked him."

Jamie rubbed his temples. "You just baited Ed Sheeran into talking about a celebrity with candle-related OCD. If that clip makes headlines tomorrow, his label is going to hate us."

"But they'll still send us his next single," Nelly pointed out, cueing up the next track. "They always do."

Jamie sighed in defeat. "You're a nightmare."

Nelly grinned. "I am the charts, Jamie. This is what the people want."

Jamie muttered something under his breath that sounded suspiciously like "you're an absolute menace," but before she could respond, the next track was already rolling. She glanced at the clock. 6:09pm. Almost there.

The adrenaline was still running high in her veins, and she knew that once she was off-air, it would come crashing down in a tidal wave of exhaustion, reality, and probably a stiff drink. But for now? For now, she was on top of the world.

Even if, deep down, she knew it was only a matter of time before she came crashing down with it.

****

CHAPTER 6 – The Pepsi Paradox
Friday 20th September 2019

It had been nearly a week since her last UK40Chart, and Dr Nelly Vixen knew it was only a matter of time before the media did what they did best—turned her into either a fallen icon or public enemy number one.

She had barely opened her eyes when her phone began vibrating violently against the nightstand. It wasn't an alarm—no, that had been silenced hours ago, somewhere between the fourth and fifth gin-and-tonic. This was something else.

Groaning, she reached out blindly, grabbing the phone and squinting against the brightness of the screen.

24 missed calls.

17 from Jamie.

6 from Kyler.

1 from a number she didn't recognise.

And then she saw it. The notification that made her sit bolt upright, hangover be damned.

A headline from the Daily Mail.

"SHOCK JOCK SHAME – OFCOM PROBES DR NELLY VIXEN AFTER RADIO RANT"

She tapped the link with a sinking feeling, the loading wheel spinning just long enough to send her heart into her throat. And then, there it was.

A full-page spread, her face splashed across the article like some kind of disgraced reality TV contestant.

"SHOCK JOCK SHAME – OFCOM PROBES DR NELLY VIXEN AFTER RADIO RANT

By Saddam Bashir, Media Editor for Mail Online"

Nelly had to chuckle, as she knew the reporter in question, as he had been a fellow University student who had done the same PhD as her, a PhD in Film and Media, and she knew that he had wanted to get into film, and was a producer for some ITV dramas as well as an occasional journalist for the Mail.

"Foul-mouthed radio host Dr Nelly Vixen, whose real name is Dr Eleanor Robinson, has sparked nationwide outrage following a series of offensive remarks made during her Sunday chart show on Manic Radio. OFCOM has confirmed an investigation into her conduct after receiving over 3,000 complaints, making it one of the most controversial broadcasts of the year.

The controversial Manic Radio host stated that "if you don't know the rules because you live on a rock or are mentally retarded,"

The comment, made live on air during her UK40Chart programme last Sunday, has ignited widespread backlash, with disability rights groups calling for immediate disciplinary action.

OFCOM has since launched a formal investigation into whether Manic Radio breached its broadcasting guidelines, citing concerns over the use of discriminatory language and repeated breaches of impartiality.

Dr Vixen, 30, is no stranger to controversy, having built a reputation as radio's most unpredictable voice. But critics argue that this latest incident goes beyond her usual brand of 'shock jock' bravado.

Calls for her removal have intensified, with high-profile figures weighing in. Speaking to The Mail, disability campaigner Francesca Willoughby said: "It's appalling that in 2019, a national broadcaster is allowing language like this to be aired without immediate consequences. This is not just an 'edgy' comment—it's offensive, outdated, and harmful. If Manic doesn't take action, OFCOM must."

Dr Vixen's comments have sparked a major backlash on social media, with thousands calling for her immediate sacking. The Manic Radio presenter, known for her brash on-air style, has a history of pushing boundaries, but critics argue this time she has gone too far.

Former BBC broadcaster Simon Mayo tweeted: 'There's a difference between being edgy and being outright offensive. This is unacceptable.'

Meanwhile, TalkRadio's Julia Hartley-Brewer defended the presenter, calling the controversy 'a classic case of people looking for something to be outraged by.'

Among those demanding action is Global Media's Deputy Head of Legal, James Jenkins, who in 2018 fought against Manic on behalf of Samantha Greene, a Manic Radio host who had been at the centre of a gender pay dispute that rocked the commercial radio industry. Jenkins, who now oversees compliance for Global, stated that "Manic Radio has a long history of disregarding broadcasting standards, but this is a new low. The industry has a responsibility to ensure that presenters with a platform of this scale do not abuse it. OFCOM needs to take decisive action. If this was a Global or Bauer presenter, they would have been off-air by Monday."

Mr Jenkins, 35, of Surrey, a leading figure in the broadcasting legal sector, has called on advertisers to pull their funding from Manic Radio until disciplinary action is taken.

"Major brands need to consider whether they want their advertising money supporting a station that repeatedly flouts OFCOM regulations and employs presenters who show blatant disregard for professional standards," he added.

Despite mounting pressure, Manic Radio has remained silent on the matter. Dr Scott Bennett, CEO of Manic Radio Group, declined to comment when approached by The Mail. However, sources inside the station suggest that management is divided on whether to back Dr Vixen or cut ties to avoid further scrutiny.

A statement from Manic Radio's official social media channels, posted late Thursday night, read: "Manic Radio acknowledges the complaints made regarding last Sunday's UK40Chart broadcast and is cooperating fully with OFCOM's review. We remain committed to delivering bold, engaging content while upholding our responsibilities as a broadcaster."

However, insiders say Dr Vixen has so far refused to issue a personal apology.

One source close to the station told The Mail: "This isn't just a rogue presenter running her mouth. This is Manic Radio's entire brand—they thrive on controversy. The only reason she's still on air is because their ratings are through the roof. But if advertisers start pulling out, that's when we'll see how much loyalty they really have to her."

Industry experts say the scandal could have wider repercussions for commercial radio.

Former Capital FM boss Richard Park commented: "This is exactly the kind of reckless behaviour that makes advertisers nervous about investing in radio. If OFCOM comes down hard on Manic, it won't just be them that feels the heat—it'll be the whole industry."

Despite the backlash, Dr Vixen still has a loyal fanbase defending her online. Hashtags like #IStandWithVixen and #ManicMadness are trending on Twitter, with supporters arguing that radio should be allowed to push boundaries.

One tweet, liked over 5,000 times, reads: "Nelly Vixen is the only reason I even listen to the charts. Radio is meant to be entertaining, not boring. Get a grip."

Others, however, are less forgiving.

A counter-hashtag, #SackVixen, is also gaining traction, with thousands demanding her immediate removal.

With pressure mounting from all sides, the question remains: will Manic Radio stand by its most notorious presenter, or will Dr Nelly Vixen finally face the consequences of her words?"

Nelly had to chuckle at how James bloody Jenkins waded in like an uninvited guest at a wedding, making it all about him. Typical Global legal brass—acting like Manic was a rogue pirate station broadcasting from an illegal transmitter in the North Sea rather than a multimillion-pound network with backing from Russian oligarchs and a CEO who thrived on media outrage.

Still, she had to admit, the scale of the backlash was impressive. Over 3,000 complaints to OFCOM? That was practically record-breaking. Only Jeremy Vine had managed to piss off that many people in a single broadcast, and he was usually discussing the ethics of leaving a shopping trolley in the middle of a car park.

She scrolled through Twitter, the chaos unfolding in real time.

"I don't even listen to the charts, but if Nelly Vixen gets sacked, I'm boycotting Manic. We need more unfiltered radio, not less! #IStandWithVixen"

"The fact that this woman is still on air is a disgrace. Manic Radio needs to act NOW. #SackVixen"

"Ofcom, we're waiting. Do your job. This is unacceptable."

"Nelly Vixen's entire career is just one long attempt to see how many fines Manic Radio can pay before they go bankrupt."

"I swear to God, if Capital try to poach her, I will set my own radio on fire."

She exhaled, running a hand through her tangled hair. Well, this was a mess, even by Manic's standards.

Her phone buzzed again. This time, it was a message from Jamie.

Jamie Wise: *You up? Don't pretend you're asleep. Have you seen the Mail? Boss is putting a statement out saying 'IDGAF what Global thinks' and is refusing to suspend you. Call me before Kyler does something stupid."*

Nelly groaned, tossing her phone onto the bed before rubbing her temples. She needed caffeine. She needed paracetamol. She needed someone to explain to her why Scott Bennett thought goading Global and OFCOM simultaneously was a good idea.

She hauled herself out of bed, pulling on an oversized hoodie and stumbling towards the kitchen. She'd barely switched on the kettle before her phone buzzed again. This time, it was Kyler.

Kyler Thompson: *"Mate, Bennett's just posted a statement. You're gonna love this. Call me when you're done laughing."*

Nelly frowned, grabbing her phone and opening Twitter.

Right at the top, in bold, defiant caps, was the official statement from Manic Radio Group.

"Manic Radio is aware of the ongoing media speculation surrounding Dr Nelly Vixen. Let's be clear: we are not here to make Global or Bauer executives comfortable. We are here to entertain and engage our audience. OFCOM has a process, and we will cooperate fully, as we always do. Until then, Dr Vixen remains on air, because we don't let the Daily Mail tell us how to run a radio station. See you on Nelly's new show, the NEW Official Pepsi Chart, every Sunday at 4pm. #ManicMadness"

Nelly had to do a double take at the new name of her show.

The Pepsi Chart?

The last time Pepsi had sponsored a chart show in the UK, it was the early 2000s, and Dr Fox was still on air. Pepsi? Corporate, polished, mainstream as hell. It was the antithesis of everything Manic stood for.

The fact Gazprom had also joined the sponsorship lineup made it even more surreal. The Russian energy giant backing a chart show? It was like pairing a McDonald's Happy Meal with a bottle of Grey Goose.

The irony that the owner of Manic was linked as a shareholder in the Russian state energy company made the whole thing even more ridiculous. It wasn't just that Manic Radio thrived on controversy—they monetised it. While Global and Bauer were busy trying to polish their brands and appeal to advertisers who wanted 'safe' content, Manic had doubled down and sold her scandal to the highest bidder.

Nelly took a slow sip of her coffee, staring at the tweet in a mixture of awe and disbelief when her phone rang.

Nate.

Her husband.

The number, however, was from a US sim card that he kept for his constant trips to the States. She hesitated for a moment before answering, knowing full well this conversation was going to be a headache she didn't need before noon.

"Nate," she said, voice still hoarse from sleep.

"Jesus Christ, Nell," came the exasperated voice of Dr Nathaniel Robinson, esteemed plastic surgeon, currently calling from some overpriced Miami hotel where he was likely sipping espresso while networking with B-list celebrities and reality stars. "I wake up to find my wife is the centre of a full-scale media scandal, trending worldwide, and somehow, you still manage to one-up yourself?"

Nelly exhaled, rubbing her temple. "Oh, come on, it's hardly my fault the Mail decided to do a full-blown hit piece. Bit dramatic, don't you think?"

"I dunno, love," Nate said, his voice dripping with sarcasm. "They've only called you a 'shock jock disgrace', got OFCOM sniffing around, and now you've got bloody Gazprom and Pepsi sponsoring your show like it's Eurovision meets a Russian oil crisis. But no, nothing dramatic about that at all."

Nelly chuckled, taking another sip of her coffee. "Babe, the network's doubling down. I'm not getting sacked. I'm getting a pay rise. I'd say that's a win."

"You seriously think this is a good thing?" Nate snapped. "Do you know how many bloody WhatsApp messages I've had from colleagues over here? People I work with are asking if I've seen the headlines. One of them actually asked me if I was embarrassed to be married to you."

Nelly bristled, her easy smirk slipping slightly. "Oh, well, forgive me for damaging your pristine reputation, Dr Robinson," she shot back. "Didn't realise my career choices were inconveniencing your Botox consultations."

There was silence on the line. Then, a slow inhale from Nate. "Jesus, Nell," he muttered. "I'm not asking you to be a saint. But could you just... for once, not turn everything into a PR disaster?"

She rolled her eyes. "You married me, mate. If you wanted a wife who played it safe, you should've gone for one of your influencer clients."

Another sigh. "Look, I have to go, but just... be careful, alright? Bennett might back you now, but if advertisers start walking? You will be the one they throw under the bus."

Nelly huffed. "Noted."

She ended the call before he could say anything else, tossing her phone onto the kitchen counter. Typical Nate—acting like her entire career was some ticking time bomb. But then again, was it?

The Mail article had put more pressure on Manic than even she had expected. She knew the station was used to handling scandals, but there was a difference between a few OFCOM fines and a full-scale advertiser revolt. If brands started pulling their money, she'd go from radio's golden controversy queen to an expendable liability.

It was then that she realised that there was the sound of aircraft on the line when she and Nate had spoken. That wasn't just a hotel lobby. He was at an airport.

Her stomach twisted. Nate wasn't just calling from Miami—he was leaving.

And then she remembered, his conference ended a few hours ago, and his flight, first class of course, would have already been booked in advance. He was on his way back to the UK.

Nelly swore under her breath.

Nate wasn't one for dramatic gestures. He was the type to let things simmer, to bite his tongue and roll his eyes, but if he was flying home early, it meant one thing—he was coming back to deal with her.

She took another sip of her coffee, trying to push the thought aside. There were more immediate problems at hand. Like the fact that she was about to be the host of The Pepsi Chart, a name that hadn't been relevant since the early 2000s, and now had the financial backing of both an American soft drink empire and a Russian energy conglomerate.

If nothing else, she had to respect the sheer audacity of it.

Her phone buzzed again. Jamie.

She groaned, knowing she had to answer this one.

"Alright, alright, I'm up, stop harassing me," she answered, voice still hoarse from sleep.

Jamie, ever the long-suffering producer, wasted no time. "Have you seen the boss's statement?"

"Yeah. 'We don't let the Daily Mail tell us how to run a radio station,'" she repeated, smirking. "Honestly, that's going on a t-shirt."

Jamie exhaled sharply. "You realise what this means, right? They're making you the face of the UK's biggest chart show. They're doubling down. This isn't just keeping you on air. They're locking you in. You're the brand."

Nelly paused. She hadn't actually thought of it like that.

Manic wasn't just defending her—they were staking the station's identity on her. And if that was the case, they weren't going to drop her, not unless they absolutely had to.

She let out a low whistle. "Bloody hell."

"Yeah. Bloody hell." Jamie sighed. "But it also means you've got to rein it in a bit, at least for the next few weeks. The last thing we need is another OFCOM investigation before the first episode of The Pepsi Chart even airs."

Nelly rolled her eyes. "Come on, Jamie. You really think I'm capable of reining it in?"

"No," he admitted flatly. "Which is why I'm dreading the next three months."

She laughed, but deep down, she knew he wasn't wrong. Manic was betting everything on her, and while that gave her security, it also meant something else—she had nowhere to hide. If the advertisers stayed, she'd be untouchable. But if they bailed?

She was done.

"You alright?" Jamie asked, his tone softer now.

Nelly hesitated, running a hand through her hair. "Yeah. I'm fine."

It was a lie, but it was an easy one to tell.

"Good," Jamie said. "Because you've got a live show in two days, and I'd really rather not have to deal with another crisis before then."

Nelly smirked. "Come on, Jamie, where's the fun in that?"

He groaned. "Just… don't get us all fired before Sunday, yeah?"

"No promises."

She hung up before he could argue and took another sip of her coffee, staring out of the window. The city outside was waking up, but she felt like she was still stuck in a weird limbo, teetering between triumph and disaster.

The Pepsi Chart.

Manic was making her the face of their most mainstream product yet, tying her name to two corporate giants who probably didn't even know what they'd just signed up for.

Nelly smirked, tossing her phone onto the kitchen counter as the reality of the situation sank in. She had just been handed the biggest platform of her career, but it came with a leash—one made of corporate sponsorships, OFCOM investigations, and the looming shadow of industry pressure.

Her hangover was still clawing at the edges of her skull, but there was no time to dwell on that now. She had to get ahead of the narrative before it consumed her.

The first thing she did was open Twitter.

#Vixen was still trending, sitting comfortably in the UK's top three topics, just behind #BrexitShambles and #RugbyWorldCup. That was a small victory in itself—she had outlasted a Tory scandal, which, considering their frequency, was no small feat.

She scrolled through the tweets, skimming past the outrage and the praise, looking for something she could use. The ones defending her were predictable—"radio needs personalities, not robots"—but the attacks were more interesting.

"Dr Vixen is the Katie Hopkins of radio. It's embarrassing that she still has a platform."

"The fact Manic hasn't sacked her proves they have no moral compass. Imagine if this was a BBC presenter."

"This woman is a walking disaster. Hope she enjoys the Daily Mail ending her career."

Nelly smirked. The Mail? Ending her career? She had survived student radio, a plagiarism scandal which caused her to get sacked from Breeze Media, and of course the immediate signing by Manic. The Daily Mail was nothing.

Still, there was no denying the scale of the backlash. If this had been any other station—Bauer, Global, hell, even the BBC—she would have been pulled off-air by Monday morning. But Manic wasn't any other station. Manic was playing a different game entirely.

And now, she was their star player.

And she was going to enjoy it.

****

CHAPTER 7 – Industry Games Over Wine & War

Saturday 21st September 2019

Nelly swirled the wine in her glass, leaning back against the booth in the restaurant she and her husband, Dr Nate Robinson, a Cheshire born plastic surgeon who she had met when her sister, Carla, had wanted to get a nose job and he had come highly recommended by a friend. They had hit it off immediately—Nate had found her irreverence refreshing, while Nelly had appreciated his calm, measured approach to life. He wasn't in media, which was a blessing; he didn't care about radio politics, or who was feuding with whom in the industry. His life was about scalpel work and aesthetics, not OFCOM complaints and station mergers. It made their relationship blissfully devoid of the nonsense that usually defined her professional life.

It was half past 3, and the couple were sat in one of those sleek, overpriced bistros in Manchester's Spinningfields—the kind that catered to footballers, minor celebrities, and media types looking to be seen. The kind of place where a bottle of wine cost more than a week's groceries, and yet here she was, idly sipping at a glass of Sancerre.

"Nelly, babes, how are ya?"

Nelly groaned as she saw Lisa Devonport, a media manager at Communicorp UK, who were based at the nearby XYZ Building, a media powerhouse that controlled a handful of regional stations across the UK.

Lisa was the kind of person who thrived on industry gossip, always armed with the latest rumours, half-truths, and barely veiled digs about her competitors. She was also, unfortunately, someone Nelly couldn't completely avoid—Communicorp still had ties with Global, as it was, in Nelly's mind, Global's pet franchisee, having been forced by the Competition and Markets Authority to operate Capital and Heart under licence rather than outright ownership.

Unlike Manic and Bauer, who were the second and third biggest commercial radio groups in the UK, Communicorp was a curious entity—technically independent, but inextricably linked to Global's branding and operations. It meant that people like Lisa Devonport operated in a strange limbo, both part of the industry's biggest player and yet forever outside the decision-making powerhouses in Leicester Square.

Nelly didn't particularly like Lisa, but she tolerated her. Mostly because Lisa was useful. And because Lisa's presence meant she wouldn't be the one paying for the next bottle of wine.

And Lisa was married to a Hits Radio Programme Director, which meant that the incestuous ties within the British radio industry were as tangled as ever. If there was gossip worth knowing, Lisa would have it.

"Lisa," Nelly drawled, placing her glass down with a deliberate slowness. "Didn't expect to see you here. Thought you'd be in your bunker, prepping for Global's eventual world domination."

Lisa smirked, sliding into the booth uninvited. Nate, ever the diplomat, gave her a polite nod before returning his attention to his steak, wisely staying out of the inevitable media bickering that was about to unfold.

"You know me, babe," Lisa said, flagging down a waiter and ordering a gin and tonic without missing a beat. "Always got my ear to the ground.

"It's no wonder you don't get hit by a car," Nelly muttered so quietly that Lisa couldn't hear. Instead, Lisa was already launching into her usual routine—smirking like she knew something no one else did, her tone dripping with the kind of glee that only someone who thrived on professional chaos could manage.

Nelly knew that Lisa's husband was a Bauer employee, a Hits Radio Programme Director, which meant that the incestuous ties within the British radio industry were as tangled as ever. If there was gossip worth knowing, Lisa would have it.

Lisa leaned in, fingers curling around the stem of her newly arrived G&T like she was about to deliver a sermon. "So, babes," she began, her tone deliberately casual but laced with anticipation, "tell me, how does it feel knowing half the industry wants your head on a pike while the other half wants to sleep with you?"

Nelly smirked, leaning back against the booth with the languid confidence of someone who had been fending off industry vultures for years. "Oh, Lisa," she drawled, "you make it sound like that's a new development. The moment I stopped sounding like a safe, sanitised BBC presenter, people either wanted to fuck me or fire me. Nothing's changed."

Lisa let out a delighted laugh, sipping her drink. "Oh, but it has changed, darling. This time, the heat's coming from all sides. Even Global's bigwigs are apparently sweating over your 'influence.'" She placed a theatrical emphasis on the last word, like it was something dirty.

Nelly snorted. "Oh, please. Global pretending to have standards is the funniest thing I've heard all week. They'd have me on Capital in a heartbeat if they thought I'd bring in the RAJARs."

Lisa tilted her head in consideration. "Mmm... not so sure about that, love. Jenkins would rather gnaw his own arm off than let you step foot in Leicester Square. There again he's been shuttling between Leicester Square, here and Leeds. My bosses at Communicorp are fed up of the Global lot keep making unannounced visits to do 'compliance' or 'brand assessments'. There's rumours that Jenkins is making our contracts that tight, not even a nun's pussy would be as sealed shut. You know he personally gave that Greene kid a job at Communicorp?"

Nelly raised an eyebrow, taking a slow sip of her wine as she processed that last bit of information. Samantha Greene? The ex-Wool City Echo presenter who had exposed Manic's pay gap scandal and subsequently found herself blacklisted from half the industry?

Lisa smirked at her expression. "Oh yeah, babe. Greene's now at Communicorp's Leeds hub, doing Drive for Heart. Apparently, she's ATK's golden girl now. Jenkins made sure of it. It's like Global's little pat on the head for being a very well-behaved whistleblower."

Nelly let out a low whistle, tapping her nails against the table in thought. "So, let me get this straight," she said, stretching out her words as she processed the latest bit of radio industry chaos. "Samantha Greene—the same woman who went nuclear on Manic, who got blacklisted, who had to fight tooth and nail just to be taken seriously again—has now been tucked neatly under Global's wing via their pet franchise? And Jenkins is personally making sure she stays locked down?"

Lisa nodded, taking a slow sip of her gin and tonic, eyes gleaming with the satisfaction of delivering a particularly juicy piece of gossip. "Exactly. Her boyfriend, that Jake Harris bloke, is her co-host on Heart. They're getting paid more than half the veterans because, according to my boss, they were Global Academy products before they joined Manic, and Jenkins sees them as a way to 'reclaim' talent Global lost to Manic. It's all about optics, babe. They get to parade them around as proof that Global 'nurtures talent' while making sure they never step out of line again. Trust me, there's no way Greene's pulling another exposé while she's cashing those Leicester Square-approved pay cheques."

Nelly smirked, swirling her wine lazily in its glass. "Christ. That's a proper leash, isn't it? So, they go from exposing Manic's bullshit to becoming Global's obedient little show ponies? I almost feel bad for them. Almost."

"Oh, you want to know the best bit... you know his wife is HR Lead at Bauer Audio UK, right?" Lisa leaned in conspiratorially, lowering her voice just enough to make it clear this was the bit of gossip she had been saving.

Nelly raised an eyebrow, intrigued. "Carly Jenkins?" she asked, swirling her wine. "The same Carly Jenkins who helped that kid take Manic to court?"

Lisa gave her an exaggerated wink. "Got it in one, babes. Yvonne Bauer doesn't make power moves without a plan. And if she's promoting Carly to HR lead for all of Bauer Audio UK, that means they're getting ready to pounce on Manic's mess. They're watching you, Vixen. Waiting for the house of cards to come tumbling down."

Nelly exhaled slowly, rolling her head back against the plush booth. "Jesus. It's like the bloody Cold War, except instead of nuclear warheads, we're throwing OFCOM fines and talent poaching at each other."

Lisa cackled. "Exactly! And you, my dear, are the Cuban Missile Crisis."

Nate, who had thus far remained diplomatically detached from the radio politics swirling around him, finally cleared his throat. "And what does that make Jenkins in this scenario?" he asked dryly, cutting into his steak.

Lisa's grin widened. "Oh, he's the smug bastard sitting in Washington, waiting for the whole thing to implode. You know, according to him, Global has a god given right to have a monopoly, not Manic. In his mind, they're just correcting a mistake."

Nelly let out a low, throaty laugh, shaking her head. "God, what a sanctimonious little twat. He acts like he's protecting the moral integrity of the industry when really, he's just making sure Global's got the only deck of cards left to play."

Lisa smirked, setting her glass down. "Babe, you know how this industry works. Morality's just a branding exercise. And right now, Jenkins is making sure Global's brand stays squeaky clean while Manic sets itself on fire for the sake of 'edginess.'"

Nate sighed, finally pushing his plate aside. "Is there anyone in this business who isn't playing some ridiculous game of chess?"

Lisa and Nelly exchanged amused glances before Nelly answered. "Community radio, maybe. But even then, I bet someone's fighting over the last tin of biscuits in the station kitchen."

"Oh, and have you heard about your old boss, the Breeze CEO who got sacked when Manic and Breeze merged earlier this month?" Lisa said with a chuckle.

Nelly's interest piqued as she swirled the last of her Sancerre. "Oh, please tell me Alan Carter's found himself in some tragic, humiliating new gig."

Lisa's grin widened. "Oh, babe, it's better than that. Alan Carter is now 'Special Advisor for Commercial Radio Affairs' at OFCOM."

Nelly choked on her wine. "You are shitting me."

Nate, who had just taken a sip of his own drink, coughed slightly. "Wait, your old boss—the same one who sacked you when you had your… PhD issue… back in Worcester, the same Alan Carter who wouldn't know talent if it smacked him in the face—is now working for OFCOM?" Nate finished, setting his glass down with an incredulous expression.

Lisa nodded, her smirk practically radiating smug satisfaction. "Oh yeah. And guess who's in charge of overseeing all compliance investigations into Manic Radio?"

Nelly groaned, running a hand down her face. "You have got to be kidding me. Alan bloody Carter? The man who allowed dinosaurs like Gary fucking Holloway to play whatever he wanted as long as it wasn't an explicit track and fit Hot AC audiences like a glove? The same Alan Carter who thought that networking stations was the devil's work until he got booted out of Breeze Media and now suddenly wants to be the gatekeeper of broadcasting standards? Christ, Lisa, you couldn't write this. He makes Phil Riley look like a bloody visionary."

Lisa practically cackled into her gin and tonic, nodding in agreement. "Oh, babe, it's poetic. Carter went from moaning about 'preserving local identity' at Breeze to licking the boots of the very suits he spent years whining about. The man spent half his career pissing on Manic, and now he gets to 'regulate' you lot? You just *know* he's going to have a vendetta."

Nelly exhaled sharply, pressing her fingers against her temples. "Well, this is just bloody fantastic. Alan Carter, the beigest man in British radio, now has the power to throw the book at Manic? That man's got the spine of a

Greggs sausage roll, but I bet he's rubbing his hands together at the thought of getting me blacklisted for good."

"Well, you did call half of Britain mentally retarded on-air last week," Nate said dryly, raising an eyebrow. "Not exactly making it hard for him, are you?"

Nelly groaned, letting her head fall back against the plush booth. "Oh, give me a break. It's not like I went on some Andrew Tate-style rant. It was one comment, a slip of the tongue, and now I'm public enemy number one while half the industry pretends they've never said worse after three pints in a VIP lounge at the Radio Festival."

Lisa, still smirking, topped up her gin and tonic. "Yeah, but babe, you *know* Carter is going to make this personal. He's got a grudge the size of Birmingham and now he's got the legal means to fuck you over with a big shiny OFCOM letterhead."

Nelly drummed her nails against the table, contemplating her next move. The fact that Alan Carter, of all people, was now in a position to oversee Manic's compliance was the sort of cruel twist of fate only radio could deliver. It was no secret that he had despised everything Manic stood for—he was a dinosaur, clinging to the 'good old days' of local, advertiser-friendly radio, the kind where presenters read out obituaries and local news bulletins about lost cats. The sort of bloke who thought networking was the death of the industry, right up until he got sacked and decided regulation was his new calling.

And now? Now he had the power to hammer Manic with fines, to push OFCOM to finally throw the book at them, to make sure *she* was the cautionary tale every other presenter was told when they got a bit too bold with the mic.

Nate, sensing the wheels turning in her mind, sighed. "Nell, whatever you're planning, don't. Just ride it out, keep your head down for a few weeks, and let this blow over."

Lisa snorted into her drink. "Oh, love. You *know* she's not going to do that."

Nelly smirked, swirling her wine again. "Of course not. Where's the fun in that?"

Lisa cackled. "That's what I love about you, Vixen. You've got the survival instincts of a cockroach in a nuclear bunker."

Nelly tilted her glass in mock-toast. "Cheers, babe. Anyway, where's that husband of yours?"

"He's probably giving Paul Keenan a blowjob and polishing Bauer's RAJAR spreadsheets," Lisa finished with a wicked grin, taking a slow sip of her G&T. "You know he's scrapping the penultimate local show on Free Radio this week. Andy Goulding's getting shipped to the new brand that's replacing Free Radio '80s, that Greatest Hits Radio. Only JD, Roisin McCourt and Dan Morrisey are staying at Free and Drive is getting done from Monday from here."

Nelly let out a low whistle, shaking her head as she absorbed Lisa's latest bombshell. "Jesus Christ. So, Bauer's finally gutting Free Radio, then? That was inevitable. They've been holding on by their fingernails for years."

Lisa nodded, stirring the ice in her G&T. "Oh, babes, you'll love this even more... they're scrapping the shows being named as the presenters shows, and having it as Hits At Breakfast, keeping it with JD and Roisin doing Coventry and Hereford plus Worcester, and Dan just doing the Black Country and Brum. The plan, according to my dear hubby, is to go pan-regional in the next couple of years."

Nelly let out a low, throaty laugh, shaking her head. "Oh, Lisa, your husband must love being a corporate hatchet man. First, they gut Free Radio, now they're pretending 'pan-regional' is some revolutionary concept rather than 'we can't be arsed keeping it local anymore.'"

Lisa smirked. "Oh, babes, you know how it is—whenever Bauer pulls the plug on something, they dress it up like they're innovating rather than just slashing costs." She took a leisurely sip of her G&T before continuing, her tone dripping with amusement. "Oh, and my lovely shag bunny told me this in confidence, but the CMA is going to drag the ratification of Bauer's purchase of the Wireless network out a bit, but secretly they're giving the nod to it as they don't see it as a 'substantial lessening of competition.'"

Nelly practically cackled into her wine glass. "Oh, that's rich! So, let me get this straight—Bauer gets to swallow up Wireless, gut Free Radio, and basically create one giant beige blob of 'Greatest Hits' and 'Hits Radio' across half the UK, and the CMA's just nodding along like it's fine?"

Lisa gave her a knowing look. "Of course they are, babes. The CMA only cares if Global tries to do it. If Bauer does it, it's just 'market efficiency.' Of course, guess who at Global is threatening to take the CMA to court?"

Nelly grinned, already knowing the answer. "James bloody Jenkins."

Lisa clinked her glass against Nelly's in mock celebration. "Ding, ding, ding. Give the girl a prize! Jenkins is fuming. Apparently, he's been running around Leicester Square all week, ranting about how the CMA is 'institutionally biased' against Global and how Bauer is 'getting away with murder' while Manic 'runs a pirate operation'. Also, Farage is getting a new TV show. Some Yank channel which Trump is highly in talks with about some kind of post-election media empire."

Nelly groaned, rubbing her temple as she downed the last of her wine. "Jesus Christ. Global's throwing a fit, Bauer's gutting Free Radio, OFCOM's now got my ex-boss on a vendetta mission, and Farage is about to be unleashed on American TV? This is like a fever dream."

Lisa cackled. "Welcome to British media, babes. It's all just one big, incestuous, messy disaster."

Nate, ever the outsider in these conversations, exhaled slowly and signalled for the bill. "And yet you lot choose to work in it."

Nelly smirked, leaning back in her chair as the waiter placed the receipt on the table. "Oh, Nate, where's the fun in a normal career?" She shot Lisa a knowing glance. "Besides, if I was worried about OFCOM investigations, boardroom backstabbing, and corporate radio pissing contests, I'd have stayed in academia."

Lisa snorted. "Babe, you'd have been banned from university campuses within a month."

"Exactly," Nelly said with a wicked grin. "And at least in radio, when they try to get rid of me, they have to pay me to leave."

Lisa clinked her glass against Nelly's. "To that, my dear, I'll drink."

As the three of them rose from the table, Nelly checked her phone one last time. A notification flashed up from Twitter.

#Vixen – Still trending.

She smirked. Whatever the industry was planning next, whatever OFCOM and Alan Carter thought they could throw at her—she was still here. Still on air. Still making headlines.

And, as long as she kept them talking, she was winning.

****

CHAPTER 8 – Powered by Pop, Politics, and Pure Chaos
Sunday 22nd September 2019

Nelly Vixen had survived another week.

The scandal was still raging, the tabloids were still circling, and Twitter was still eating itself alive over whether she was the worst thing to happen to British radio since Chris Moyles' ego or the last true personality on the airwaves. But crucially, she was still on air.

It was an hour until her show started, and she had been asked by the PR team to create some new promo links for the final half hour across the network for the newly branded Pepsi Chart. A rebrand that still made her want to laugh.

The fact that Gazprom was also a sponsor, and had equal billing to Pepsi, despite being sanctioned by both the US and UK Governments, was the kind of craziness and absurdity that only Manic Radio could pull off.

Then there was the script, which was as bipolar as a goldfish with short-term memory loss. Half of it was corporate-friendly, polished nonsense that sounded like it had been lifted from a mid-2000s MTV Europe promo to satisfy the suits at Pepsi, and the other half, which played at the madness that was a Russian energy giant that was sanctioned by the British government co-sponsoring a pop chart in 2019.

Nelly skimmed through the lines on the script in front of her, her manicured nails tapping against the paper as she muttered them under her breath.

"The Pepsi Chart, fuelled by the freshest hits, and brought to you by the taste of a new generation! Powered by Gazprom, the Kremlin's finest purveyor of gas and sanctions."

The fact that the latter half was a direct dig at the ridiculousness of their corporate sponsors made her smirk. This was what she loved about Manic—they never shied away from leaning into the chaos. Any other station would have buried the Gazprom angle under a mountain of PR spin, but Manic? Manic was actively taking the piss out of it.

She cleared her throat, leaned into the mic, and hit record.

"You're listening to the Manic Radio Network, and I'm Dr Nelly Vixen. Join me at 4 for the hottest new chart show, the Pepsi Chart—bigger, bolder, and now with even more questionable sponsorship choices! That's right, pop music and global energy politics in one unholy cocktail. The Official Pepsi Chart, proudly powered by Gazprom— because nothing says 'fresh hits' like Russian gas and soft drinks."

The irony that she was literally reading the script verbatim, and not deviating from the approved copy, yet it still sounded like satire, made her smirk. The sheer absurdity of it all was exactly why she loved working at Manic. It was the only network in the UK that would knowingly take a sponsor that half the government wanted nothing to do with and then actively mock it in their own branding.

She clicked stop, replaying the audio to make sure the delivery was perfect. Crisp, dripping with just the right amount of sarcasm.

"That's good, Nell," Rex Cotton, who was covering for Jamie in the production booth as Jamie was off sick, having gotten a hangover from going clubbing in the Northern Quarter in Manchester the previous night, muttered through the talkback. "I love how PR are taking the piss out of how we have a literal Russian energy giant backing a pop chart. It's like something out of Black Mirror."

Nelly chuckled, leaning back in her chair. "Mate, it's beyond Black Mirror. This is full-on dystopian satire. I half expect the next sponsor to be North Korean Airlines."

Rex snorted. "Give it six months and we'll be launching The Kim Jong-un Breakfast Show, live from Pyongyang."

Nelly smirked, flipping through the rest of the script. "Alright, let's bang out the next one before I get too tempted to go completely rogue."

She cleared her throat again, hitting record.

"Manic Radio presents The Official Pepsi Chart, your soundtrack to Sunday. The biggest tracks, the hottest new entries, and the finest imported energy from Eastern Europe. The Pepsi Chart—refreshing, explosive, and legally questionable in at least three major jurisdictions!"

Pressing stop, Nelly chuckled as she read the next one to herself.

"You're listening to Manic's Official Pepsi Chart, Vladimir Putin's favourite export after oil and misinformation campaigns. Join me, Dr Nelly Vixen, for three Gazprom hours packed full of the latest Top 40 tracks, power plays and borscht."

Rex practically wheezed with laughter through the talkback. "Oh my God. You do realise if this gets past compliance, it'll be the most unhinged thing ever broadcast on a UK chart show?"

Nelly grinned, stretching in her chair. "Mate, if compliance had any actual power at Manic, I'd have been off-air two years ago." She tapped her nails on the desk, glancing at the remaining promo lines. "Anyway, what's left? 'The Pepsi Chart—powered by Gazprom, because who needs free speech when you've got fossil fuels'?"

"That and "The Official Pepsi Chart, proudly fuelled by Gazprom—because nothing says 'banger after banger' like totalitarian energy policy!"," Rex said with a grin. "Mate, this is comedy gold. You realise that if we ever get properly cancelled, it'll be because we're too entertaining for the regulators to handle?"

Nelly smirked, rolling her shoulders before leaning back into the mic. "Right, one last take before I go and pretend to care about Ed Sheeran's latest single."

She hit record, her voice dripping with amusement. "The Official Pepsi Chart—brought to you by the finest pop stars, the biggest tracks, and a corporate deal that probably raised a few eyebrows in Westminster. That's right, it's pop music and geopolitical instability in one convenient package. Join me, Dr Nelly Vixen, as we count down the UK's most played tracks, powered by Pepsi, Gazprom, and the kind of radio management decisions that would make a BBC executive burst into tears."

She pressed stop and exhaled dramatically. "That's a wrap. If that doesn't win us a Sony Award, nothing will."

Rex chuckled, finishing the final mix and exporting the promos to the playout system. "You're an absolute menace, Vixen. Seriously, who else could make a Sunday chart show sound like a James Bond plot?"

Nelly stood, stretching with a smirk. "Oh please, Bond wouldn't last five minutes in commercial radio. He'd get eaten alive by the sales team before he even made it to breakfast." She grabbed her phone, checking the time. "Right, let's see how much damage I can do in three hours of live broadcasting."

Rex saluted her playfully. "Try not to start a diplomatic incident, yeah?"

Nelly winked as she sauntered out of the production booth. "No promises, mate. No promises."

As the clock struck half past 3, Nelly knew that she had half an hour until her show started, and she knew, from the running order, that Ed Sheeran had, yet again, retained the top spot on the chart for a seventh consecutive week.

Of course he had.

It was 2019. If it wasn't Ed Sheeran, it was Dua Lipa, or Lewis Capaldi, or some sad lad with a guitar whining about lost love while being streamed 500 million times on Spotify.

She sighed, walking towards Studio 1, already mentally preparing herself for the inevitability of pretending to be excited about it.

The fact that Studio 1 was the awkward studio, as the production office, where she had left, didn't have a direct door to Studio 1, but required her to walk into the corridor, down 3 steps, turn left, then into the studio as it was on a par with the newsroom and sports department, only added to her minor irritation. Studio 2, which was the 'local' studio for the Liverpool feeds and Studio 3, which was the 'local' studio for the Chester and Wirral feeds, were integral studios, where production and presentation was all in one space.

But Studio 1? Studio 1 was formerly the Broom Closet, where news originally presented from, and its production office was the office of the former CEO, a Scouser named Terry McBride, who had been in charge when Fenway Sports Group had its short term of ownership of Manic in the early 2010s before selling it off to its current Russian-backed investors. The irony wasn't lost on Nelly—this station had gone from a Scouse-run independent to a chaotic, corporate-sponsored, politically dubious empire, and somehow, she was still here, still standing, still on air.

As she stepped into Studio 1, she was greeted by DJ Manic, or Tom Brown, a 21 year old host who presented the networked (for the none-Breeze stations) Sunday

Throwback Show. Normally a resident of Studio 2, because he preferred the integrated setup, he had been temporarily booted to Studio 1 due to an engineer "tweaking" something in Studio 2 that was apparently taking longer than expected.

Nelly knew that Tom was a fan of the corporate lines that they had to do on air, the 'Trigger Lead In, Provocative Point, Dazzling Details, Power Out' style patter that Manic had drilled into them all at the Boot Camps, like the one that had happened a fortnight ago.

It was then that Nelly realised that it had been nearly a fortnight since the death of Jenna Kilmare, a death which Nelly had almost completely buried under a mountain of chaos, media scandal, and industry politics.

"And that was S Club 7 with their absolute classic Reach, bringing back all the Y2K vibes on your Sunday afternoon. You're with DJ Manic on the networked Sunday Throwback Show, and coming up, I've got some Britney, some Robbie, and—because we legally have to include it at least once per hour—an early-2000s Craig David banger. First up though, we've got the Mistress of Mayhem, the Doctor of Disruption herself, Dr Nelly Vixen, here in the studio, Nelly, good to see you here on the Manic Radio Throwback, ready to cause yet another nationwide incident. How's the outrage machine treating you this week?" Tom grinned, swivelling slightly in his chair as he turned to face her.

Nelly smirked as she slid into the seat across from Tom, adjusting her mic level with the ease of someone who had spent years effortlessly walking the tightrope between radio chaos and outright cancellation.

"Oh, you know how it is, Tom," she drawled, kicking her feet up on the spare chair. "One minute, you're the voice of a generation, the next you're being discussed in Parliament as a threat to national stability. Business as usual."

Tom snorted, flicking a switch on the console to cue the next track underneath their chat. "I mean, let's be real—if you're not at least one Daily Mail headline away from exile, are you even presenting at Manic?"

"Exactly," Nelly said with a grin. "And besides, if Manic actually wanted me to behave, they wouldn't have handed me a Pepsi-sponsored chart show alongside a Russian gas giant. I'm just doing my civic duty and making sure people realise how utterly ridiculous this all is."

Tom chuckled, shaking his head. "Oh, don't worry, love, we all realise it. I mean, when Pepsi signed off on this deal, do you think they envisioned their brand being sandwiched between Ed Sheeran and literal Kremlin propaganda?"

Nelly tapped her fingers on the desk thoughtfully. "I like to imagine some poor Pepsi executive sitting in a boardroom in Atlanta, listening to my promos, slowly realising they've made a terrible mistake."

Tom leaned into the mic with mock sincerity. "Speaking of terrible mistakes, we should probably acknowledge the absolute state of this week's chart, shouldn't we? A bit of a spoiler for those who are waiting for number one, Ed

Sheeran and Stormzy got the top spot again. Because of course, they did."

Nelly groaned dramatically, leaning back in her chair. "Wow, great, take my thunder why don't you?" she said, rolling her eyes. "How do you know who's got the top spot?"

Tom grinned, and Nelly knew the answer already, but they were telling the story for the listeners who were listening to the show live. "Mate, this is Manic. We don't do mystery—we do data mining. The overnight figures are right there. Also, let's be honest, if Ed Sheeran isn't number one, it's only because Dua Lipa's staged a coup."

Nelly rolled her eyes, stretching her arms above her head lazily. "Honestly, at this point, I think the Official Charts Company just hands Ed the number one spot out of habit. Like, they're too scared to let someone else have it in case they disrupt the fragile balance of the pop music ecosystem."

Tom chuckled, flicking a few buttons on the desk to prepare for his next link. "Well, speaking of fragile balance, I should probably remind our lovely listeners that, unfortunately, I am legally required to play a Craig David track before I'm allowed to leave this booth."

Nelly grinned, leaning into her mic. "It's contractual, isn't it, for your throwback show, to play Robert Miles, Dario G, Benny Benassi, and at least one song from the Born to Do It era every single week?"

Tom nodded solemnly. "It's the law, mate. The Throwback Show code. If I don't play a Craig David track, OFCOM will personally come down here and revoke my broadcasting licence. Or worse, the entire industry will collapse in on itself. Anyway, here's Fill Me In by Craig David. Because what is British radio without at least one Craig David classic per show?"

The opening notes of Fill Me In played out across the studio, and Tom leaned back in his chair, giving Nelly an exaggerated look of mock exhaustion.

"Right, that's my contractual obligation fulfilled. I'm safe from industry exile for another week."

Nelly smirked, twirling a pen between her fingers. "See, that's the difference between you and me, Tom. You follow the radio laws. I break them for sport."

Tom snorted. "Mate, you don't break them. You run them through a shredder and then set the pieces on fire in the middle of Leicester Square."

"They'd probably get an injunction against me for that, too," Nelly quipped, stretching. "You up for a quickie as we've got 10 minutes of music on your end and then it's my show in here."

Nelly knew that, despite being married, she and Nate had a bit of an open relationship, and she suspected that Nate often slept with his Cheshire housewife clients while she was too busy navigating the minefield of commercial radio. Their arrangement worked—it was honest, it was practical, and neither of them pretended to be the sort to play at traditional marriage roles.

That the currency at Manic was cocaine, alcohol and sex meant that she and Tom had already crossed that line before, more than once, in between shifts when the station corridors were quiet. It wasn't serious—it was just what Manic was. A place where boundaries blurred, professionalism was a loose concept, and the station's mantra of play hard, work harder wasn't just a slogan; it was a survival mechanism.

Tom smirked, leaning back in his chair as he eyed Nelly with a mixture of amusement and intrigue. "Ten minutes? You really think that's enough time to deal with me?" he teased, his voice laced with cocky bravado.

Nelly rolled her eyes, amused. "Please, I've done more damage in less time. You're not special, Brown."

Tom let out a mock gasp, placing a hand over his chest in faux outrage. "Ouch. Wounded, truly. And here I thought I was at least in the top ten of your extracurriculars."

Nelly smirked, pushing herself up from her chair, stretching lazily. "You're probably in the top five," she admitted, watching his grin widen. "But only because Jamie is absolutely useless when he's drunk, and Kyler talks too much."

Tom chuckled, adjusting the fader levels on the desk as Craig David's Fill Me In drifted towards its final chorus. "Fair. Jamie drinks like he's still a fresher at Manchester Met, and Kyler's got the stamina of an overcaffeinated labrador, but the self-control of a Tory MP on a night out in Soho."

Nelly snorted, stepping around the desk towards him, her movements deliberate but unhurried. "And you? What's your USP?" she asked, tilting her head.

"Apart from having a 12 inch dong, Vixen…" Tom said, undoing Nelly's trousers and standing the 30 year old up. Nelly knew that Tom filled her quim up quite snugly the past 5 times that they had been together in Studio 1, and this time was no exception.

The next thing Nelly knew, she was bent over on the mixing deck, her breasts, which she had gotten enhanced 3 years earlier to a 44F cup pressing against the cool surface of the console as Tom pushed himself into her from behind. She let out a low moan, biting her lip to keep from being too loud—after all, there were still a handful of staff roaming the corridors, and the last thing she needed was someone barging in mid-session.

Tom wasn't the best shag she'd ever had, but he was convenient, and at Manic, convenience was king. Although, Nelly had to admit, the 12 inches of his man meat more than made up for his lack of creativity. He wasn't a talker, which suited her just fine—no pointless pillow talk, no attempts at feigned intimacy, just pure, unfiltered release before they both had to get back to pretending they were professionals.

The cold surface of the console sent a shiver through her, contrasting deliciously with the heat of his body pressing into hers. One hand tangled in her hair, the other gripping her hip, controlling the rhythm with the same confidence he had when he was behind the mic.

"Fuck, Vixen," Tom grunted, voice husky. "You really don't waste time, do you?"

Nelly smirked, arching her back slightly, pushing herself against him. "Why would I? Got a number one to announce in—" she gasped as he thrust deeper—"seven minutes."

Tom chuckled, his fingers tightening their grip on her waist. "Seven minutes? Think we can squeeze in a second round?"

"Oi, don't flatter yourself, Brown," she teased, biting her lip to suppress a moan. "You get me off once before we go live, and you should consider it a job well done."

She could feel him smirk against her shoulder, his breath hot against her skin. "Challenge accepted."

The sounds of Craig David's Fill Me In faded into the next track, and Nelly half-registered the knowledge that the song had about three minutes left before Tom had to jump back on air. Not that he seemed particularly concerned.

Her head dropped against the mixing desk, fingers gripping the edge as he increased his pace. He was rough, but not careless—just the right amount of pressure, just enough control to push her closer, but not let her fall over the edge too soon.

"You know," she gasped, voice breathy, "if you keep this up, I might actually have to put you in the top three."

Tom chuckled, biting lightly at the back of her neck. "If I'd known I was being ranked, I would've put in extra effort the first time."

"Just shut up and—" her words dissolved into a muffled moan as he shifted the angle, hitting just the right spot to make her toes curl.

Tom grinned against her skin, clearly revelling in the reaction. "Oh yeah, that's it, isn't it?" he murmured. "That's the spot."

"Fuck, yes," Nelly groaned, fingers gripping tighter, nails scraping against the console. "Don't stop."

Her breathing grew more ragged, body tightening, the pleasure building to an inevitable crescendo. Tom knew it too—he could feel it in the way she tensed beneath him, the way her moans became more desperate, more uncontrolled.

And then, with a final, perfectly timed thrust, the dam broke.

Nelly bit down on her own wrist to stifle the cry that threatened to escape, her body shaking as waves of pleasure crashed through her. Tom wasn't far behind—he buried himself deep, groaning low and guttural as he finished inside her, fingers digging into her hips.

For a moment, all that filled the studio was the sound of their heavy breathing, the distant hum of the station's automation, and the lingering bassline of whatever early-2000s banger was currently playing on Tom's show.

Then, with a chuckle, Tom pulled back, fixing his trousers as he leaned against the desk. "Well, that was a productive use of company time."

Nelly, still catching her breath, reached for a tissue from the desk and wiped herself off before fixing her own trousers. "Corporate efficiency at its finest," she quipped, smoothing down her shirt as if nothing had happened.

Tom checked the clock, grinning. "Two minutes to spare. You're welcome."

Nelly rolled her eyes but smirked as she grabbed her headphones from the chair. "Yeah, yeah, don't get cocky. Now go pretend to be a respectable radio host while I get ready to announce yet another painfully predictable number one."

Tom saluted her playfully before sliding back into his chair, adjusting his mic just as his final throwback track faded out. Nelly watched, amused, as he slipped seamlessly back into his presenter voice, his casual, cocky swagger returning as if he hadn't just had his cock inside her against the mixing desk.

"And that, my lovely listeners, was your ultimate Sunday throwback session. I've been DJ Manic, you've been brilliant, and coming up next—whether OFCOM likes it or not—it's the chaos queen herself, Dr Nelly Vixen, with the brand-new Pepsi Chart. Will Ed Sheeran still be clinging to the top spot like a cockroach in a nuclear apocalypse? Probably. But you'll have to stick around to find out. Stay tuned, legends."

The moment the fader went down, Tom turned to Nelly with a wink. "Try not to get us all sued before the first hour's up, yeah?"

Nelly smirked, slipping her headphones on as she settled into the presenter's chair. "No promises, mate."

As Tom grabbed his things and strolled out of the studio, leaving the scent of cheap aftershave and ego in his wake, Nelly took a deep breath, cracked her knuckles, and leaned into the mic.

"Alright, you little radio gremlins, buckle up. It's Sunday, it's Manic, and this is the brand-new, highly questionable, potentially OFCOM-inducing Pepsi Chart. Powered by Gazprom, because apparently, we're in an actual dystopian novel now. Let's get started."

She pressed play, and with that, another week of beautiful, chaotic radio anarchy began.

****

CHAPTER 9 – OFCOM, Outrage & One-Way to Malta

Wednesday 16th October 2019

Nelly had to chuckle as she lurked on Radio Today, the gossip rag for the radio industry. If you wanted to know who'd been sacked, who'd been poached, and who had just spectacularly torched their career on-air, this was the place to be. The fact that 99% of the industry, from the CEOs to the part-time weekend jocks, pretended they didn't read it religiously was the biggest open secret in British radio.

And there it was. Right at the top.

"OFCOM to Investigate Manic Radio's Pepsi Chart Following Complaints Over Host's Conduct"

Nelly exhaled sharply through her nose, shaking her head as she skimmed through the article.

"Dr Vixen, known for her sharp tongue and irreverent broadcasting style, stated on air that "Dance Monkey sounds like watching a group of mentally retarded geriatrics avoiding euthanasia."

A spokesperson for OFCOM stated: 'We have received a significant number of complaints regarding comments made by Dr Vixen on Manic Radio's Pepsi Chart. As part of our standard procedure, we are assessing whether these remarks breached our broadcasting code, particularly with regards to harmful and offensive content. If the case is taken forward, Manic Radio could face regulatory action.'

Manic Radio, who is owned by Ilya Koslov, a Russian businessman with alleged ties to various Kremlin-affiliated enterprises, has thus far declined to comment. However, sources within the station suggest that CEO Dr Scott Bennett is refusing to cooperate with OFCOM beyond the legal minimum, allegedly stating in an internal memo that 'if Global and Bauer want us to play by their boring rules, they can pry the faders from our cold, dead hands.'"

Nelly snorted, leaning back in her chair. That sounded about right. Bennett had spent the last decade turning Manic into the biggest thorn in the side of the British radio establishment, gleefully throwing Ofcom fines into the station's expenses like they were just another utility bill. And yet, this time, things felt different.

Flipping over to the other gossip playground, the Digital Spy Radio Forums, a hotbed of nerds, industry insiders, and bitter ex-presenters, Nelly had to admit that she was one of the middle category, the industry insiders who occasionally spilt the tea on what was really going on behind the scenes. She rarely posted, but she lurked. Everyone did. It was where the real banter happened, away from the polished PR statements and corporate wank.

And sure enough, the thread was already 17 pages deep.

OFCOM Investigating Manic's Pepsi Chart – Will This Be The End Of Dr Vixen?

Trainbasher: *Looks like Nelly Vixen is being investigated. I hope she gets dumped off Manic. Ever* *since they took over Midlands Manic last month, its gone to shit.*

RadioHead77: *This was inevitable. Honestly surprised it's taken this long. You can't say 'mentally retarded geriatrics' on air in 2019 and expect no fallout.*

DABisTheFuture: *Manic's been getting away with murder for years. The industry's patience has run out. Global and Bauer are lobbying behind the scenes, guaranteed.*

CommunityRadioLad: *And yet, somehow, she's still on air. Proves one thing: controversy equals RAJARs.*

JohnnyOnTheWireless: *Say what you want about Vixen, but she makes radio actually interesting. You think people are tuning into Heart Breakfast with Jamie the Bland to hear a real personality?*

JustForTheRAJARs: *If OFCOM actually had balls, they'd revoke Manic's licence. But we all know how this ends – another slap on the wrist, another fine, and another 200k bump in listeners for Vixen.*

SimonMayoFan89: *The real story here is Gazprom. The sponsorship deal alone should be a scandal, let alone the fact she's openly taking the piss out of it on air.*

Nelly chuckled at the name of the original poster, a user named Trainbasher, who's profile picture was a bus in some Midlands street, no doubt some ageing ex-radio presenter who'd spent the last decade ranting about how digital radio had ruined everything or some nerd who posted about missing 100.7 Heart FM and 97.2 Beacon

FM, two Midlands stations which got absorbed into Global's Heart network and Bauer's Hits Radio network respectively. The Midlands lot were always the most bitter. They'd never quite gotten over the slow strangulation of their local radio scene, and Manic's aggressive takeover of Midlands Manic last month had only poured fuel on the fire.

The irony that she was a Selly Oak girl, and so technically one of them, wasn't lost on her. But she'd long since stopped caring about regional loyalty in an industry that had systematically gutted everything local for years. Manic was at least honest about what it was—a corporate monster with no illusions about authenticity. The others? They pretended they still cared while networking everything to hell.

She scrolled further, her eyes skimming through another dozen posts.

AirCheckLegend: *OFCOM's going to investigate, sure, but Bennett isn't stupid. They'll stall, drag it out, get some lawyers involved, and then pay the fine like it's a parking ticket. Rinse and repeat.*

RAJARstats4lyfe: *More to the point, what happens if they actually pull her off air? Would Manic even survive it?*

DrivetimeDan: *Vixen IS Manic. If she goes, they're done. The brand is controversy—without it, they're just another Kiss FM clone with fewer ads and more coke-fuelled presenters.*

ClassicILR: *I miss the days when radio wasn't this much of a mess. You wouldn't have had this kind of scandal in the 90s. Bring back proper presenters who knew how to keep it professional.*

JohnnyOnTheWireless: *Mate, the 90s had Smashie and Nicey, Chris Evans pissing off BBC execs weekly, and DLT being a nightmare. Professionalism my arse.*

Nelly snorted. The rose-tinted nostalgia for 'proper radio' never failed to amuse her. The industry had always been a chaotic bin fire—the difference now was that social media made every tiny scandal a national talking point before breakfast.

Logging into her Digital Spy account, she debated for a moment whether to post or just lurk in the shadows as usual. A well-placed comment here could send the thread into a tailspin, but she wasn't sure she could be arsed dealing with the inevitable backlash.

But then again, she thought, *I might as well give the gits a piece of my mind.*

With a smirk, she clicked Reply and started typing.

VixenChartShow: *Oh wow, lads. You'd think I'd committed a war crime the way you lot are carrying on. Can't wait to see OFCOM's grand ruling: "Naughty girl, here's a fine, now go make us another record-breaking RAJAR quarter". Also, big love to "ClassicILR" for pretending the 90s were some golden age of professionalism. Mate, the decade that gave us Chris Evans waving his dick about on TFI Friday and Bam Bam getting fired for telling a listener to set themselves on fire?*

Pipe down. And Trainbasher, you saddo, I bet you still wank over old BRMB jingles and cry about how the 'death of local radio' ruined your life. Maybe if you spent less time crying over long-lost RDS codes and more time getting laid, you wouldn't be so pressed about a woman having a personality on air. PS: If Global really wanted me gone, they'd have put a better bribe in my inbox. Try harder, losers.

Within minutes, her Digital Spy post had set the forum ablaze.

Trainbasher was back in full force, frothing at the mouth.

Trainbasher: *"Oh wow, Vixen herself descending from her ivory tower to insult the people who actually care about radio? Nice try, love. You might be riding high on controversy now, but let's see how smug you are when OFCOM actually grows a spine and pulls your licence."*

ClassicILR: *"No one's pretending the 90s were perfect, but at least presenters had respect for the industry. You, Vixen, are nothing but a symptom of how far commercial radio has fallen. A cheap headline-grabber who thinks she's untouchable. Your days are numbered."*

JustForTheRAJARs: *"LMAO, I can't believe she actually posted. This is why I love Manic. No other presenter would wade in like this. Peak radio carnage."*

SimonMayoFan89: *"Nah, but why is she right though? Bam Bam did literally tell someone to set themselves on fire and got away with it for months."*

Nelly smirked as she refreshed the page, watching as the reactions flooded in. Half of them were clutching their pearls, screaming about how she was a disgrace to the industry, while the other half were practically worshipping her for keeping radio interesting. Exactly the kind of split she thrived on.

Looking at her phone, she noticed a text message from Dr Scott Bennett, which was less of a telling off and more of an encouragement of her maverick ways.

Scott Bennett: *Fucking hell, Vixen. Remind me to never let you near our corporate Twitter account. That was the single best way to piss off every radio nerd in the country. Top notch shithousery.*

Nelly smirked as she read Bennett's message. Of course, he wasn't going to tell her to rein it in. That wasn't how Manic operated. If anything, she'd probably just secured herself another pay rise.

Nelly tossed her phone onto the desk, leaning back in her chair with a self-satisfied smirk. The industry was frothing at the mouth, Twitter was eating itself alive, and she was still very much on-air. If OFCOM thought they could make an example out of her, they clearly hadn't done their homework.

Looking round her home, she knew that Nate was at a Real Housewife's home, giving yet another private consultation on a nose, lip or boob job, while she was left to her own devices, stirring up chaos in the industry one tweet at a time. Getting up, she grabbed her car keys and headed to the garage, where Nate's Aston Martin and her

Jaguar normally parked side by side, a perfect metaphor for their marriage—one was sleek, refined, and designed for appearances, the other was fast, unpredictable, and, like a fox, ready to pounce on its next victim.

Sliding into the leather driver's seat, Nelly felt the softness of the Jaguar F-Pace's Siena Tan perforated Windsor leather performance seats with Ebony/Siena Tan interior, the Carpathian Grey exterior of the car gleaming under the dim light of the garage. She revved the engine slightly, smirking as she pulled out onto the quiet Cheshire road, heading towards the M56. If she was going to deal with this OFCOM nonsense, she might as well do it on her own terms—with a coffee, a cigarette, and a long drive just to get out of the house.

Tuning into Radio 4, Nelly knew that Women's Hour was set to start, meaning that she had a front row seat to whatever middle-class outrage was currently gripping the BBC's flagship feminism-adjacent talk show. Not that she had anything against Women's Hour—some of it was quite interesting—but there was something almost amusingly predictable about how they picked their battles. If they weren't clutching their pearls over some Daily Mail-fuelled panic about school uniforms, they were dissecting the latest cultural trend like it was the Rosetta Stone of female oppression.

Sure enough, the host was already in full flow.

"Coming up next: should controversial broadcasters like Dr Nelly Vixen be allowed such large platforms, and what does it say about modern media when female shock jocks are encouraged to push boundaries in a way that their male counterparts once were?"

Nelly almost choked on her laughter. Oh, this is rich.

She turned the volume up slightly as a smooth-voiced guest, likely some former editor of The Guardian or a media academic from a red-brick university, launched into an impassioned speech about the "toxicity of performative controversy" and "whether female broadcasters should be expected to play into the same aggressive radio culture that men established decades ago."

"I think what we're seeing here is a deliberate attempt to frame Dr Vixen as some sort of rebellious figure when, in reality, this is just a rebranding of the same old shock-jock misogyny," the guest intoned, "except now it's coming from a woman, which allows Manic Radio to shield themselves from criticism under the guise of 'progressiveness'."

Nelly raised an eyebrow. Oh wow, I'm a Trojan horse for corporate gender-washing now? That's a new one.

The host hummed in agreement. "And, of course, we can't ignore the fact that Manic Radio is owned by Russian investors. There are broader ethical concerns here. When we have a major British broadcaster operating under financial interests that align with foreign oligarchs, should OFCOM be taking a stronger stance?"

Now that was interesting. The Kremlin angle was always lurking beneath the surface, but so far, no one had been bold enough to outright suggest Manic was some kind of propaganda arm. Sure, it was owned by a Russian billionaire, but so were The Independent and the entire Premier League. That didn't mean she was suddenly an undercover FSB agent smuggling coded messages into the Top 10.

Then again, that would be a hell of a plot twist.

"But surely people like Dr Vixen, who speak their mind freely and therefore are able to prove to the male dominated industry that is radio can still be an exciting and dynamic space, are actually proof that there's still room for genuine personalities?" A second guest cut in, their voice less polished but more animated. "Look, I'm not saying she's a feminist icon—far from it—but you have to admit, no one's talking about the safe, sanitised presenters on Global's stations, are they? They're talking about her."

Nelly smirked, letting the words wash over her. Finally, someone in this discussion with half a brain.

And then there was the court case which, earlier this year, forced Manic to give backpay to over 200 of its female employees, a mixture of on-air talent, producers as well as support staff. The pay gap scandal had rocked Manic to its core, but unlike the BBC, which had at least pretended to care, Manic had simply thrown money at the problem and doubled down on its usual strategy—making controversy its brand.

The court case, led by James Jenkins, acting on behalf of Samantha Greene, had been one of the biggest PR disasters in Manic's history. Yet, instead of caving to the pressure like a respectable media company might have, Manic had taken an entirely different approach.

Scott Bennett, ever the agent of chaos, had issued a statement that was equal parts defiant and completely unhinged. "We acknowledge the legal ruling and will, of course, comply with the order for backpay. However, we would like to remind everyone that Manic Radio has always been an equal opportunities employer. We discriminate against everyone equally. Our male employees are underpaid, overworked, and frequently traumatised. Our female employees are underpaid, overworked, and frequently traumatised. We pride ourselves on our consistent commitment to making life difficult for all staff, regardless of gender. This is what true equality looks like."

The media had gone feral. Even The Guardian had struggled to decide whether they were outraged or begrudgingly impressed by the sheer audacity of the statement. James Jenkins, predictably, had gone on The Media Show to decry Manic's "blatant disregard for broadcasting ethics."

As the Women's Hour host and her guests continued their discussion, Nelly rolled her eyes and flicked the volume down. It was always the same cycle—moral panic, pearl-clutching, and an eventual resigned acceptance that nothing was going to change. The BBC could wring their hands all they liked, but the truth was, Manic Radio was too big to ignore, and she was too embedded in its DNA to be easily removed.

Seeing that she was coming to the A555 junction, the Manchester Airport Eastern Link, Nelly decided that she was going to make a spontaneous trip for a couple of days to the Mediterranean before this OFCOM nonsense started getting serious. If there was one thing she had learned in the industry, it was that nothing pissed off regulators and corporate watchdogs more than looking completely unbothered.

"Siri, book me a flight from Manchester to Malta, business class, departing as soon as possible, returning on Saturday," she said, knowing that, despite not having any clothes, she had her credit card, and that she could obtain anything she needed once she landed.

"Siri, book me a flight from Manchester to Malta, business class, departing as soon as possible, returning on Saturday," she said, knowing that, despite not having any clothes, she had her credit card, and that she could obtain anything she needed once she landed.

As Siri confirmed her booking, she smirked. Nothing like a last-minute escape to the Mediterranean while the industry frothed at the mouth over her latest so-called scandal. If they thought she was about to sit at home, biting her nails, waiting for OFCOM to come knocking, they clearly didn't know her well enough.

She parked her Jaguar F-Pace in the premium parking at Terminal 2, stepping out with a smug satisfaction that only came from knowing you were about to dodge every single person demanding an explanation from you. As she strode through the terminal, sunglasses perched on her head, she checked her phone one last time before switching it to aeroplane mode.

"Shit, an hour layover at Frankfurt and an hour at Munich, just because I'm going on bloody Lufthansa," she muttered as she checked in using the online check-in.

Nelly sighed, rolling her eyes. Lufthansa was fine—efficient, comfortable, German to a fault—but she would have preferred a direct flight. Still, considering she had booked the trip in less time than it took for OFCOM to draft a press release, she supposed she couldn't be too picky.

She knew that her passport, which was always in her handbag, was valid, as she had renewed it earlier in the year when she'd briefly considered doing a summer stint in Dubai radio, before realising that working under UAE media laws would be the equivalent of putting a straitjacket on her personality. She had no interest in sanitising her on-air persona to fit some squeaky-clean corporate mandate, let alone one enforced by an actual government.

As she moved through Terminal 2, she glanced up at the departure board. Her Lufthansa flight was still on time, with the expected layovers in Frankfurt and Munich before she'd finally land in Malta. A pain in the arse, but worth it for the sheer pettiness of disappearing right when the industry was at peak hysteria over her.

Heading through the terminal, Nelly knew that she had fast track security access because of her husband's frequent flyer status, which meant she could bypass the hordes of bleary-eyed tourists and stressed-out business travellers fumbling with their laptops at security. She breezed through the process with the practised ease of someone who spent far too much time in airports, barely flinching as she tossed her designer handbag onto the conveyor belt.

Hearing her phone ring, Nelly looked at the caller to see that it was her husband, who had obviously seen the transaction on the credit card app, as, despite her being a second cardholder, she knew that Nate kept a close eye on their spending. She sighed and answered.

"Nate, before you start—yes, I just booked a last-minute flight, yes, it's on Lufthansa, and no, I'm not fleeing the country in disgrace," she said, cutting off whatever tirade he had been preparing. "Anyway, you're probably shagging one of your mistresses, so you don't get to judge my spontaneous holiday choices."

There was a pause on the other end of the line before Nate chuckled. "Nah, I was going to say that I'm going away myself for a week, as I've got a client who's moved to Abu Dhabi and wants me to do some private consultations out there. Thought I'd let you know before you started a conspiracy theory that I was in some Real Housewife's en-suite performing backdoor Botox injections."

Nelly snorted as she moved past Duty-Free, resisting the temptation to grab an overpriced bottle of gin. "Well, it wouldn't be the most absurd thing you've ever done. So, what you're saying is, neither of us are going to be home this week?"

"Looks like it," Nate replied smoothly. "I'll be in the Emirates, you'll be in Malta, and OFCOM will be left shouting into the void wondering where you are."

"Perfect," she drawled, stepping onto the escalator towards the premium lounges. "I assume you're paying for all this, by the way?"

"You already booked it on my card, love," he deadpanned. "So yes, I suppose I am."

"Excellent," Nelly said cheerfully. "Enjoy Abu Dhabi, don't get caught up in any international scandals, and if your clients insist on flying you over in first class, remind them that you're a man of the people."

"Yeah, because nothing says man of the people like flying Emirates First," Nate replied dryly. "Look, just don't say anything too career-ending while you're over there, yeah?"

Nelly smirked. "Nate. Darling. Have you met me?"

"Unfortunately," he said. "Try not to start a diplomatic crisis with the Maltese government, at least. I'd like my wife to return home without being persona non grata."

"I make no promises," she replied sweetly, before hanging up as she arrived at the entrance to the Escape Lounge.

****

CHAPTER 10 – Three Years On:
Fired, Famous, and Still a Menace
Friday 1st November 2019

Three years.

That was how long it had been since Nelly had been sacked by Breeze Media off their Worcestershire Beats station, effectively nuking what should have been a safe, steady career in regional radio. Three years since she'd been hauled into Alan Carter's office, told she was "no longer a good fit for the brand," and escorted out of the building like some rogue intern who'd stolen a few promotional keyrings.

The fact it had been for fraud, as she had plagiarised her thesis, the Film and Media Studies PhD at the University of Worcester that she had, admittedly, copied half of the thesis she had wrote from an obscure academic journal that she had been convinced no one would ever bother reading—was beside the point. As far as she was concerned, the real crime had been getting caught.

She had been part of the 'Worcestershire Breakfast Zoo' on Worcestershire Beats, a three man show that had tried desperately to inject some chaos into the deeply uninspiring landscape of regional radio. Her co-hosts, Mark Daniels and Lisa Roberts, had been the perfect foils—Mark was the lovable rogue, the kind of presenter who could charm a pensioner into calling in about their neighbour's cat while still managing to crack an innuendo that went over management's heads. Lisa, meanwhile, was the 'responsible one'—or at least, that's what the listeners were meant to believe. In reality, she was just as much of a liability as the rest of them, except she hid it behind a well-practised, smooth professionalism.

Not that Mark and Lisa were perfect, that they had no skeletons in their closets. In fact, Mark and Lisa had been fired from Coventry's Sunshine FM, a station which went under nearly a year after they'd been booted out. Their crime? Being the sacrificial lambs in a rigged competition scandal that had nothing to do with them and everything to do with the suits upstairs panicking about OFCOM fines.

The rest of Broadwave Networks had sold out to Global not long after Sunshine collapsed, when Ashley Tabor was hoovering up every independent station that he could get his hands on in his never-ending quest to turn commercial radio into a personality-free, brand-safe wasteland. At the time, Worcestershire Beats was owned by Woody Bones as part of a 12 station Central England network that Broadwave, Manic and Bauer all wanted, but, despite its limited networking and relatively small footprint, it had managed to avoid the corporate reaper's scythe for a little while longer.

While Beacon FM, BRMB, and its 3 sibling stations, Nottingham's Heart 106, Wyvern FM and Mercia FM, they all were forced to be sold off to another company, which was Orion Media, in 2009, due to competition rules, and then Orion became part of Bauer in 2016. The Bones Network got sold in 2010 by Woody Bones to Breeze Media, a small media group similar in size to Orion Media, whose ethos was more on local broadcasting and less on corporate streamlining. Breeze had prided itself on keeping things local, at least on the surface. In reality, it was like every other independent operator—desperate to stay afloat in a market where the only way to survive was either to sell out to Global or hope Manic or Bauer eventually swallowed you up.

For a while, it had worked. Worcestershire Beats had been a fun, scrappy station where Nelly had free rein to be as much of a troublemaker as she liked—within reason, of course. She and Mark had once convinced a local councillor that a housing estate in Kidderminster had been taken over by a cult (it hadn't), and Lisa had nearly gotten them sued after she called the CEO of a local dairy farm a "cheese pimp" on air. It had been chaotic, reckless, and exactly the kind of radio Nelly loved.

And then, of course, she'd fucked it all up.

The plagiarism scandal hadn't just gotten her fired from Breeze—it had made her unemployable. The moment the story broke, every major broadcaster shut their doors. No one wanted to touch a presenter who had been caught committing academic fraud, especially not when the tabloids had framed it as some grand deception, like she'd been running a black-market dissertation empire instead of just being too lazy to write her own thesis.

And Alan Carter had relished it.

That smug, sanctimonious bastard had sat across from her in his office—his cheap suit, his thinning hair, that unbearable air of self-importance—and delivered the news like he was passing down a royal decree.

"Nelly," he had said, in that condescending tone of his. "I'm afraid this isn't something we can overlook. Worcestershire Beats has a reputation to uphold."

She had nearly laughed in his face. A reputation? For what? Playing the same five Olly Murs songs on repeat and sponsoring the local garden centre's annual gnome festival? But she had kept her mouth shut, because even then, she had held on to the faint, misguided hope that she could talk her way out of it.

She couldn't. Carter had already made up his mind.

"You're no longer a good fit for the brand," he had told her, with all the self-satisfaction of a man who had never taken a risk in his life. "We'll, of course, ensure you leave with dignity."

That had been the real kicker. With dignity. As if being marched out of the building while her former colleagues watched in awkward silence was dignified. As if having her pass deactivated before she'd even reached the car park was dignified. As if the Daily Mail running an entire article on her fall from grace—complete with a particularly unflattering photo from a station promo shoot—was dignified.

Back then, Manic had been an oddity in the Fenway Sports Group, only purchased it because Jürgen Klopp had been pranked into recording a station ident for Manic a year into his management of the Liverpool squad, and someone at Fenway had decided it would be a laugh to own a radio station. It was 2016 at the time when FSG brought Manic, and for two whole years, the Scouse based station, as its origins being in Garston's Manic FM, a small, scrappy competitor to the Emap owned Radio City, had suddenly found itself with the financial backing of the same people who owned Liverpool Football Club. And for a while, that had meant chaos. The kind of chaos that suited Nelly perfectly.

Manic had been desperate for talent at the time, especially someone who could shake things up and give them an edge over their bigger, more sanitised competitors. The fact that Nelly came with baggage? That was a bonus. In an industry where Global and Bauer were vacuuming up every station and personality worth having, Manic thrived on controversy. A sacked presenter with a scandalous backstory? Perfect.

McBride, the then-CEO, had practically hired her on the spot.

"You've got a mouth on you," he'd said during her 'interview,' which had mostly been a pub meeting in the Baltic Triangle over pints of Guinness. "I like that. Radio needs more gobshites."

Within a fortnight, she was on air at Manic's networked late-night show, *Up All Night with Dr Nelly Vixen*, and by the time Fenway decided they couldn't be arsed running a radio station anymore and sold it off to its current Russian backers, Nelly was already an institution. The sacked breakfast jock with a PhD scandal had somehow become the loudest, most infamous voice on commercial radio.

And now, three years to the day since Alan Carter had sat her down and ended her career in regional radio, she was sitting in her Cheshire home, sipping an overpriced Pinot Noir, while that same Alan Carter was overseeing OFCOM's compliance investigations into her.

The irony was delicious.

She scrolled through her phone, idly skimming through Twitter, where the latest Digital Spy threads were already debating whether OFCOM would finally 'get rid' of her. She knew the answer. They wouldn't. Scott Bennett and the Manic legal team would throw just enough money at the problem to keep her on air. They always did.

But she wasn't stupid. Carter had it in for her. He'd been given a new lease of life as a 'regulator' now that Breeze Media had been swallowed up and he was out of the game. This was his chance to finally crush the thorn in his side—the woman who had gone from an embarrassing footnote in his career to the most recognisable name in British commercial radio.

The bastard would love to see her fail.

Her phone buzzed, and she glanced down to see a message from Lisa Roberts.

Lisa Roberts: *Happy sacking anniversary, babe. Can't believe it's been three years since Carter pulled the trigger. And now he's trying to regulate you? You literally could not write this shit.*

Nelly smirked, typing back a quick reply.

Nelly Vixen: *I know, right? Next thing you know, he'll be running the whole damn industry. Actually, scratch that. Tabor would never let someone with his lack of charisma near Global HQ.*

Lisa replied instantly.

Lisa Roberts: *LMAO, true. You know Mark and I are still down at Worcestershire, and Mark keeps pissing himself laughing when he hears your promos for the new Pepsi Chart.*

Nelly knew that Worcestershire Beats was now part of the Manic network, and that Mark and Lisa, having stayed behind through all the buyouts and ownership changes, were still holding down the breakfast show there.

Unlike Global, who would go straight for the rebranding to Capital and cut the local teams, or Bauer, who would inevitably shove it under the Hits Radio network identity and cut it down to Breakfast—there again, Nelly knew that as Bauer owned Free Radio, which was Worcestershire Beats' competitor, they wouldn't have been allowed to fully take over Worcestershire Beats anyway—Manic had opted for keeping it as it was. The branding was still local, the imaging was still recognisable to the old audience, and the schedule, at the moment, apart from her Chart show and some of the Breeze network shows, were mostly untouched. That was the Manic way—network what could be networked, but keep just enough of the local identity intact to prevent an outright listener rebellion.

She knew that most of the Breeze hosts, like Pete Smith and the Fermanagh FM hosts, were dinosaurs, and wouldn't take change if it bit them on the arse. They were old-school, clinging to the last vestiges of the ILR era, the days when local stations had actual personalities rather than faceless voice-tracked nobodies reading liner cards written by interns. Some of them, like Pete, had even started actively campaigning against Manic's changes, making passive-aggressive jabs on air and ranting about the "death of real radio" in industry WhatsApp groups.

But Mark and Lisa? They weren't stupid. They had seen several of their friends in the industry get made redundant from Global's purchases of Galaxy and Heart, and of Orion's purchases of Wyvern FM, Beacon, Mercia, and BRMB. They knew that the alternative to Manic taking over wasn't some idyllic return to local radio's golden age—it was being swallowed whole by a corporate machine that didn't give a toss about presenters who weren't already on a national playlist.

Lisa's next message popped up on Nelly's screen.

Lisa Roberts: *Mark reckons you should send Carter a 'Happy Sacking Anniversary' card. Maybe one of those massive Moonpig ones with your face on it. Just for the banter.*

Nelly snorted, nearly spilling her wine. It wasn't the worst idea in the world.

Nelly Vixen: *I should send one with 'Thanks for the Career Upgrade' on the front.*

Lisa Roberts: *Or better—'Hope You're Enjoying Your Shiny New OFCOM Desk, You Spineless Cockweasel.'*

Nelly Vixen: *"Might need to work on the wording a bit, but I like the energy."*

Nelly knew that deep down, Mark and Lisa probably envied her. They would never admit it, but they had played it safe. They had stuck to their comfort zone, riding the wave of every buyout, merger, and rebrand, while she had taken a gamble—one that had almost destroyed her career before Manic had salvaged it. And now? Now she was the biggest name in commercial radio, while they were still waking up at 4 AM to do local breakfast in the West Midlands.

Her phone buzzed again.

Johnny Paulson: *Hey, Nell, fancy covering the 7-10pm slot? Behzinga and KSI are doing their Sidemen stuff and none of the cover lot fancy doing it. Boss says triple pay if you do.*

Nelly knew that Johnny, the Network Director of Programming, was keen to throw the cash around when it came to getting last-minute cover. Manic might be chaos, but one thing they did right was rewarding presenters who could step up at short notice. Triple pay for three hours of radio? She'd be an idiot to say no.

Nelly Vixen: *Triple pay for three hours? I'd have taken it for double. Stick me on the rota. The usual Sidemen Evening Show, right?*

Nelly knew that the Sidemen, a group of YouTube influencers who Manic had got on contract for a new evening show, had been a wildcard move even by Manic's standards. Getting KSI, Behzinga, and the rest of them to do a weekly radio slot had been a stroke of genius from a marketing perspective—young listeners who normally wouldn't touch FM or DAB radio with a ten-foot pole were suddenly tuning in just to hear their favourite YouTubers chat nonsense in between chart hits.

Unlike Capital, who filled their roster's prime slot, the breakfast slot, with a legacy hire in Roman Kemp, whose father was Spandau Ballet royalty, and the Hits network, who had Wes Butters and Gemma Atkinson for their drive show, Manic had decided to throw caution to the wind and bet big on the digital generation. It was a high-risk, high-reward move—either it cemented their reputation as the station that actually understood Gen Z, or it completely blew up in their faces. So far, the gamble was paying off.

Nelly took another sip of her wine, smirking as she glanced at the time. The 7-10 slot would be an easy gig. It wasn't her usual chaos-fuelled chart show, but it was still prime-time. Plus, it would give her the perfect opportunity to mess with the corporate sponsors who were probably still panicking over her latest antics.

****

"You're listening to the Sidemen Evening Show, and I'm Nelly Vixen, in for KSI and Behzinga, because apparently, being multi-millionaire influencers means you can just not show up to your own radio show and still get paid. What a life, eh?"

Nelly leaned back in the studio chair, her lips curling into a smirk as she let her words settle in. She knew that the social media platforms, the Twitter, TikTok, Facebook and Instagram algorithms would already be churning out clips of her opening link within minutes. The Sidemen fans were rabid—anything related to KSI and his crew had a guaranteed viral factor, and Nelly had no doubt that by the time she was done with the show, there would be at least three trending hashtags dissecting every word she said.

She adjusted her mic level and carried on.

"Anyway, since the lads are off doing whatever it is YouTube millionaires do on a Friday night—probably bathing in AdSense money or challenging Jake Paul to a cage fight—I'll be keeping you company for the next three hours. Don't worry, I promise not to pretend I know what 'no cap' means. We've got some tunes, we've got some chaos, and if we're really lucky, we might even make a sponsor nervous. Stick around, legends as leading our show is bloody Ed Sheeran and Stormzy with their collab track Take Me Back to London, because of course it is. If Ed Sheeran isn't on your playlist at least twice an hour, is it even commercial radio?"

She let the track roll in, stretching her arms and glancing over at the text screen, where the first batch of listener messages was already flooding in. Most were just excited Sidemen fans who had tuned in expecting KSI and Behzinga and were now trying to figure out why they were getting a fast-talking radio gobshite instead.

@Jaden_YT: *Where's KSI???*

 Not my queen Vixen taking over the Sidemen slot, LOL. This is gonna be chaos.

@ChelseaFCfanboy: *If Nelly makes another Gazprom joke, I will actually lose it.*

She grinned. Oh, the temptation.

As the track faded, she hit the mic fader and leaned in.

"Alright, so for anyone just tuning in, no, you haven't wandered into an alternate universe. This is still the Sidemen Evening Show, but KSI and Behzinga are off doing… whatever it is YouTubers do when they're not in this studio. Probably counting stacks of money and ignoring their WhatsApp messages from producers. But don't worry, because you've got me, Dr Nelly Vixen, a woman who, according to OFCOM, is a *serious threat to broadcasting standards*."

She made sure to say it in her most dramatic voice, just to make it extra ridiculous.

"So, we've got three hours together. We could do what the Sidemen normally do, which is mostly chat nonsense, play some bangers, and occasionally read out texts that say 'KSI is the GOAT.' Or—and hear me out on this— we could cause some mild but legally permissible levels of chaos. Up to you, really."

The text screen *exploded.*

@ManLikeHarry: *VIXEN WANTS CHAOS, WE GIVE HER CHAOS.*

@NotLoganPaul: *Mild? Nah, we go full nuclear.*

@GamerGirlRox: *If this show doesn't end with an OFCOM complaint, did it even happen?*

She smirked, leaning back in her chair.

"You lot are terrible influences. I love it. Right, here's the deal. You tell me what we should do tonight. Let's make this interactive. Do I give you actual quality radio content, or do I go rogue and see how many sponsors I can annoy before management start calling my mobile? You decide."

The messages flooded in, and Nelly knew, before even glancing at them, what the overwhelming consensus would be.

She chuckled. "Alright then, you absolute goblins. Let's play."

****

CHAPTER 11 – Frequency of Fury
Monday 18th November 2019

Nelly, being bored while at her Cheshire home, was browsing Instagram when she found Capital Liverpool's latest post—an aggressively filtered promo shot of Dan Kilmare, grinning like a budget boyband reject.

@Capliverpool: *NEW HOST ALERT! Welcome Dan Kilmare to the Capital Liverpool Drive Show! Mornings just got BIGGER, BOLDER and BETTER! #WakeUpWithDan #CapitalLiverpool*

Nelly burst out laughing.

BIGGER, BOLDER, BETTER? Dan Kilmare? The same Dan Kilmare who was, until now, a Wessex Soundwave drive host, one of the former Breeze Media local hosts who had been absorbed into Manic during the buyout? The same Dan Kilmare who had spent the last two months sulking because Manic had overlooked him for a better slot? The same Dan Kilmare who had let her fuck him like a bored housewife in the middle of a midlife crisis, and then his late wife, Jenna, the same day in the bar in Liverpool tried to rip her head off for it?

Nelly snorted, sipping her G&T as she scrolled through the comments under Capital Liverpool's post. As expected, it was a mix of clueless listeners hyping him up and ex-Breeze presenters pretending to be supportive.

@radiofanatic98: *YESSSSSS!!! Dan is the best! Capital finally getting some proper talent!*

@exbreezerocks: Good luck, Dan! You deserve this! #TeamBreeze

@realradioinsider: Manic to Capital? Bit of a downgrade, mate. Have fun hitting the same six songs on repeat. #sellout

Nelly smirked. Someone *got it.*

Then she saw it—one particular comment that made her sit up a little straighter.

@dankilmareofficial: "Thanks for the love, everyone! And to the haters—keep watching this space. Some people think they can get away with anything... but not for long. #PapersBeingServed #JusticeForJenna

"Oh, fuck off," Nelly muttered under her breath.

The audacity. The sheer, steaming audacity of this man. Two months ago, he'd been crying over his wife's unconscious body in a Liverpool bar. And now he was throwing thinly veiled threats at *her?*

She refreshed the page, just to see if anyone had picked up on it. A few comments had—one ex-Breeze lackey responded with a string of clapping emojis, while some nosy bastards had started asking questions.

@manicfanboy: Go on, @dankilmareofficial, who's this about?

Nelly's pulse quickened. The bastard was baiting her. After two months of silence, Dan Kilmare was suddenly acting like some kind of righteous avenger, all because

Global had handed him a shiny new job at Capital Liverpool.

She tapped out a quick reply before she could think better of it.

@drnellyvixen: *You always were good at pretending, Danny boy. Enjoy the playlist of ten songs and zero personality. Let's hope your presenting skills are better than your legal threats. #SeeYouInCourt*

She hit send. Petty? Absolutely. But Dan had made the first move, and she wasn't about to sit there and let him paint himself as some kind of grieving widower seeking justice.

Her phone buzzed almost immediately. Jamie Wise.

"Jesus Christ, Nelly," he groaned as soon as she answered. "What did I tell you about not poking the bear?"

Nelly rolled her eyes, stretching out on the plush velvet sofa in her Cheshire home, one leg dangling lazily over the armrest. "Oh, come on, Jamie. You saw his post—what was I supposed to do? Let him chat shit unchecked?"

"You could've, I don't know, not responded?" Jamie's exasperation was palpable through the phone. "Maybe not goad a man who's already looking for an excuse to take you down?"

"Mate, he's already made up his mind," Nelly said, swirling the ice in her glass. "You think he got that Capital slot purely on 'talent'? Please. He sold them a sob story—

grieving widower, evil Vixen, tragic radio romance—it's like a fucking ITV drama."

"To be fair, Nell, you did tombstone his wife, and made the Undertaker look like he was a lazy rookie while doing it," Jamie shot back. "I mean, seriously, I thought you were gonna start rolling your eyes back and summoning the druids."

Nelly snorted. "Yeah, well, Jenna started it."

"You're really gonna use that as your legal defence? 'She threw the first slap, Your Honour'?" Jamie sighed. "Look, I know you think you're untouchable, but this isn't just some radio Twitter spat. If Dan's hinting at legal action, Global's backing him. They'd love nothing more than to take you and Manic down a peg. Remember who Global have as the Deputy Head of Legal."

Nelly's smirk faltered for just a second. She knew exactly who Jamie was talking about.

James Jenkins.

The same James Jenkins who had been behind Global's legal warfare for years, the man who had spent the better part of a decade dismantling rivals with surgical precision. The same James Jenkins whose wife, Carly Jenkins, was now Head of HR at Bauer, and the same James Jenkins who had, once upon a time, written a blog exposing Manic's own misogynistic past at one of its stations in the South East of England.

Yeah. That James Jenkins.

And now, he had a direct reason to come for her.

Nelly exhaled sharply, sitting up properly for the first time that evening. The warm buzz from her G&T faded slightly as reality sank in. This wasn't just Dan Kilmare being a bitter little weasel. This was him pulling the levers at Global, getting them to fight his battles. And James Jenkins? He'd love an excuse to take down someone like her. Someone who had made a career out of pissing off the establishment.

She hated to admit it, but Jamie had a point.

"Nate, love," Nelly said, muting the phone, summoning her husband who was in the entertainment room with some of his fellow plastic surgeons, watching a re-run of the Brazilian Grand Prix while drinking overpriced whiskey. "Get in here. Now."

A moment later, her husband, Dr Nate Robinson, appeared in the doorway, a tumbler of Macallan in hand, wearing the expression of a man who knew whatever he was about to hear was going to give him a headache.

"Get that lawyer friend of yours on the phone, I need him here on the double," Nelly said, her voice sharper now. "Dan Kilmare's making moves, and if Global's backing him, we need to get ahead of this before it spirals."

Nate let out a low groan, taking a slow sip of his whiskey. "Jesus, Nelly. What now? Did you call his dead wife a slag on Twitter or something?"

"No, but now that you mention it—"

"Nelly." His tone was flat. A warning.

She rolled her eyes. "I didn't. But Dan's making noise, and he-"

And as predicted, it was the Royal Mail, with 6 parcels, plus a stack of envelopes in his hand. Nelly knew that her husband had his business bills and some of his equipment delivered to the house instead of to his surgery, as he claimed it was a tax loophole, though Nelly never cared enough to find out if that was actually true.

Opening the door, Nelly chuckled as she saw the Louis Vuitton box, a suitcase and some jewellery from the Les Gastons Vuitton collection that she had saw, a total of nearly £20,000 in purchases made purely on impulse.

The fact that she recognised that specific parcel purely because the LV monogram tape was enough to make her smirk. "Merry bloody Christmas to me," she murmured, signing for the packages without even glancing at the rest of the post.

"Bit early for that, love," the postman chuckled, handing over the stack of letters with an amused shake of his head. "You lot in these Cheshire mansions must keep Harrods in business single-handedly."

Nelly gave him a wink. "Someone has to."

She grabbed the rest of the post and shut the door, carrying the haul back into the living room where Nate was still standing, watching her with mild irritation. "Are you done with your little Selfridges spree, or are we actually dealing with whatever PR disaster you've cooked up this time?"

Nelly ignored him, flipping through the envelopes absently, half-expecting to see the usual mix of credit card statements, PR invites, and glossy, oversized charity gala requests.

Then she saw it.

A thick, cream-coloured envelope, unmistakably official. A legal notice. The return address?

A thick, cream-coloured envelope, unmistakably official. A legal notice. The return address?

Potter and Associates, 30 St Mary Axe, London.

Nelly stopped dead in her tracks, staring at the envelope as if it might explode in her hands.

Potter and Associates.

A top-tier, cutthroat legal firm that did class action lawsuits, private prosecutions, and, most worryingly, media litigation.

Nelly's stomach tightened. This was it. The first official shot fired.

She flipped the envelope over and tore it open with one manicured nail, her pulse quickening as she pulled out the neatly folded letter. The firm's expensive letterhead gleamed in embossed black ink at the top.

"Re: Private Criminal Prosecution - Dr Eleanor Robinson.

Dear Dr Robinson

We are instructed by our client, Mr Daniel Kilmare, to initiate private criminal proceedings against you in relation to an alleged act of grievous bodily harm (GBH) under Section 20 of the Offences Against the Person Act 1861 and murder, contrary to common law. The allegations concern an incident at The Merchant Bar, Liverpool, on the evening of 10 September 2019, wherein it is claimed that you inflicted serious injuries upon our client's late wife, Ms Jenna Kilmare, contributing to her subsequent medical complications and distress.

In accordance with legal procedure, we will be presenting this matter before the Magistrates' Court in the coming weeks, seeking a summons for you to attend a preliminary hearing.

Additionally, we are advised that our client reserves his rights in pursuing a separate civil claim for damages, the details of which will be outlined in due course.

We recommend that you seek independent legal representation at your earliest convenience.

Yours sincerely,

Potter & Associates

30 St Mary Axe, London"

Nelly stared at the letter, the weight of its words settling like a stone in her chest. Grievous bodily harm? Murder? Murder?

For a moment, the entire world narrowed to that single accusation. Her mind, usually sharp as a scalpel, stalled completely. Then, like a dam breaking, the outrage surged.

"This is fucking ridiculous," she muttered, shaking the letter as if it might shake loose some logic.

Jamie's voice crackled through the phone, forgotten in her other hand. "Nelly? What's going on?"

She pressed the phone to her ear, her other hand still clutching the legal notice. "Dan's actually gone through with it. The prick's trying to privately prosecute me. For GBH and murder."

There was a beat of stunned silence on Jamie's end. Then: "I… I'm sorry, what?"

"I killed Jenna, apparently."

Nate, who had been watching her with growing concern, snatched the letter from her hands and skimmed it. "Oh, for fuck's sake." He pinched the bridge of his nose. "This is some next-level bullshit."

Nelly exhaled sharply, pacing the length of the living room, her designer slippers scuffing lightly against the floor. "Jamie, you need to call Scott. Get the Manic lawyers on this yesterday. If Global thinks they can weaponize this pathetic sob story to take me down, they've got another thing coming."

"This isn't Global, Nell," Nate said, looking over her shoulder and sighing. "This smells of a case where the law firm has got insurance against it, and they're trying to make a name for themselves. They want a settlement, not a conviction."

Jamie let out a low whistle. "GBH and murder? Jesus Christ, Nell, I knew Dan was bitter, but this is some next-level American true crime bullshit."

Nelly clenched her jaw, trying to contain the rising anger bubbling in her chest. She wasn't the panicking type—far from it—but the sheer audacity of Dan Kilmare, the sheer stupidity of this entire circus, was making her hands shake.

She slumped onto the sofa, the ridiculous amount of expensive post still piled beside her, the unopened LV suitcase now a stark contrast to the legal document she was gripping so tightly that her nails were digging into the paper.

"It's a bluff," she said finally, though the words felt unconvincing, even to her. "No way does this actually hold up in court."

Nate exhaled sharply, running a hand through his neatly styled hair. "You better hope it's a bluff, love, because even if it doesn't hold up, this is the kind of PR nightmare that could bury you alive."

Jamie hummed in agreement. "Even if it gets laughed out of the Magistrates' Court, the damage is already done. It's the allegation that sticks in people's minds. Not the verdict."

Nelly scoffed. "Please. Like I haven't survived worse scandals."

"Yeah," Jamie shot back. "But none of those involved a murder charge, babe."

Silence. The room suddenly felt very cold.

Nate sighed, taking another sip of his Macallan. "We need to be smart about this. First things first, you don't say a fucking word online. No Twitter, no Instagram digs, no cryptic 'lol, I'm untouchable' posts. You love poking the bear, Nelly, but right now, the bear has a fucking legal team."

Nelly pursed her lips, resisting the urge to argue. As much as she hated to admit it, Nate had a point.

Jamie cleared his throat. "I'll get in touch with Scott. Manic's lawyers are ruthless when it comes to protecting their own, especially since they know Global would love to sink their teeth into this mess. But Nelly... if this actually makes it to court, you're gonna need to lawyer up. Like, properly lawyer up."

Nelly let out a slow breath, running a hand through her blonde extensions. Lawyer up. It felt ridiculous, even hearing it aloud. This was Dan fucking Kilmare—Dan. A man whose biggest career achievement until now had been doing Men at Work Mondays on Wessex Soundwave.

And now, thanks to Global throwing their weight behind him, he was making a play to take her down.

No. Not happening.

"Fine," she said, pushing herself up from the sofa, her spine straightening. "Call Scott. I'll get my own lawyers on standby too." She turned to Nate. "And you're coming with me when I meet them. No offence, darling, but I trust your people more than I trust Manic's corporate lapdogs."

Nate sighed, swirling the whiskey in his glass before downing it in one. "I'll set up a meeting."

Jamie exhaled down the line. "Alright, that's a start. But Nelly, seriously—don't underestimate how much Global wants this to blow up. James Jenkins has been dying to get back at Manic for years, and this? This is gold for him."

Nelly's lips curled into a smirk, though there was something darker behind it now. "Well then," she murmured, "it looks like I've got a war to win."

****

CHAPTER 12 – Jackpot Justice
Wednesday 20th November 2019

Paul Barrington, Nelly decided, was a right bastard—but a bastard that Nate was paying a fortune to have on retainer, both for his business affairs and, now, her impending legal war.

Barrington was a tall, wiry man in his mid-forties, with the permanent air of someone who had seen too much and been paid too well to care. His suit was as sharp as his legal mind, and he had the unnerving ability to make you feel like you'd already lost a case before he even opened his mouth.

He glanced over the paperwork in his Mayfair office, his expression unreadable. The floor-to-ceiling windows behind him framed the City of London in all its capitalist glory, but Nelly was too preoccupied with the legal document in his hands to appreciate the view.

"So," Barrington finally said, placing the document down on his sleek, minimalist desk. "You're being privately prosecuted for GBH and murder."

Nelly crossed one leg over the other, feigning indifference. "Allegedly."

Barrington raised an unimpressed eyebrow. "Private prosecutions aren't just for show, Dr Robinson. This isn't some Twitter spat with a Capital FM DJ. If it moves forward, it will be in a courtroom, and if a magistrate allows it, you'll be standing trial in front of a jury. And if you're convicted of GBH under Section 20?" He leaned back in his chair. "Five years, minimum."

Nate, seated beside her, let out a slow exhale. His usually relaxed posture was noticeably tenser, one hand clasped around his whisky tumbler like it was the only thing keeping him grounded. "This is ridiculous," he muttered. "Everyone knows it was a bar fight. The woman had a heart attack. Nelly didn't murder her."

Nelly exhaled sharply, her fingers tapping impatiently on the armrest of the leather chair. "Exactly. This isn't some calculated assassination; it was two pissed-up women in a bar who had a scrap. And now, because Dan Kilmare's a bitter little prick with a saviour complex, I'm apparently a criminal mastermind."

Barrington's lips twitched in what might have been the shadow of a smirk. "Nevertheless, this is serious. Your name, your career, your reputation—everything is on the line here. If we go to trial, the media will have a field day. 'Dr Nelly Vixen, the Femme Fatale of British Radio.'" He drummed his fingers on the desk. "They'll frame it as if you strangled her with a microphone cord, and Kilmare will lap up every second of it."

Nate swirled his drink, his jaw tight. "And if it does go to trial?"

Barrington exhaled through his nose. "It depends on the judge. If we're lucky, they'll throw it out before it even reaches a jury. If we're not…" He shrugged. "You'll need the best barrister money can buy. And I mean, *the* best."

Nelly leaned forward, her eyes gleaming with something dangerously close to amusement. "Well, then, I suppose it's a good thing I married a man who likes to throw money at problems, isn't it?"

Nate shot her a warning look. "This isn't a joke, Nelly."

Barrington clasped his hands together. "Indeed. Now, as the event happened over a month ago, and the police cleared you of all charges, there is no CCTV at the bar in question, meaning that this case hinges entirely on witness testimony."

Barrington's voice was smooth and unbothered, but his words carried weight.

"Which means," he continued, adjusting his silver cufflinks, "if even one witness paints a convincing enough story, it gives the prosecution a foundation to argue that Jenna Kilmare's death was a direct result of your actions. And since private prosecutions don't rely on the Crown Prosecution Service, we're looking at a completely different beast. I assume that the witnesses in this case are split on the events and their own view of what happened that night?"

Nelly scoffed, rolling her eyes. "Oh, absolutely. The Manic lot are firmly in my corner and the ex-Breeze lot have made me out to be Jack the Ripper."

Barrington gave a slow, measured nod. "That's what I assumed. If it comes down to a battle of testimonies, it won't just be a question of what happened that night. It'll be a question of character. The prosecution will paint you as a reckless, egotistical, violent woman with no regard for consequence."

Nelly smirked. "So… me, then."

Nate groaned, rubbing his temples. "Nelly, for Christ's sake."

"Nate, you know I'm a chaos gremlin, and I'm not about to start pretending I'm Mother Teresa now," Nelly quipped, drumming her manicured nails against the armrest of the chair.

"Mother Teresa wouldn't be able to cope with the mayhem on your chart show," Barrington remarked dryly. "Unfortunately for you, courts don't respond well to 'chaos gremlins' with a history of on-air controversy, tabloid scandals, and public bar brawls."

Nelly rolled her eyes. "Brilliant. So, what's our move?"

Barrington steepled his fingers together, his expression one of quiet calculation. "We have a few options. First, we attempt to have the case struck out before it reaches trial. If the magistrate rules that there is insufficient evidence to proceed, the case collapses before it even begins. However, given the press attention surrounding this, I suspect the court may be inclined to let it run its course."

"Because it makes for a good headline," Nate muttered, his grip tightening on his glass.

"Exactly." Barrington gave him a knowing look. "Which brings us to option two. We fight it in court. As the opposition is using another City firm, one which, thankfully, Global Media don't use, means that its not being backed by their employer, that it's a privately funded case. This means two things: one, Dan Kilmare is either personally paying for this, which is unlikely given his previous salary and current financial standing, or two, someone else is bankrolling him. Someone with a vested interest in seeing you crash and burn. Now, it's useless asking if you have any enemies, isn't it?"

Nelly smirked, crossing her arms as she leaned back in her chair. "Enemies? Darling, I have a fan club dedicated to hating me. Shall I send you a list?"

Barrington didn't react beyond a slow blink. "Who, specifically, would want to see you publicly humiliated, legally ruined, and, ideally, out of a job?"

Nelly chewed on her lower lip, her mind whirring through the possibilities. "Well, the obvious answer is Global. But if they were behind it, they wouldn't be using Potter & Associates. They'd be using someone from their usual legal team—someone like James Jenkins."

Barrington nodded. "Exactly. Which means this isn't an official Global vendetta. It's personal."

Nate exhaled, rubbing his jaw. "Dan doesn't have the money for this. So, who the hell does?"

"Well, unless Dan's won the lottery, then I don't know," Nelly said, chuckling.

Barrington didn't laugh. Instead, he tapped a long finger against the desk, his expression unreadable. "There's always someone willing to fund a personal grudge," he said smoothly. "And if Kilmare is playing the part of the grieving widower-turned-hero of justice, then whoever is backing him is equally invested in seeing you fall."

Nelly leaned forward, her tone laced with impatience. "So how do we find out who's behind this?"

Barrington allowed a small smirk to form on his lips. "Leave that to me."

Nate shifted in his seat, his body language radiating discomfort. "This is insane," he muttered. "It's been two months, and suddenly, he's got the backing to launch a private prosecution. Someone is pulling the strings here."

Nelly drummed her nails against the armrest. "And I want to know who."

Barrington nodded. "I'll make some enquiries. In the meantime, you keep your head down."

Nelly scoffed. "Darling, I don't do 'head down.'"

Barrington merely raised an eyebrow. "Then learn. Because the more you poke at this, the worse it will get."

Nate exhaled sharply and stood, draining the last of his whisky. "Come on, Nelly. We've got enough to process for one day."

Nelly hesitated for half a second before following suit, rising gracefully from her chair. "Fine," she conceded. "But if this turns into a public circus, I'm not going to sit quietly."

Barrington smirked. "Oh, I'd never expect you to."

As they left his Mayfair office and stepped out onto the pavement, the crisp November air cutting against her skin, Nelly's phone buzzed in her pocket. She pulled it out, her brows furrowing as she saw a notification.

@dankilmareofficial: *Yes, I have to get it off my chest… I won the Euromillions last week, all £135million of it. But that doesn't affect my @Capitalliv show, as I'm still going to be making you Scousers laugh every weekday on drive!* # *LiverpoolsHitMusic*

Nelly stared at the tweet for a full ten seconds before bursting into laughter.

"Are you actually kidding me?" she exclaimed, shoving the phone towards Nate, who was rubbing his temple like he was already nursing a migraine. "This bastard won the bloody Euromillions?!"

Nate took one look at the tweet and exhaled sharply. "Well, that answers one question. Looks like Kilmare is paying for this himself."

"You know, Nate... if this was America, we'd be getting a Netflix docuseries out of this," Nelly finished, shaking her head in amused disbelief. "Making a Murderer—but make it Making a Radio Presenter."

Nate let out a weary sigh, pinching the bridge of his nose. "Or maybe just Making a Bloody Mess."

They stood on the pavement outside Barrington's office, the sharp chill of a November evening settling around them. London's elite scurried past in tailored coats and expensive shoes, oblivious to the absolute circus unfolding in the world of commercial radio.

Nelly scrolled through Twitter, watching as the comments under Dan Kilmare's ridiculous Euromillions announcement piled up. Predictably, Capital's listeners were buzzing with excitement, the usual 'You deserve this, Dan!' and 'Omg congrats!' flooding in.

But then there were the others. The ones from the industry.

@realradioinsider: *So, let me get this straight. Dan Kilmare won £135 MILLION and is still doing Capital Liverpool Drive? Commitment or insanity?*

@manicfanboy: *Lmfaoooo Manic pays minimum wage, so I'd get why he'd want to stay. But Capital? He's literally being paid in Greggs vouchers.*

@exbreezerocks: *Maybe he just really loves being on air. Radio isn't just a job, it's a passion!*

@pepsichartthrowback: *Oh please. Dan Kilmare is still bitter as hell over Nelly Vixen. And now he's rich enough to fund a bloody legal case? You know he's gonna milk this for all it's worth.*

Nelly snorted at the last one. "Someone gets it."

Nate, however, was less amused. "I don't like this, Nelly. Not one bit."

She rolled her eyes, tucking her phone into her coat pocket. "You don't like a lot of things. What's new?"

"What's new," Nate said tightly, "is that this idiot now has unlimited resources to throw at you. Before, we assumed someone was bankrolling him. But now? He can throw cash at this case like it's a Saturday night at bloody Annabel's. And do you know what happens when someone has nothing to lose and more money than sense?"

Nelly smirked. "They get annoying?"

"They get dangerous," Nate corrected, his expression darkening. "You need to take this seriously."

"I am taking it seriously," Nelly argued, folding her arms. "I just refuse to panic over it."

"You should panic," Nate muttered. "Because I've met people like Kilmare before. They're not dangerous because they're smart—they're dangerous because they're stupid and rich. And that is a terrifying combination."

Nelly hesitated. She hated to admit it, but he had a point.

She was used to handling people like Scott Bennett—the Manic CEO who thrived on chaos but had a business brain sharper than a knife. Or James Jenkins—the Global lawyer who played the long game, dismantling his opponents piece by piece.

But Dan Kilmare?

Dan Kilmare was an emotional wreck with £135 million in his bank account and a personal grudge driving him forward.

And that? That was a wildcard.

"Let's get a drink," she said abruptly, shaking off the uneasy feeling creeping into her chest.

Nate raised an eyebrow. "You think getting pissed is the answer?"

"I think it's my answer," Nelly shot back. "Come on, I know a place that does a dirty martini that could solve world peace."

Nate sighed but followed her lead as she flagged down a black cab.

****

Walking around Harrods, Nelly decided that she wanted to do what she did best when under pressure—spend an obscene amount of money on things she didn't need.

Nate, who had agreed to tag along only because he needed a distraction from the absolute mess unfolding around them, was already regretting it. He trailed behind her as she strolled through the designer section like a queen surveying her kingdom, plucking up items with the casual ease of someone who knew price tags were irrelevant.

"You're stress-shopping," Nate muttered, watching as she picked up a silk Gucci blouse without so much as glancing at the price.

"I am," Nelly admitted, holding it against her frame and giving an approving nod before passing it to the assistant. "And it's working."

Nate pinched the bridge of his nose. "You do realise spending ten grand in Harrods isn't going to make Kilmare's legal case disappear, right?"

"No," she said breezily, moving onto the display of Balenciaga sunglasses. "But it'll make me look fabulous while I fight it. Anyway, who said anything about ten grand? Your bank balance is over a million, so you can afford what I've got planned."

Dragging Nate to the escalators, Nelly took him to the technology department, where she knew they sold a Bang & Olufsen Beosound Balance Speaker, a £3,000 masterpiece which she absolutely did not need but suddenly couldn't live without.

"Let me get this straight," Nate sighed, watching as she gestured at the assistant with the practised ease of someone who was far too used to getting what she wanted. "You're under a private prosecution for GBH and murder, you're about to be dragged through the legal system by an emotionally unstable radio presenter who just won the bloody Euromillions, and your solution is to drop a small fortune on a speaker?" Nate finished, rubbing his temple like he was on the verge of an aneurysm.

Nelly flashed him a sweet, saccharine smile. "Not just any speaker, darling. A statement piece."

The Harrods assistant—a well-groomed man in his late twenties who clearly recognised the particular brand of chaos he was dealing with—remained professionally neutral as he nodded. "An excellent choice, madam. The Beosound Balance is one of our finest wireless speakers, offering room-filling sound with a sleek, minimalist design."

Nate groaned. "Christ, don't encourage her."

Nelly turned to the assistant, all charm. "Can you have it delivered to my Cheshire address? And charge it to my husband."

"Of course, madam," the assistant replied smoothly, already punching the details into his tablet.

"Good, and do you do the Therabody Theragun G4 PRO as well?" Nelly asked, flashing a knowing smirk at Nate. "Because if I'm going to be stress-shopping, I may as well invest in something to massage away all the tension you're giving me."

The assistant nodded eagerly. "Yes, madam, we do have the Theragun G4 PRO in stock."

"Excellent. Add it to the order," she said with a flick of her wrist.

Nate sighed deeply, rubbing his temples again. "You are actually insane."

"I'm retail therapy-ing," Nelly corrected, eyeing up an Ember Smart Mug, a luxury temperature-controlled mug that she definitely didn't need but suddenly had an overwhelming desire for. "You should try it sometime, Nate. It might do wonders for your stress levels."

Nate groaned. "Nelly, this isn't therapy. This is you spending an obscene amount of money on things you'll forget about in a week."

"Incorrect," she said, handing the mug to the assistant with a dazzling smile. "I'll remember them every time I use them to drown out the sound of my impending trial. Now, I need a new MacBook Pro, as my old one has seen better days, and if I'm going to be dealing with lawyers, PR disasters, and the absolute circus that is my life right now, I might as well do it on a laptop that doesn't crash every time I try to open a Google Doc."

Nate, at this point, had fully resigned himself to his fate. He crossed his arms, watching as she sashayed over to the Apple section with all the confidence of a woman who had just declared financial war on her own husband's bank account.

"I swear to God, Nelly, if this ends with you trying to expense 'fighting a murder charge' as a legitimate reason for blowing through a five-figure sum—"

"Relax, darling." Nelly turned to him with a wink. "It's an investment. Besides, if I do go to prison, at least I'll have some nice things to remember my freedom by."

Nate let out a long, slow sigh. "You are actually insufferable."

"I know," she replied cheerfully, tapping at the MacBook display. "I'll take this one. The 16-inch, fully specced. And do you have the AirPods Pro in stock? I'll take those too."

The assistant, who had clearly worked in Harrods long enough to recognise a customer with no budgetary concerns, nodded smoothly. "Of course, madam."

Nate turned to the assistant with a defeated expression. "Do you have any discount for husbands who are being financially exploited?"

The assistant's lips twitched, but he remained professionally neutral. "I'm afraid not, sir."

"Figures."

Nelly watched as an Arab Sheikh walked past her with an entourage of security detail and three personal shoppers trailing behind him, each carrying a different designer bag. She smirked, turning back to Nate with a playful gleam in her eyes.

"See? I could be worse. At least I'm not demanding a crocodile Hermès Birkin and a Rolls-Royce Phantom."

Nate exhaled sharply. "Not yet."

She grinned, nudging him lightly as she moved to the checkout area, where the Harrods assistant was efficiently processing the ludicrously expensive haul.

"Right, darling," she said, linking her arm through his as they waited. "Since you're already suffering, you might as well take me to dinner."

"You've just bankrupted me," Nate deadpanned. "And now you want dinner?"

"Oh, please, don't be dramatic," Nelly scoffed. "You're a bloody plastic surgeon in Cheshire. Half your clients are WAGs and reality stars who pay you obscene amounts to keep their faces from melting. You'll survive."

Nate pinched the bridge of his nose but didn't argue. "Fine. Where?"

She pretended to ponder, tapping a manicured finger against her chin. "Somewhere expensive. Somewhere with overpriced steak and a wine list so pretentious it comes with a sommelier who frowns at you if you mispronounce 'Châteauneuf-du-Pape'. Failing that, the Savoy at the Ritz. I've got a fancy for Aylesbury Pekin Duck."

Nate stared at her, expression somewhere between exasperation and resigned amusement. "You want me to take you to the Savoy at the Ritz after you've just spent the GDP of a small country in Harrods?"

Nelly batted her eyelashes at him. "You're the one who said I should take this seriously. And honestly, I can't think properly on an empty stomach. This is a crisis, Nate. And in times of crisis, one must eat well."

Nate exhaled sharply but gestured for her to lead the way. "Fine. But if you order the most expensive bottle of wine on the menu, I'm charging you interest on this little shopping spree."

She beamed, looping her arm through his as they left Harrods. "Darling, I would never."

Nelly noticed her husband groaning at how she had just effortlessly drained his bank account, but she chose to ignore it. He'd survive. He always did. Besides, if she was about to face the fight of her life, she was going to do it wrapped in silk, sipping vintage wine, and listening to Bang & Olufsen-quality sound.

"You know I do love you, Nate," Nelly said, holding her husband's hand as they stepped into the cab waiting outside Harrods.

Nate let out a long sigh, rubbing his temple with his free hand. "I know, Nelly. I also know you only say that when you've just done something that's either financially ruinous or legally dubious."

Nelly laughed, leaning her head on his shoulder as the cab pulled into the busy London traffic. "Darling, if I was legally dubious, I wouldn't be sitting in the back of a black cab, would I? I'd be halfway to Monaco by now, sipping champagne and watching you try to find a lawyer willing to take me on."

Nate didn't dignify that with a response, instead glancing at her shopping bags with a mix of exasperation and reluctant admiration. "You do realise if this all goes to court, you're going to be scrutinised for every single thing you've ever done, right? This is a dangerous game, and you're playing it like it's just another radio stunt."

She sat up, suddenly serious. "Oh, I know exactly how dangerous this is." Her blue eyes darkened, her playful smirk replaced by something sharper. "But here's the thing, Nate. If Dan Kilmare thinks he can outmanoeuvre me in the press, he's in for a very rude awakening."

Nate arched an eyebrow. "You've got a plan?"

Nelly smirked, reaching for her phone. "Of course I do."

She pulled up her Instagram story, staring at the perfect opportunity to set the tone before Dan Kilmare got to spin his sob story to the tabloids. A picture from earlier, taken while trying on sunglasses in Harrods—a casual, effortless image of luxury, captioned:

"When life hands you lemons, make a very expensive gin and tonic. Cheers, darlings."

She hit post, ignoring Nate's groan beside her.

"You really don't know when to back down, do you?" he muttered.

Nelly grinned, slipping her phone back into her bag. "Oh, darling, backing down is for people who don't know how to win."

And with that, she leaned back against the seat, already mentally crafting her next move.

Dan Kilmare had fired his first shot. Now it was her turn.

And she never played fair.

****

CHAPTER 13 – A Shot of Gin, A Twist of Revenge

Friday 22nd November 2019

Of all the gin joints in all of the world, Nelly, walking into Liverpool Gin Distillery, didn't expect Dan Kilmare to be there, filming content for Capital's Instagram.

Nelly had to bite the inside of her cheek to stop from laughing. Of course he was here. Of course Capital Liverpool had sent their newest drive-time darling to a gin distillery for some half-baked, brand-friendly social content. Because nothing said Liverpool's Hit Music like a bloke who had just won £135 million pretending to care about locally distilled spirits for the sake of engagement metrics.

She clocked him immediately—slicked-back hair, spray-on jeans, and a Capital-branded bomber jacket that screamed I am a corporate puppet now. He was perched at the bar, clutching a gin glass like it was a prop in a West End production, chatting animatedly to a pint-sized Capital producer holding a stabiliser-mounted iPhone.

The fact he was still wearing his wedding ring as if he hadn't just spent the last few days weaponizing his dead wife's memory for legal clout made Nelly's blood boil. But instead of giving him the satisfaction of a reaction, she smirked, adjusted the cuffs of her camel-coloured Burberry trench coat, and strode to the bar with the air of someone who had absolutely no intention of acknowledging his existence.

"And that's what I've made, thanks to the guys here at Liverpool Gin Distillery," Dan was saying, his voice projecting the kind of false enthusiasm reserved for people who had been media-trained into oblivion. "Buy the special edition Capital Gin only at Liverpool Gin Distillery—just in time for Christmas—while it's still in stock!"

Nelly rolled her eyes so hard she nearly sprained something. Capital Gin? Christ, they really would slap their logo on anything. What next—Capital-branded Weatherspoons?

"That's good Dan," the producer said, and Nelly groaned, as she had, for Manic, done her own fair share of promo shoots in random locations with sponsors who had about as much relevance to her show as she did to the Radio 4 shipping forecast. The difference was, at least when she did it, she had the self-awareness to take the piss out of herself in the process.

She leaned against the bar, catching the bartender's attention with a raised eyebrow. "Large gin and tonic, heavy on the gin, minimal on the tonic." She said it loud enough that she knew Dan would hear.

Listening in, Nelly then heard Dan talking on the phone, and it wasn't talking to a colleague or boss, but, by the sound of it, talking to his solicitor.

Nelly turned slightly, pretending to check her phone while tilting her head just enough to catch snippets of the conversation. She had long since mastered the art of passive eavesdropping—a skill honed from years of navigating the cutthroat world of radio, where gossip was currency and information was power.

"Yeah, yeah, I know," Dan muttered, his voice just low enough to sound secretive but just loud enough to carry across the bar. "She walked in as if she owns the bloody joint while I'm doing my job for Capital. Surely she can't be allowed to influence a witness or harass the victim of a crime. After all, the bitch killed my wife."

Nelly almost snorted into her gin and tonic. Oh, this was rich. Dan Kilmare, suddenly the grieving widower-slash-moral crusader, painting himself as the victim when he was the one weaponizing Jenna's death for a courtroom spectacle? It would have been laughable if it wasn't so utterly pathetic.

The irony that she had slept with him before the incident, the fight where Jenna Kilmare had died of a heart attack and not, in Nelly's mind, because of the tombstone piledriver or the other wrestling moves Nelly had used in self-defence, was almost too much to bear. She knew Dan was spinning a narrative, one that conveniently left out the fact that Jenna had come at her first, clawing and shrieking in a drunken rage, throwing punches that Nelly had simply been better at dodging. Jenna had been unhinged, and Nelly had been the unfortunate target. But now, thanks to Dan's vendetta and his newfound Euromillions-backed legal war chest, the entire story had been rewritten into some Shakespearean tragedy where Nelly was the villain.

Taking a slow sip of her gin, she leaned ever so slightly closer, tilting her head to hear more.

"I just want this to be over, mate," Dan was saying, voice laced with performative exhaustion. "I want justice, and I want her to pay for what she did. That woman… she's a monster. She's walking around, drinking gin like she doesn't have blood on her hands. I want a restraining order banning her from being within… well, whatever the maximum distance that she can be from me. 500 metres? A kilometre? Whatever keeps that psycho out of my life. She killed my Jenna, and she deserves to rot in prison for it."

Nelly gripped her gin glass so tightly that the stem threatened to snap. Rot in prison? Oh, Kilmare was really going for it now. The absolute nerve of this man. A bloke who, just two months ago, had been riding her like she was a fairground attraction, was now standing in a gin distillery, publicly declaring her the second coming of Harold Shipman.

She took a slow, measured breath. She wasn't stupid—losing her temper here, in public, while Kilmare was conveniently on camera, was exactly what he wanted. He wanted her to cause a scene, to give him the perfect clip to parade around in court as proof that she was unhinged.

Instead, she smiled.

A slow, calculated, downright murderous smile.

Time to remind Dan Kilmare that he wasn't the only one who could play dirty.

She turned on her heel, sauntering up to him like a lioness approaching a wounded gazelle.

"Ah, Danny boy," she drawled, her voice dripping with faux sweetness as she plucked the gin glass from his hand before he could react. She took a slow, deliberate sip, maintaining eye contact the entire time, then placed it back on the bar. "Lovely to see you. What's this I hear about you getting a Capital-branded gin? How very… on-brand for a sellout."

"I'm only doing my job. After all, I refuse to work for a company that helps murderers keep their jobs and profit off the controversy," Dan shot back, puffing out his chest in a poor attempt at looking intimidating. "Unlike you, some of us actually have standards."

Nelly let out a bark of laughter. "Standards?" she echoed, eyes gleaming with amusement. "Dan, sweetheart, you work for Capital FM. Your entire job is to read out time checks between the same ten songs on repeat and pretend to care about Little Mix's latest single. You are quite literally a playlist monkey in a bomber jacket."

Dan's face reddened. "At least I have a job that doesn't involve being a professional train wreck."

"Oh, please." Nelly took another sip of her gin, leaning lazily against the bar. "You'd still be grovelling for an off-peak slot on Wessex Soundwave if you hadn't won the bloody Euromillions. And now you've decided to spend your newfound fortune on launching a vendetta against me instead of doing something actually productive—like, I don't know, buying a private island and retiring in peace."

Dan clenched his jaw, his fists twitching at his sides. "You can mock me all you want, but it doesn't change the fact that you're a killer, and I'm going to make sure the world knows it. I loved Jenna, and you murdered her in cold blood."

"So says the man who fancied a cheap shag in the bogs at the M&S Bank Arena during the Manic Boot Camp and then got found out by his wife."

"Oh, piss off Vixen," Dan's producer, a blonde woman who was wearing the usual Capital corporate uniform of an oversized branded hoodie and leggings, interjected. "You can't just waltz in here and start harassing our talent while we're working."

"Oh, piss off Vixen," Dan's producer, a blonde woman who was wearing the usual Capital corporate uniform of an oversized branded hoodie and leggings, interjected. "You can't just waltz in here and start harassing our talent while we're working. Anyway, you're just pissed off because you can't get RAJAR #1 for your chart show while The Big Top 40 with Will Manning is battering you in the ratings," she finished, folding her arms across her chest with all the smugness of a middle manager who'd just been given a free Greggs voucher at a team-building exercise.

Nelly's smirk didn't falter, but internally, she had to fight the urge to roll her eyes. Oh, this was precious. A Capital producer trying to come for her over RAJAR figures? The same Capital that had been haemorrhaging local audiences ever since they axed regional breakfast shows?

The same Capital whose entire strategy was now just "put Roman Kemp on everything and hope for the best"?

"Bless your heart," Nelly purred, swirling her gin with theatrical nonchalance. "Tell me, darling, do they actually teach you to say that in Capital FM producer school, or do you all just absorb the corporate Kool-Aid through osmosis?"

The producer's smugness wavered for a fraction of a second before she recovered, scowling. "Face it, Nelly, your shock-jock act is tired. Nobody wants some has-been controversial presenter on a chart show. People want feel-good, family-friendly, professional radio, and that's why Dan is on the rise while you're on your way out."

"Ah, yes," Nelly nodded sagely. "Professional radio. You mean the kind where presenters are encouraged to be so generic and interchangeable that they could be replaced by a voice-tracked AI and nobody would notice?" She took a slow sip of her gin. "Sounds riveting."

Dan stepped forward, shoulders squared, attempting to regain some of his earlier bravado. "Laugh all you want, Vixen. But I'm not the one on trial. You are. And when the courts see you for what you really are—a bitter, violent, washed-up bitch who plagiarised her PhD thesis and killed a pregnant woman. You know the autopsy found she was two months pregnant, so it's not just my wife you killed."

For a moment, Nelly felt the air in the room shift.

She had always known Dan Kilmare was a pathetic little worm, a second-rate presenter who had clawed his way up the radio ladder by sheer force of ego and opportunism rather than talent. But this?

This was new.

This was nuclear.

She stared at him, her usual smirk frozen in place, though inside, something dark and sharp and *dangerous* curled in her chest like a coiled snake.

"Two months pregnant?" she echoed, her voice deceptively light. "And you're just bringing this up now?"

Dan's nostrils flared. "Because I didn't know until I got the autopsy report back, did I?"

Nelly hummed, swirling the last of her gin in her glass. "That's interesting, considering your wife was off her face on double vodka Red Bulls and screaming at me like a banshee before she dropped dead. But sure, let's go with the narrative where I'm a cold-blooded murderer."

Dan's face darkened. "You don't even care, do you?"

"Oh, sweetheart." Nelly finally placed her glass on the bar with a soft clink. "If I didn't care, I wouldn't still be standing here, listening to you flounder around for the most tragic-sounding angle you can find. First, I was a drunken thug who lashed out. Then I was some calculated assassin. Now I'm a—what? A baby killer? Is that the angle you're going for?"

Dan's jaw tensed.

The Capital producer took a cautious step back, realising this was spiralling into something well beyond the standard banter they were used to throwing at Manic presenters.

Nelly tilted her head. "Tell me, Danny boy, did she even know? Because if you're trying to sell me this sob story about your poor, saintly, pregnant wife, I'd really love to know if she ever got the chance to tell you—or if this is just another convenient little detail you're trotting out for maximum sympathy points."

Dan's lips pressed into a thin line, his eyes darting away for the briefest moment.

Gotcha.

The bastard hadn't known.

Nelly almost pitied him. Almost.

"I don't need to explain anything to you," Dan finally spat. "The courts will see the truth. The public will see the truth. I don't care how many snarky little one-liners you throw around—your career is done. You're done. And the best bit is, it's not reliant on the taxpayer for the prosecution, meaning, you murdering bitch, that I'll be seeing you in court no matter what. You see, the CPS may have not charged you because Jenna had a heart condition, and the Judicial Review failed, I still can, according to my lawyer, take you for wrongful death. And with my new fortune, I can throw everything at you until you're ruined."

Nelly regarded him for a long, slow moment, her expression unreadable. Then, finally, she let out a short, dry laugh.

"Oh, Danny boy," she sighed, shaking her head as if she was genuinely disappointed in him. "You really should've stopped when you were ahead."

Dan scowled. "What's that supposed to mean?"

"It means," Nelly said, stepping forward until there was barely a breath of space between them, her voice dropping just enough that only he could hear, "you've just admitted, on camera, in front of witnesses, that this whole prosecution isn't about 'justice'—it's about revenge."

Dan froze.

His eyes flickered to the Capital producer, who chuckled. "I didn't record it, Dan, so don't worry, mate." She shook her head with amusement. "But, I mean… you probably shouldn't have said that out loud."

Nelly smirked, watching Dan's confidence flicker for just a second. The Capital producer might not have recorded it—but the entire room had heard him. And in a case built on public perception as much as legal technicalities, that little outburst was as good as handing her defence team a gift-wrapped present.

"Looks like you've been caught monologuing, Kilmare," Nelly murmured, brushing past him to pick up her glass again. "I'd say 'better luck next time,' but let's be honest—there won't be a next time. You've played all your cards, and now you're stuck with a very expensive legal case and a very public meltdown."

Dan's face darkened. "You think this is funny? You won't be laughing when the judge sees the evidence."

Nelly tilted her head, looking at him like he was a particularly slow-witted child. "Oh, Danny. If you had real evidence, you wouldn't be launching a private prosecution, would you? You'd have the CPS backing you. But they didn't, did they? Because even they knew this was a waste of everyone's time."

Dan clenched his fists. "You got lucky."

"No, love," she said, voice light, almost conversational. "I got good lawyers."

He stared at her, jaw tightening, his entire body radiating frustration. Nelly had seen this look before—on men who had lost, but didn't yet have the emotional intelligence to accept it.

"You think, just because I'm a Bristolian and got my start on a Breeze station, that I'm just some thick regional lad who doesn't know how to play the game?" Dan spat, his voice rising slightly.

Nelly arched an unimpressed eyebrow. "Oh no, darling, I think you're a thick regional lad who thinks he knows how to play the game. And that's much more tragic."

Dan's nostrils flared. He was trying so hard to maintain his composure, but the cracks were starting to show. It was all over his face—the twitch in his jaw, the way his fingers flexed like he was itching to throw something.

And then it happened.

His producer pulled her phone from her pocket and dialled a number.

"Yes, Police please," the producer said with calm authority. "I'd like to report an incident of harassment. Yes, we're at the Liverpool Gin Distillery. The suspect is Dr Eleanor Robinson, also known as Nelly Vixen."

Nelly let out an incredulous laugh, raising her hands in mock surrender. "Oh, come on," she drawled, eyes flickering between the producer and Dan, who was now looking distinctly pleased with himself. "This is a bit dramatic, even for you lot."

The bartender, who had been watching the exchange with mild interest, exhaled through his nose. "Alright, everyone, let's keep it civil, yeah? No need for all this aggro."

Dan folded his arms, smirking. "You walked in here, Vixen. You made your move. Now you deal with the consequences."

"Oh, spare me," Nelly shot back, her patience wearing thinner than Capital FM's playlist. "If anything, you started it by slandering me all over your little phone call. But sure, let's pretend I'm the problem here."

She took another sip of her gin, deliberately slow, before placing the glass back down on the bar with a soft clink.

"So, what's the plan, then? You want me carted out of here in handcuffs? Bit of a bold move, considering there's CCTV, and I haven't actually done anything."

The producer narrowed her eyes. "You harassed Dan while he was working."

"Oh, sweetheart," Nelly cooed, tilting her head. "If I wanted to harass him, he'd be crying by now."

Dan bristled, but before he could respond, the producer was already talking into the phone again. "Yes, she's still here," she said. "Blonde, mid-thirties, wearing a Burberry trench coat. Yes, that Nelly Vixen."

Nelly let out a low whistle. "Wow. You really want this PR disaster, huh? I mean, sure, call the cops. Let's see how that plays out in the press. 'Radio Presenter Arrested for Ordering a Gin and Tonic Near a Colleague.' Sounds riveting."

The bartender looked from Nelly to Dan, unimpressed. "Mate," he said to Dan. "She's literally just standing here, having a drink."

Dan opened his mouth, then closed it. His producer, however, was still committed to the bit. "Yes, she's causing a disturbance. Yes, we'd like her removed."

Nelly grinned, folding her arms. "Love, if you think a couple of Merseyside cops are going to turn up to arrest someone for ordering a drink in a gin distillery, you are deluded. They've got actual crimes to deal with."

The bartender sighed, rubbing his temple. "Right, listen—both of you, take it outside if you wanna scrap. Otherwise, order your drinks and keep it peaceful."

Dan, whose bravado was waning, shot Nelly one last glare before muttering, "Let's just go," to his producer.

The producer hesitated. "But the police—"

"Hang up the bloody phone, Chloe," Dan snapped, rubbing his face with one hand. "She's not worth it."

Nelly clapped her hands together, grinning. "Oh, I love that I'm living in your head rent-free."

Dan said nothing. Instead, he grabbed his coat and stormed towards the exit, his producer trailing behind him, still looking mildly disappointed that she wouldn't get her viral "Nelly Vixen ARRESTED" moment.

As they disappeared out the door, Nelly exhaled, shaking her head with amusement. "Christ," she muttered, turning back to the bar. "Right. Another gin, please. This time, double."

The bartender chuckled, already pouring. "That was something."

"That," Nelly corrected, accepting the fresh drink with a smirk, "was a man who knows he's already lost."

****

CHAPTER 14 – A Declaration of (Radio) War

Sunday 1st December 2019

It was 10 in the morning, and Nelly was getting ready for work, as it was Sunday, her usual Chart show day. The Manic UK40Chart might have been a corporate-sponsored, carefully curated list of pop hits, but for Nelly, it was her personal battleground—a place where she got to inject chaos into the airwaves and make executives at Manic sweat over her unpredictability.

Her Knutsford home was a picture of calculated excess—plush cream carpets, high ceilings, art pieces from obscure but expensive modern artists. The kind of house that screamed "I make money by talking absolute nonsense for a living."

Her husband, Dr Nate Robinson, a Cheshire plastic surgeon with a client list full of WAGs and reality stars, was standing in the bedroom doorway, arms folded, watching her get ready with a mixture of exhaustion and disbelief.

"You're really going into work after all this?" he asked, gesturing vaguely towards the mess of legal documents strewn across the dressing table—the latest barrage of paperwork from Dan Kilmare's lawyers.

Nelly, adjusting the strap of her black Agent Provocateur bra under her silk blouse, scoffed. "Darling, if I stayed at home every time someone tried to sue me, I'd never leave the house."

Nate exhaled sharply, pinching the bridge of his nose. "Nelly, this isn't some tabloid scandal you can just sass your way out of. This is a private prosecution for GBH and murder."

"And?" she replied breezily, stepping into her Louboutin stilettos. "It's not like I actually did murder her. Even if I had, you know I'd have done a much better job of covering it up."

Nate groaned. "Christ, Nelly."

"Oh, relax," she smirked, fixing her blonde waves in the mirror. "I'll be on air in an hour, reading out the nation's favourite pop songs while Capital Liverpool's most tragic presenter continues to fling legal shit at the wall, hoping something sticks. Let him embarrass himself."

Nate was unimpressed. "And if this goes to trial?"

She turned to face him, her expression hardening just a fraction. "Then we fight it. Properly." Her voice dropped slightly. "Dan Kilmare has spent two months rewriting history, painting me as some villain in his grief-stricken revenge saga. I let him have his moment. But that moment is over."

Nate studied her, jaw tightening. He knew this version of Nelly well. This wasn't the brash, reckless chaos-goblin that the tabloids loved to dissect. This was Dr Eleanor Robinson, radio's unkillable cockroach, the woman who had survived more industry scandals than most people had hot dinners. The woman who never lost.

"…Alright," he muttered finally, rubbing his temples. "Just… don't make it worse."

Nelly chuckled, as she knew that she was the average chaos goblin and would provoke anyone for anything, and that provoking Dan Kilmare on-air today was almost inevitable. "Darling," she said, pressing a kiss to Nate's cheek as she grabbed her handbag, "I only ever make things better."

Walking out the house, Nelly headed to the garage, where Nate's Aston Martin and her Jaguar normally parked side by side, a perfect metaphor for their marriage—one was sleek, refined, and designed for appearances, the other was fast, unpredictable, and, like a fox, ready to pounce on its next victim.

Sliding into the leather driver's seat, Nelly felt the softness of the Jaguar F-Pace's Siena Tan perforated Windsor leather performance seats with Ebony/Siena Tan interior, the Carpathian Grey exterior of the car gleaming under the dim light of the garage.

Even though she had six hours until her show started, and four hours until she was due to do her pre-show prep, Nelly decided she was going to have a little drive around Cheshire before heading into the Manic Radio studios in Speke. She needed to clear her head, strategize her next move, and most importantly—figure out just how much she could push Capital, and their owner, Global Media, on-air today without her boss, Scott Bennett, threatening to pull the plug.

The car roared to life as she pulled out of the driveway, the faint hum of Radio X playing in the background—purely so she could hear what wasn't being played on her chart show today. As she weaved through the quiet country lanes, her phone buzzed in the centre console.

Jamie Wise.

Of course.

She hit the Bluetooth button.

"Jamie, darling," she drawled, pressing a little harder on the accelerator. "How nice of you to check in on me before I singlehandedly destroy Manic's legal department with my latest antics."

Jamie sighed. "Nelly, don't. Just... don't."

Nelly smirked. "Don't what?"

"Don't do whatever it is you're thinking of doing. Look, I know Kilmare's winding you up, I know you want to clap back, but for once in your life, can you just... behave?"

She snorted. "Darling, you say that like I have ever behaved."

Jamie groaned. "I mean it, Nell. We had a meeting this morning—Scott's already dealing with Global sending 'concerns' to OFCOM about your show. Apparently, your tone last week was 'antagonistic' and 'distasteful'."

Nelly let out a sharp laugh. "Oh, I love that. 'Tone.' Is that what we're calling a perfectly executed takedown of Dan Kilmare's Capital-driven sob story?"

"You called him 'a failed local DJ cosplaying as a tragic hero' live on air!" Jamie exhaled. "Nelly, this isn't just banter anymore. This is war. And Global love a good war."

She took a corner a little too fast, the thrill of speed matching the heat bubbling under her skin. "Well, then, I suppose I'll have to win, won't I?"

Jamie groaned. "Fucking hell, woman. Just don't poke the bear."

Nelly rolled her eyes. "Jamie, sweetheart, I am the bear. Anyway, I'm heading to Sale for a bit before my show, as I fancy shagging Kyler Thompson... after all, he's a good fuck for a skanky Manc boy."

There was a sharp silence on the other end of the line.

Jamie Wise, long-suffering producer of The Manic UK40Chart, sounded like he'd just swallowed his own tongue.

"...I'm sorry, what?"

Nelly grinned, switching lanes as she glided onto the M56 towards Greater Manchester. "Oh, come on, Jamie. Don't pretend to be shocked. You know me. You know I've got a type."

Jamie let out an incredulous laugh, the kind that was half amusement, half sheer exasperation. "Kyler Thompson? Nelly, he's literally a human embodiment of a Wetherspoons at closing time. He wears North Face gilets unironically. His entire aesthetic is 'former Academy player who peaked at 19'."

"And he's also a Manic host, one of us, meaning that he's internal, not an outsider, so he understands the chaos that is Manic. Anyway, he's got that Toni Green under his spell, and, although he's a walking red flag, he's a good fuck."

Jamie let out an exaggerated groan. "Christ, Nelly. You're not just playing with fire—you're bathing in it."

Nelly smirked as she flicked on the cruise control, adjusting her oversized sunglasses as she sped past a lorry. "Darling, I set the fire."

Jamie huffed. "Fine. Whatever. Just don't end up on the front page of the Mail tomorrow, yeah? The last thing we need is 'Manic Shock Jock in Sex Scandal with Colleague While Facing Murder Trial.'"

Nelly pouted. "Oh, but think of the ratings."

Jamie muttered something unintelligible under his breath before regaining his composure. "Look, just… remember the rules today, alright? No direct mentions of Kilmare, no legal threats, and for the love of God, don't openly encourage listeners to spam Capital's socials again."

Nelly sighed theatrically. "So, essentially, I'm not allowed to have fun?"

"Correct."

"Ugh, fine," she said dramatically. "I suppose I'll have to find other ways to cause mischief."

Jamie groaned again. "That's what I'm afraid of."

With that, Nelly ended the call and pressed down on the accelerator.

She had a trip to Sale to make.

****

"Up next, its Nelly Vixen," Nelly heard DJ Manic, or Tom Brown, the host of DJ Manic's Sunday Throwback Show, announce over the air. Sitting in Studio 1, while Tom was in Studio 2, Nelly knew that this was it—the moment her chaos truly began.

The Manic UK40Chart was her playground, and today, she was going to play dirty.

As Tom's voice continued over the airwaves, she leaned back in her chair, smirking as she adjusted her mic levels. The soundproof glass separating the studio from Jamie in the producer's booth, as Studio 1 was the awkward studio, was positioned perfectly to see Jamie giving her the three minute countdown that the ads, news and station jingles would run for.

Nelly's fingers drummed against the desk as she watched the countdown tick down. She could already feel the anticipation in her veins, the electric charge that always surged before she went live.

She was ready.

As the jingle faded out, she leaned into the microphone, her voice sliding through the airwaves with the effortless smoothness of someone who had done this a thousand times.

"Well, well, well… it's that time of the week again, darlings. Welcome to the Manic UK40Chart—your weekly dose of the best music in the country, as decided by what you losers listen to on Spotify and what we at Manic play. The algorithms have spoken, the mathematicians have done the sums, and Gupta in the scamming department has made a phone call from India to steal a million rupees from a pensioner in Hull, but most importantly, I am here to provide you with two things— bangers and absolute chaos."

She paused for dramatic effect, letting the sound of the station bed hum beneath her voice.

"Now, before we dive into the chart, a little public service announcement. This week, I was going to be a good girl. My producer, the ever-suffering Jamie Wise, specifically told me not to go rogue, not to be antagonistic, and definitely not to say anything that could get us another complaint from a certain conglomerate that owns Snooze, Fart, Crapital and London's Boring Conversations… but honestly, darlings, where's the fun in that?"

"And Jamie's just shot himself at the mention of me saying that. Oh, bless him. You see, dear listeners, every week I promise him I'll behave, and every week he somehow believes me. Isn't that adorable?"

She could see Jamie through the glass, furiously gesturing for her to stick to the script. She smirked, leaning back in her chair, entirely unbothered.

"Anyway, for number 40, it's the lad I still want to lick whipped cream off his abs in the Ritz in London, Sigala and Ella Henderson with 'We Got Love'. Now, I don't know about you lot, but if I had abs like Sigala's, I'd be contractually obliged to never wear a shirt. I'd turn up to Tesco in just a pair of designer joggers and a smug expression. Actually, that's a lie—I don't go to Tesco, I prefer Waitrose and Booths, being married to a plastic surgeon in Cheshire and all that. But you get the point."

The moment she finished speaking, the first notes of We Got Love filled the studio, and Nelly leaned back, smirking as she locked eyes with Jamie through the glass. He was rubbing his temples, visibly exhaling through his nose like a teacher who had just caught their most difficult student setting fire to the school rulebook.

Jamie pressed the talkback button, his voice cutting through her headphones. "Nelly. For fuck's sake."

Nelly sipped from her water bottle, looking far too pleased with herself. "What? I stuck to the chart. I introduced number 40. I even complimented Sigala's abs, which, frankly, is a public service."

"You mentioned Global, you dragged Capital, and you implied we employ scammers in India."

"I implied nothing. I merely pointed out the reality of our wonderful media landscape."

Jamie groaned. "Just… for the love of God, no more rogue comments about Global."

Nelly grinned. "I'll do my best, darling. But you know how it is—once a woman's accused of murder, she just stops caring about consequences."

Jamie looked like he wanted to bash his head against the mixing desk.

Sipping some vodka from a bottle she had in her handbag, not a cheap brand like Grey Goose, but a properly premium, handcrafted artisan vodka imported from some obscure Nordic country that only people who read Tatler had heard of, Nelly leaned back in her chair and sighed contentedly.

The chart was rolling. The chaos had begun.

And she wasn't stopping now.

As the last chorus of We Got Love faded, she leaned back into the mic, her voice honeyed with amusement.

"That was Sigala and Ella Henderson, starting us off at number 40. A wonderful track to ease us in… or, in my case, to soundtrack the moment I realise just how many complaints I'm about to get before this show is over. But hey, what's radio without a little controversy?"

She flicked her gaze up to the producer's booth, where Jamie was mouthing something that looked suspiciously like I will actually kill you.

She smirked.

"Now, before we move on, I just want to give a quick shoutout to all the wonderful people over at Global Media. I know you lot are tuned in, keeping tabs on me, probably foaming at the mouth over my mere existence. It's touching, really. You could be listening to your own station, but instead, you're all here, giving me your undivided attention. Love that for me."

She let the silence hang for a second, just long enough for Jamie's headset to nearly fall off his head as he frantically motioned for her to cut it out.

"Anyway!" she continued, flipping through her script like she hadn't just insulted the most powerful media company in British radio. "Time for number 39, and its Ron Weasley… sorry, Ed Sheeran and Stormzy, because our algorithm thinks Tom Walker's Better Half of Me, which Radio 1 are about to say is their #39, is at number 41 and shouldn't be played. And let's be honest, darlings, even I can only stomach a certain amount of beige singer-songwriters in one sitting. So, without further ado, here's Take Me Back to London—or as I like to call it, The One Where Ed Sheeran Tries to Convince Us He's Hard."

As the track started playing, Nelly noticed that Jamie had officially given up.

From the producer's booth, he was rubbing his temples so aggressively that Nelly half-expected him to develop premature wrinkles—though, lucky for him, she was married to a man who could fix that for an extortionate price.

"Nelly," Jamie's voice crackled through her headphones as soon as she muted the mic, "do you have a death wish?"

Nelly grinned, crossing her legs as she swirled her water bottle—still very much filled with premium vodka. "Darling, you say that like it's news."

Jamie inhaled sharply. "We are ten minutes into the show, and you've already implied Global are monitoring us like MI5, dismissed Capital's entire playlist as corporate beige, and—oh yeah—called Ed Sheeran 'Ron Weasley'."

"Which is factually correct," Nelly pointed out, taking a sip. "Gingers in British media are either Prince Harry, Ron Weasley, or Mick Hucknall. It's the law."

Jamie let out a strangled noise of frustration. "Can you just stick to the chart?"

Nelly smirked. "I am sticking to the chart. I'm just providing context. Anyway, I can't wait to make our big announcement, can you?"

Jamie froze. His hands, which had been mid-air in an exasperated gesticulation, dropped to his sides.

"What announcement?" his voice crackled through the talkback, laced with a very specific kind of producer panic.

Nelly swirled the vodka in her water bottle, gazing innocently into the mic.

"You know, Jamie. The announcement." She let the silence stretch just long enough for him to start twitching.

"Nelly. For the love of all things holy, we do not have an announcement."

Nelly tapped her perfectly manicured nails against the desk, watching the countdown timer tick towards the end of Take Me Back to London.

"Didn't you read the brief? The statement that Dr Bennett released to the internal newsletter on Connect? That this show is going on the road for the Christmas number 1?"

Nelly noticed Jamie frantically logging into Connect, the internal website for Manic which had all of the internal announcements, schedules, and chaos management strategies that Scott Bennett sent out in an attempt to keep Manic's loose collection of radio anarchists somewhat under control. She knew that, for the weekend where they'd be announcing the Christmas number 1, they'd be in an Outside Broadcast van with a stage and a full production team, parked right outside Global's headquarters in Leicester Square.

Jamie's face drained of colour as he finally found the internal announcement.

"Oh, for fuck's sake," he muttered, rubbing his temples. "Scott's gone off his rocker, having us do our show from right outside Global's HQ?" Jamie let out an exasperated laugh. "Jesus Christ, Nelly, you're going to get us shut down."

As the sweeper for number 38 went over the air following the last beats of Take Me Back to London, and the system played out the next track, Taylor Swift's Lover, Nelly looked at the PlayoutONE screen, and noticed that her next link was after a song by Poundz called Opp Thot, meaning that she had chance to go to the loo before having to do her next link.

She pulled off her headphones and strolled towards the door of Studio 1, pausing just long enough to shoot Jamie a wicked smirk through the glass. "Don't worry, darling," she cooed. "I'll keep it mostly legal."

Jamie's response was muffled by the soundproofing, but she could tell it wasn't complimentary.

Nelly stepped out into the corridor, the buzz of the Manic Radio studios humming around her. Down the hall, some poor soul was wrangling a technical issue in the news booth, while a runner from production scurried past, balancing a tray of overpriced oat milk lattes. The usual controlled chaos.

****

"And that was Ride It by Regard, which means we're down to the..." Nelly said, as the sweeper that announced it was the final trio of tracks in the chart, bringing an end to the week's countdown. "That's right, darlings, we've made it to the final three. You've spent the last nearly three hours of your life listening to me waffle on about this week's most-streamed songs, and now we're finally at the business end of things."

She paused, letting the tension build, her voice lowering into that signature honeyed drawl that kept even her most ardent haters glued to their radios.

"Now, before we get into it, I just want to say a huge thanks to all my lovely listeners who keep making this show the most talked-about chart in the country, which is why I have some good news. This year, we're announcing the Christmas number 1 as usual, but not here at our studios in Speke. Instead, we're going to be live from London and outside the Empire in Leicester Square... yes, we're going to be live from the heart of the entertainment district of London, and you lovely people will get to meet me in person, live from the Manic Stage that will be parked there."

Nelly grinned, leaning back in her chair as the phones predictably lit up. Listeners were already calling in, social media was already exploding, and somewhere in London, she imagined some poor Global executive had just spat out their Pret flat white in horror.

"And don't worry," she continued, her voice dripping with faux innocence. "We're bringing the full showbiz treatment—big stage, flashing lights, and of course, the highest quality sound system money can buy, so our dear friends inside the Global building can hear every single note of the Christmas number one announcement."

Through the soundproof glass, Jamie was waving his arms in what could only be described as pure producer panic, his mouth moving rapidly into the talkback mic. A second later, his voice crackled through her headphones.

"Nelly! What the actual fuck do you think you're doing?!"

Nelly grinned, barely containing her amusement as she leaned into the mic. "Oh dear, I think my producer's having a bit of a breakdown. Let's all take a moment to send Jamie our thoughts and prayers."

Jamie's muffled swearing in the background only made her grin widen.

"Right, back to business, darlings. Your number three track this week, it's a brand new entry—"

The usual sweeper that signified that it was a brand new entry, and as the drumroll played in the background, Nelly leaned in, grinning as she made the big reveal.

"It's none other than Everything I Wanted by Billie Eilish. A moody little number from everyone's favourite Gen Z queen of the existential crisis. Honestly, if I was 18 and painfully online, I'd probably be writing cryptic Tumblr posts about this song right now."

As the track faded in, Nelly leaned back in her chair, smirking at Jamie through the glass. His expression had gone from panicked to absolutely murderous. She could see him frantically typing, likely sending an emergency email to Scott Bennett, or maybe even bracing for the inevitable legal cease and desist from Global.

She knew, however, that she was merely following the instructions that Bennett had emailed her quickly during the second half of the show, that she had to announce the event before the final song, ensuring maximum chaos before the curtain fell on this week's Manic UK40Chart.

The moment Billie Eilish's melancholic vocals filled the studio, Jamie stormed into Studio 1, his headset still wrapped around his neck, his face an alarming shade of crimson.

"Nelly," he hissed, yanking her headphones down so she had no choice but to hear him directly. "Are you out of your mind?"

She glanced at him, utterly unbothered, and reached for her vodka-laced water bottle. "Probably," she mused, taking a sip. "But you knew that already."

Jamie scrubbed a hand down his face. "You just declared war on Global. Again."

"Oh, darling," she crooned, stretching her legs out as if this was all just a casual Sunday brunch chat. "I've been at war with Global since the day I stepped into this industry. This is just the next battle."

"You announced the Christmas number one OB live outside their headquarters. Do you have any idea what kind of shitstorm that's about to unleash?"

Nelly waved a dismissive hand. "Scott approved it."

Nelly chuckled as Jamie groaned with the sound of a man who had completely given up on trying to rein her in.

"You know what? Fine," he said, throwing his hands up. "Fine. But when Global inevitably try to slap us with a cease and desist, I am not the one dealing with Legal. You can explain yourself to Scott."

Nelly beamed, raising her vodka-water in a mock toast. "Oh, don't worry, darling. I fully intend to."

Jamie let out a noise that was somewhere between a groan and a strangled laugh before storming out of the studio, presumably to either have a breakdown in the corridor or write a strongly worded resignation email that he'd never actually send.

Nelly, still entirely unbothered, turned her attention back to the show.

Billie Eilish's track was winding down, the last few moody notes fading into silence, which meant it was time for number two.

She pressed the mic button.

"Right, darlings. We're nearly at the top spot, but before we get there, let's talk about the song that's just missed out on glory this week. Coming in at number two, it's none other than Dua Lipa... yes, she's brewed up yet another bloody banger, and honestly, at this point, I wouldn't be surprised if she's got a secret lab somewhere where she just manufactures hits in bulk. It's Don't Start Now—Dua proving, yet again, that breakups are best handled with disco beats and passive-aggressive lyrics. Enjoy."

As the first pulsating bass notes of Dua Lipa's track filled the airwaves, Nelly leaned back in her chair, utterly pleased with herself. She could already imagine the panic spreading through Global's legal team like wildfire. Emails being fired off, lawyers drafting furious letters, producers at Capital scrambling to do damage control.

She glanced up at Jamie through the soundproof glass. He had his head in his hands.

Beautiful.

Her phone, sitting on the desk, buzzed violently. She flipped it over and smirked. A WhatsApp message from Scott Bennett, Manic's CEO.

Scott Bennett: *You magnificent nightmare. I assume Global will be issuing legal threats before you even get to number one. We'll handle it. Carry on.*

She grinned. Scott had spent his career baiting Global. He was, after all, the man who had built Manic on the back of pissing off the radio establishment. The fact that he was completely unfazed by her latest stunt only fuelled her even more.

She checked Twitter, where #VixenVsGlobal was already trending, and listeners were losing their minds.

@ChartFiend: *Nelly Vixen just announced Manic's Christmas Number 1 reveal is happening OUTSIDE GLOBAL HQ. We are witnessing radio warfare in real time.*

@EdSheeranFanboy97: *Did she just call Ed Sheeran Ron Weasley on national radio?*

@RadioInsiderLeaks: *Sources at Global are saying the execs are 'furious' over Manic's OB announcement. Nelly Vixen has done it again.*

@KempLover99: *I feel like Roman Kemp is going to have to spend his whole show tomorrow pretending he didn't hear this madness.*

She laughed to herself. The absolute chaos she had unleashed, and she wasn't even at number one yet.

The final beats of Don't Start Now faded, and she straightened in her chair, flicking her mic back on.

"Alright, darlings, this is it—the moment you've been waiting for. We've had 39 songs, countless complaints, and at least one producer on the verge of a breakdown, but now it's time for the big one... and I've got them on the line... hello, Tones."

The pre-recorded phone call played out, where Nelly and the Australian singer-songwriter had a quick chat about the song's success before the final announcement. Nelly had to chuckle about how her comments this week were tamer than the week it had got its first number 1 in the charts, she had said it sounded like watching a group of mentally retarded geriatrics avoiding euthanasia. Instead, she had said that sounds like the background music you'd hear in a dentist's waiting room, but, you know, in a good way.

Knowing that it was the final few minutes of the show, and that the former Breeze stations, as well as the Manic stations, would be having a "Manic Chilled Takeover" show next, one which was effectively laid back CHR tracks with links from the Glasgow station, G-Vibes, across the Manic network. Nelly decided to make her closing link count. If she was going to end the show on a high, it might as well be one that sent Global's executives spiralling into damage control mode.

She leaned into the mic, voice silky smooth.

"And there you have it, darlings. Your number one track this week, for yet another consecutive week, is Dance

Monkey by Tones and I. Which means, once again, the great British public have confirmed that they really do love a song that sounds like a bunch of circus clowns doing ketamine at an abandoned funfair. But you know what? If it works, it works."

She could already hear Jamie Wise swearing under his breath in the producer's booth.

"That's it from me, darlings. Another week of chaos, another week of me avoiding yet another OFCOM investigation. Next week its Hannah Peterson in for me as I'm having a week off, and I'll be back on the 20th for the live Christmas number 1 show from London, as I'm having a few weeks off before I cause any further national incidents. Until then, keep streaming, keep causing trouble, and if you see a Capital presenter, buy them a drink—God knows they need it."

She flicked off the mic, leaned back in her chair, and stretched, utterly satisfied with herself.

Through the glass, Jamie Wise was sitting motionless, staring blankly at his screen like a man who had just realised his entire career had been one long, unfortunate mistake.

Her phone vibrated. Another WhatsApp from Scott Bennett.

Scott Bennett: *Global's lawyers just emailed. Subject line: "Formal Complaint - Vixen's Conduct on UK40Chart." Haven't read it yet. Going to get a coffee first. Solid work, as always.*

She grinned, tossing her phone into her bag before standing up and stepping out of the studio.

Jamie followed her into the corridor, rubbing his temple like a man who had officially lost all will to live.

"You do realise you've just guaranteed that Capital will have a Roman Kemp Emergency PR Crisis segment tomorrow?"

Nelly shrugged. "I consider it a gift."

Jamie groaned. "I swear to God, one day, Global are going to sue you into oblivion."

Nelly smirked, slinging her handbag over her shoulder as she walked towards the exit. "Darling, they've been trying to do that for years. And yet—" she gestured broadly at herself, still very much standing, still very much on air.

Jamie muttered something under his breath about needing therapy before retreating into the producer's booth to presumably draft his resignation email for the tenth time this year.

****

CHAPTER 15 – Objection! Overruled! Ignored!

Tuesday 17th December 2019

Nelly was on an Emirates flight from Dubai, stretched out in first class, sipping on a flute of Dom Pérignon while the cabin lighting bathed everything in a warm, ambient glow. She had spent two weeks in Sydney, avoiding the British winter, drinking obscene amounts of expensive cocktails, antagonising Australians with her refusal to call flip-flops 'thongs,' and, of course, causing international incidents wherever possible. A few days in the UAE had been the perfect finishing touch to her and Nate's annual winter getaway—a necessary escape before the full-blown war she had walked into back home.

Now, however, she was flying straight into the fallout.

Nate, ever the picture of a weary husband married to a chaos gremlin, was reclining beside her, scrolling through his phone with an expression that hovered somewhere between resignation and mild concern.

"You do realise that Global have actually gone to court over your live from Leicester Square show this coming weekend?" he muttered, holding up a Daily Mail Online article for her to see. The headline was as hysterical as expected:

"GLOBAL MEDIA SEEK INJUNCTION AGAINST MANIC RADIO'S 'STUNT' OUTSIDE LONDON HQ

By Saddam Bashir, Media Editor for Mail Online"

Nelly groaned as she saw Saddam's name, as he was the same person who she had gone to university with back in the day—before he'd sold his soul to the tabloid machine.

"Oh, for fuck's sake," she muttered, taking Nate's phone from his hands and scrolling through the article.

Global Media have launched legal proceedings to block Manic Radio's planned Christmas No.1 outside broadcast from Leicester Square, branding it 'a blatant act of harassment' and 'an unprecedented attack on the integrity of UK commercial radio.'

Sources close to Global's legal team, led by Deputy Head of Legal James Jenkins, say they will argue in court today that Manic's stunt constitutes a 'deliberate provocation designed to incite disruption' and 'potential reputational harm' to their London operations.

Manic Radio, known for its controversial programming under the leadership of Dr Scott Bennett, has yet to comment—though host Dr Nelly Vixen, who is currently at the centre of a separate legal battle with Capital Liverpool's Dan Kilmare, has made a series of pointed remarks online suggesting she is 'excited' for the event.

"Nelly," Nate sighed, rubbing his temple. "This is not a game."

"Oh, darling," she purred, taking another sip of her champagne, "everything is a game."

"You do realise they might actually win this, right?" he pressed. "If Global get that injunction, you're not going to be anywhere near Leicester Square this weekend."

"Nate, love, Scott is a lawyer, so he knows the loopholes and how to dance through them better than anyone. If Global really think they can out-manoeuvre him, they're in for a rude awakening."

Nelly scrolled further down the article, rolling her eyes at the typical media melodrama.

"Legal experts suggest that Global's case hinges on whether Manic Radio's planned outside broadcast can be deemed an act of targeted harassment. "If the court determines that the event is designed primarily to disrupt Global's business rather than function as a legitimate public broadcast, they may have a strong argument for an injunction," said Richard Cartwright, a senior media lawyer.

Supporters of Manic, however, say that they intend to go to Leicester Square to see the Pepsi Chart Show, which is powered by Russian gas giant Gazprom and soft drinks brand Pepsi, being broadcast live from outside Global's headquarters. "It's not about harassing Global," one listener commented on Twitter. "It's about supporting independent radio and watching Nelly Vixen wind them up for sport."

Dr Nelly Vixen, the host of the Pepsi Chart, was unavailable for comment, but a spokesman for Manic Radio said, "Our Christmas Number One show is a celebration of music, and we are committed to bringing the best entertainment to our listeners. We are working with the relevant authorities to ensure the event proceeds as planned.""

Which, as Nelly knew, was PR code for: We are absolutely doing this whether Global like it or not, and Scott Bennett is already drafting five different ways to get around this injunction.

She let out a low chuckle, tossing Nate's phone back onto the armrest between them.

"See? Everything's fine. PR's got it covered. Scott's probably laughing himself sick in his office right now. Besides, it's just a bit of festive fun. Who knew Global were such grinches?"

Nate gave her a long, unamused look. "Nelly, they're literally arguing in court that this is harassment."

She sighed dramatically, stretching her legs out on the fully reclined first-class seat. "Darling, if Global think a couple of flashing lights and a stage in Leicester Square is harassment, they need to spend some time in actual reality. They're just bitter that they didn't think of it first."

Nate groaned and reached for his whisky. "I swear, one day, you're going to push this too far."

"One day," she agreed, sipping her champagne. "But not today."

Looking at the map, Nelly saw that the plane was over Brussels, meaning that Manchester wasn't too far from landing. She had a little over an hour before she was thrown back into the battlefield of British radio politics, which meant just enough time to enjoy one last peaceful glass of champagne before the madness resumed.

Nate, ever the cautious one, was already deep in thought, probably strategizing damage control for whatever fresh chaos awaited them upon touchdown. Nelly, however, was preoccupied with a far more pressing issue—how exactly she was going to make Global's injunction backfire spectacularly.

Her phone buzzed on the armrest tray. A WhatsApp notification from Scott Bennett.

Scott Bennett: *Touchdown at 11:15, right? Need you to get to London ASAP. Koslov's private jet is waiting at Aether Private Terminal for a hop to for a hop to London City. Meet me at the High Court at 2, as you've been summoned as a witness for us. Bring your A-game.*

Nelly smirked, shaking her head. Of course Ilya Koslov, the Russian oligarch who owned a significant stake in Manic Radio via Gazprom's UK interests, would swoop in with his personal jet like this was some sort of international espionage thriller. Because, really, why deal with train delays when you could fly to London in a luxury aircraft funded by Russia's biggest energy conglomerate?

Nate glanced at the screen. "Jesus Christ, Nelly. Do you even realise how dodgy this looks? You are literally about to step off an Emirates flight, get into a Russian billionaire's jet, and fly straight into a court battle with Britain's biggest media company."

Nelly grinned, finishing her champagne. "Darling, if I worried about optics, I wouldn't be me."

Summoning the steward who was polishing crystal glassware at the front of the cabin, Nelly handed him her empty flute with a satisfied smile. "Another, please. And make it quick—I've got a plane to catch after this one."

Nate groaned. "I swear, you are the only person alive who can say that unironically."

The steward, ever the picture of first-class hospitality, refilled her glass with practiced ease before gliding away. Nelly took a slow sip, already mentally preparing for what awaited her in London.

Summoned as a witness, she thought, sighing. That was an interesting development. She had assumed Scott would keep her out of the legal proceedings as much as possible—after all, she was hardly the poster girl for corporate diplomacy. But if she was being called to the High Court, it meant Scott wanted her on the offensive.

Which suited her just fine.

Her mind raced through possibilities. What was Scott's angle? If Global's legal team were arguing that this was an act of harassment, then Manic had to prove otherwise. That meant demonstrating that the event was a legitimate outside broadcast—not just an excuse to antagonise their biggest rival. And who better to sell that narrative than the *face* of the Pepsi Chart herself?

She flicked through the Daily Mail article again, smirking at the "sources close to Global" nonsense. That was James Jenkins, without a doubt. The man had spent his career cleaning up Global's messes and issuing legal threats at anything that so much as breathed in their direction. And now, he was about to square off against Scott Bennett, a man who treated lawsuits the same way most people treated minor parking fines.

****

"Comrade!" Nelly heard Ilya Koslov, the oligarch who owned Manic Radio, call out as she stepped off the Emirates plane at Manchester Airport's Terminal 3. The biting December air hit her like a slap as she adjusted her oversized Celine sunglasses, her Burberry trench coat billowing around her. Nate trailed behind, looking distinctly unimpressed with the entire situation. "Come with me to the terminal, we'll get the customs formalities dealt with quickly, and then we get you on the jet."

Nelly smirked, striding towards the sleek black Bentley waiting to whisk her away to the private terminal. Ilya Koslov, the ever-charming yet utterly terrifying Russian media mogul, clapped a firm hand on her shoulder as if they were old war buddies.

"You are causing much trouble, Dr Vixen," he said with a grin, his thick Russian accent making everything sound vaguely like a Bond villain monologue. "I like it. Keeps things interesting."

Nate, still blinking away the absurdity of the situation, exhaled sharply. "Great. Another man encouraging her terrible life choices."

"Oh, please," Nelly scoffed, sliding into the Bentley's back seat as a driver in a sharp suit shut the door behind her. "Like you didn't know what you were signing up for when you married me."

Ilya chuckled, lighting a cigarette despite the airport's strict non-smoking policy. "Scott says you are summoned as witness, da?"

"Apparently," Nelly replied, stretching her legs out. "James Jenkins is trying to get our OB shut down, but Scott's got a plan. He always does."

Ilya took a long drag, blowing the smoke out of the barely cracked window. "I assume you know what to say?"

Nelly smirked. "Darling, when do I ever follow the script?"

Nate groaned, massaging his temples. "You do realise you're walking into the High Court? Not a radio studio. Not a piss-up at the Manic Christmas party. The High. Court. Where you will be cross-examined by Global's legal team. Possibly by James Jenkins himself."

"Oh, I do hope so," Nelly grinned, adjusting her sunglasses. "I owe that smug bastard a very public humiliation."

"Do you want me to come with you, or do you want me to take our cases home, love?" Nate then said, and Nelly knew that he was already calculating the damage control required if things went south. Nate, for all his exasperation with her, always had her back when it really mattered. But there were limits, and being dragged into one of her legal catastrophes was where he drew the line.

"I will have my driver take your luggage home, Comrade Robinson," Ilya said with a dismissive wave of his hand. "Your wife, however, is coming to London. Scott insists."

Nelly chuckled at how Ilya, who she knew was a former KGB operative, still carried himself with the effortless authority of someone who could make people disappear with a phone call. Not that she minded. If she was going to fight Global in court today, it helped to have a Russian oligarch and a morally flexible CEO in her corner.

The fact that he called everyone Comrade was something that Nelly found even more amusing, as, for the 30 year old that she was, she knew that the Soviet Union had died over three decades ago, yet Ilya still carried the air of a Cold War relic who had simply adapted to capitalism like a shark adapting to warmer waters.

The Bentley glided towards Aether Private Terminal, bypassing the chaos of Manchester's main airport, where normal passengers were battling Christmas travel delays and overpriced Pret sandwiches. Nelly, meanwhile, was stepping straight onto a jet chartered by an oligarch.

Truly, life was surreal.

Walking through security, Nelly had to admit that the private terminal was more luxurious than the regular departure areas. No queues, no screaming children, and certainly no frantic business travellers jostling for space. Just a sleek, modern lounge with floor-to-ceiling windows, where a tray of champagne flutes sat untouched beside an extravagant spread of pastries that no one actually seemed to be eating.

Ilya, ever the picture of controlled power, strode through without a second glance, nodding at the staff like a man who owned the place—because, for all Nelly knew, he probably did. She followed, her Louboutins clicking against the polished marble floor, while Nate trailed behind with the air of a man who had resigned himself to his wife's bullshit.

"You'll be in London in an hour, comrade," Ilya said, ushering her towards the waiting jet. "Scott will meet you at the High Court. He says be sharp. And no—" he gave her a pointed look "—no drinking before you testify."

Nelly scoffed, pretending to be offended. "Darling, I would never turn up to court drunk. Hungover, perhaps. But never drunk."

Ilya sighed heavily, shaking his head as he waved her towards the jet. "Go. Win. Destroy them."

With a smirk, Nelly climbed the short set of stairs, stepping into the kind of luxury that only Russian oligarchs could justify—plush leather seats, a stocked bar (which she totally wasn't touching), and the faint hum of power exuding from every corner of the cabin. The flight attendant, a striking blonde woman with the kind of sharp cheekbones that suggested a past life as an FSB agent, greeted her with a polite nod.

"Champagne, Dr Vixen?"

Nelly grinned, throwing a glance over her shoulder as she settled into a seat. "Your boss says no. But I say yes."

The flight attendant, clearly unfazed by whatever geopolitical power play was happening behind the scenes, simply nodded and poured.

Nate let out a long, suffering sigh as he stepped onto the plane after her. "I swear to God, Nelly, one day this is all going to collapse around you."

"Oh, darling," she purred, sipping her champagne. "Not today."

****

The Judge, Nelly noticed, seemed to be hanging on every word that James Jenkins was spouting with the kind of interest that someone who was being bribed to be interested would have.

Nelly smirked slightly, adjusting the collar of her cream-coloured Burberry trench as she leaned back in her seat in the High Court, legs crossed, utterly unbothered. If she was meant to be intimidated, it wasn't working.

James Jenkins, Deputy Head of Legal for Global, was in full flow, pacing in his perfectly tailored navy suit, voice oozing faux concern as he laid out his case.

"My Lord, we are not dealing with an ordinary commercial dispute. We are dealing with a deliberate, premeditated act of corporate harassment. Manic Radio's plan to host their Pepsi Chart show outside our headquarters is not a legitimate broadcast—it is a calculated provocation, designed to cause disruption, reputational harm, and media embarrassment. We contend that this constitutes unlawful interference in the operations of Global Media and should be prevented by way of an injunction."

James then pulled a file from his sheaf of parchment labelled 'City of Westminster Council—Events Department' and placed it on the desk in front of him.

"As per the evidence you can see in this sheaf, the Commissioner of the Police of the Metropolis has confirmed that they would be unable to provide staffing cover to control such an event, given the potential for public disorder, and the impact on public safety in Leicester Square at one of the busiest times of the year. Furthermore, the City of Westminster Council has made no official statement supporting this event, nor has any formal approval been given for the occupation of Leicester Square for a purpose other than regular public use. This is not a case of a radio station merely hosting a promotional event. This is an act of deliberate and malicious provocation, targeting our company directly."

"Objection, my Lord," Manic's barrister from a London firm called Spencer, Hargreaves and Wood said with the authority of someone who was skilled at corporate warfare. "Does Mr Jenkins even have the Right of Audience, given his position at Global Media as their Deputy Head of Legal? He is not a barrister, nor a solicitor advocate. I understand that his Honour may grant discretion for him to speak, but this is a High Court matter, not a small claims dispute over unpaid invoices."

"So the letters QC after my name mean nothing?" Jenkins said with a smirk that suggested he relished every second of legal combat. "My learned friend, your Lordship, may have forgotten that I undertook pupillage under my father, Lord Henry Jenkins QC, and that I was appointed both Deputy Head of Legal and in-house Barrister for Global

Media in 2017, after serving in their Legal department since 2008, when Mr Tabor-King, my employer, formed Global Media."

"Christ, he's good. I wished I'd got a job for Global instead of Manic," Paul Walker, one of Scott Bennett's legal team muttered and Nelly groaned as the last thing she needed was one of their own legal team going weak at the knees for James Jenkins' theatrics.

"Overruled," the Judge said with the kind of enthusiasm that made Nelly wonder if he was an LBC listener and had already made up his mind before even hearing their side of the argument.

"My Lord," Manic's barrister, Roland Spencer, then began smoothly, his voice carrying the perfect balance of I am a serious legal professional and I know exactly how much I can wind you up without getting held in contempt, "Mr Jenkins has made a compelling argument, as always. And, as always, it is filled with delightfully misleading rhetoric. The reality, my Lord, is that this is nothing more than a Christmas broadcast. A celebration of the UK's number one single. A radio tradition that Manic Radio has every right to host in a public space."

The Judge raised an unimpressed eyebrow. "A public space directly outside the offices of your biggest commercial competitor."

Scott gave a small, knowing smile. "Leicester Square is also home to dozens of businesses. Shall we discuss whether Manic's presence outside the Empire Cinema is an attack on Cineworld? Or perhaps an attempt to undermine M&M World? I believe they are doing a two-for-one offer on chocolate reindeer at the moment—shall we summon their legal team to weigh in?"

The courtroom held its breath for a moment, the air thick with tension.

Jenkins' jaw clenched slightly. He didn't like being outmanoeuvred, and Spencer knew exactly what she was doing. She was painting Manic as the scrappy underdog, the plucky little broadcaster standing up against Global's corporate machine. It was a good strategy, but Nelly could tell Jenkins wasn't about to roll over just yet.

"The scale of the disruption is precisely the issue," Jenkins said smoothly, regaining his footing. "Leicester Square is one of the busiest areas of London, especially in December. Manic Radio has neither the logistical capability nor the necessary council permissions to host an event of this size in such a location. Their CEO, Dr Scott Bennett, has a well-documented history of antagonising Global Media, and this is simply the latest attempt. This is not about music. This is not about broadcasting. This is about harassment. Furthermore, their plans show that access to Global's Headquarters would be impeded, and therefore would breach London Fire Brigade regulations regarding fire exits and emergency access. If Manic's event were to proceed, it would create a substantial risk to both employees working in Global's building and the general public navigating the area."

That bastard, Nelly thought to herself, chuckling. *That absolute bastard got a good shot with the fire regulations.*

"Furthermore, my Lord," Jenkins added, and Nelly groaned, as she knew that he was going to go for the jugular with another devastatingly precise argument, "Manic Radio's chosen sponsor for this event— Gazprom—is currently under intense scrutiny by UK regulatory bodies. Given the geopolitical implications of a Russian energy giant funding a major public event directly outside a British media company's headquarters, there are serious national security concerns that must be considered. The Home Office has yet to issue a statement, but we are formally requesting that this be factored into your Honour's deliberations."

The courtroom buzzed with murmurs, the weight of Jenkins' argument settling over the space like a thick, oppressive fog.

Nelly, for the first time in a long time, felt the thrill of genuine challenge. Jenkins had gone straight for the nuclear option. He wasn't just trying to block their event—he was painting Manic Radio as a potential national security risk. And the bastard was doing it well.

Scott Bennett, however, remained entirely unfazed. If anything, he looked amused.

"Mr Jenkins," Scott said, his voice infuriatingly calm, "are you suggesting that the UK40Chart, which has been broadcast for decades, is now a geopolitical threat because Pepsi and Gazprom have chosen to sponsor it? Shall we ban every football match sponsored by Russian companies too? Or shall we acknowledge that your argument is a desperate attempt to weaponize foreign policy against your competitors?"

Jenkins didn't so much as blink. "We are simply stating that there are broader concerns about the optics of this event—"

"—and you didn't seem to have those concerns when Gazprom was sponsoring the UEFA Champions League," Scott cut in smoothly. "I seem to recall Capital FM running competitions for listeners to win tickets to those very matches, all while Gazprom's branding flashed proudly across stadiums worldwide. So, unless Mr Jenkins is now arguing that his own employer was guilty of engaging with a national security risk, I'd say we can drop this particular line of nonsense."

"My Lord, I would like to apply for Dr Bennett to be removed from the Court," Jenkins then said, grinning, and Nelly knew why—her boss had no right of audience as, although he was a lawyer by trade, having a PhD in Law, he was not a barrister and therefore should have been sitting quietly behind his legal team rather than engaging in verbal sparring with Jenkins.

"I've watched too many Judge John Deed episodes," Nelly muttered to herself as she saw the Judge getting irked by Bennett's constant interjections. The Judge sighed, rubbing his temple in a way that suggested he deeply regretted not taking an extended holiday over Christmas.

"Dr Bennett," the Judge said, voice dangerously calm, "if you wish to contribute to these proceedings, you may instruct your barrister to do so on your behalf. Otherwise, I suggest you remain silent, unless you wish to be held in contempt."

Scott, ever the poker-faced operator, simply smiled. "Of course, my Lord. My apologies."

Nelly shot him a glance from across the courtroom. He wasn't sorry in the slightest.

Jenkins smirked, clearly enjoying himself. "Thank you, my Lord. Now, unless my learned friend would like to suggest that Manic Radio should also be granted diplomatic immunity, I believe the facts of the matter remain clear—this event is a deliberate and calculated disruption, and Global Media is well within its rights to seek an injunction."

Roland Spencer cleared his throat, taking the floor once again. "My Lord, if I may address two key points in Mr Jenkins' argument. Firstly, the claim that this constitutes harassment is, at best, an overreach, and at worst, a fundamental misunderstanding of broadcasting law. Manic Radio, like any station, has the right to conduct outside broadcasts in public spaces, and unless Global Media wishes to argue that Leicester Square belongs exclusively to them, I fail to see how this event could possibly be deemed unlawful."

The Judge exhaled, eyes narrowing. "And the second point?"

Spencer smiled politely. "The issue of fire regulations. Manic Radio has already obtained a risk assessment from an independent safety consultant, who has confirmed that no fire exits of the Global Media building would be obstructed. Furthermore, the event will be conducted in full compliance with City of Westminster licensing regulations. In fact, I have here"—he gestured to a thick binder placed neatly on the desk—"a signed statement from the relevant local authorities confirming that no formal objections have been raised. The Commissioner of the Metropolitan Police has not issued any statement to the effect that this event constitutes an exceptional risk."

Jenkins' jaw twitched slightly, his carefully constructed argument beginning to unravel.

"As for the geopolitical concerns," Spencer continued, tone crisp, "I fail to see how a radio chart show sponsored by a soft drinks brand and a European energy company constitutes a matter of national security. Unless, of course, Global Media now considers themselves an arm of the Home Office."

A ripple of suppressed laughter ran through the courtroom. Even the Judge's lips twitched slightly.

Jenkins, however, was not done yet. "My Lord, even if we disregard the security concerns, we must consider the potential for public disorder. Given the... reputation of Manic Radio and its presenters, it is entirely foreseeable that this event will draw a volatile crowd. Dr Eleanor Robinson, otherwise known as Nelly Vixen, has made a career out of provocative, inflammatory behaviour. Her presence alone is a magnet for controversy."

Nelly raised an eyebrow. "Oh, piss off, Jenkins."

A horrified silence fell across the courtroom.

Nelly realised her mistake a fraction of a second too late. She clamped her mouth shut, but the damage was done.

The Judge's eyes slowly lifted from his papers, his expression one of pure, unfiltered disapproval.

"Dr Robinson," he said, voice like an executioner's axe, "you are a witness, not a commentator. If you interrupt these proceedings again, I will have you removed from the courtroom. Do I make myself clear?"

For once in her life, Nelly decided against pushing her luck.

"Yes, my Lord," she said, forcing herself into something resembling humility.

Scott shot her a look that was half amusement, half what the hell are you doing? Jenkins, meanwhile, looked like all his Christmases had come at once.

"My Lord," Jenkins said smoothly, "I believe Dr Robinson's outburst only serves to reinforce my point."

Spencer, ever the professional, barely flinched. "My Lord, I think we are all aware that Dr Robinson is a larger-than-life personality. That does not, however, mean that this event should be censored simply because Global Media does not like the way in which it is being conducted."

The Judge pinched the bridge of his nose. "Enough. I have heard both arguments, and I will now retire to consider my decision. The court will reconvene at 4pm."

****

"Well, that was a waste of time for us," Nelly said a few hours later, when she, Scott Bennett and the legal team for Manic were all aboard the private jet of their owner, heading from London City Airport to Liverpool John Lennon Airport.

"Don't worry, Nell," Bennett said with a grin. "I've filed for permission to appeal His Lordship's granting of an injunction. I doubt it'll go through before Sunday, but that's fine. We'll still do it anyway. The stage is being set up as it's a 3 day job, and we've got a load of G4S security on standby to keep everything running smoothly. If Global want to take us to court again, they can, but by the time the appeal process kicks in, the show will already have happened."

Nelly smirked, swirling the last of her champagne in her glass. "So we're just... doing it anyway?"

Scott gave her a look that could only be described as smug. "Of course. As we'll outside Global HQ, we'll have technically breached the injunction, but by the time they get police involved, the show will be done, and we'll be long gone. The High Court doesn't work at the speed of live radio, darling."

Nelly let out a low, satisfied chuckle. "Oh, I do love a good legal loophole."

Scott leaned back in his seat, taking a sip of his whisky. "It's not even a loophole, really. It's just... strategic application of bureaucracy. The fact is, the appeal process takes time, and we all know Global's legal team moves like a herd of frightened accountants when things don't go their way. By the time they get their act together, the Christmas No.1 will already have been revealed, the listeners will have their show, and we'll have delivered the single greatest PR stunt in Manic history."

Roland Spencer, their barrister, was less impressed. "You do realise that this means Global can take you for contempt of court? If the injunction is upheld, and you go ahead with this event, they can make an example of Manic."

Scott waved a dismissive hand. "Oh, let them try. This isn't the BBC. Nobody actually gives a shit about commercial radio law. They can slap us with a fine, and we'll pay it out of the marketing budget."

Spencer sighed, clearly aware that he was dealing with a client who viewed legal consequences as mild inconveniences rather than genuine deterrents. "Just don't expect any favours from the judiciary if you keep pulling stunts like this."

Nelly smirked. "Oh, I think Scott thrives on making enemies in high places."

Scott grinned. "It's the only way to do business."

Ilya Koslov, who had been quietly enjoying a cigar in his seat across from them, exhaled a thick plume of smoke and chuckled. "In Russia, when media company has problem, we do not go to court. We simply buy judge… or disappear him."

Scott laughed, shaking his head. "As much as I appreciate your, uh, pragmatic approach, Ilya, we do try to keep things at least slightly above board here in the UK."

Ilya smirked, swirling his vodka. "Ah, yes. British legal system. So noble. So fair. Unless you are not billionaire. Then it is just game for rich men to play."

Nelly, reclining in her seat, smirked over the rim of her champagne glass. "Well, darling, I fully intend to play and win."

Spencer sighed, rubbing his temples as if resigning himself to the inevitable. "You do realise that if Global push this to the limit, they could argue for an emergency enforcement order? They could get the Metropolitan Police involved to physically stop you from broadcasting."

Scott raised an eyebrow. "And what exactly are they going to do? Send riot cops to arrest a bunch of presenters on live radio? Because I tell you now, we'll have cameras rolling the whole time. They won't want that kind of PR disaster."

Spencer exhaled slowly. "You're gambling on the idea that they'll back down."

Scott smirked. "And I'm very good at gambling."

Nelly grinned, adjusting her Celine sunglasses as she took another sip. "Scott, darling, remind me again why we don't just go full pirate radio and broadcast from a boat in the Thames? It would be very on-brand."

Ilya chuckled. "In Soviet Union, we had pirate radio. We call it 'state media.'"

****

CHAPTER 16 – Lighting the Fuse
Sunday 22nd December 2019

There were two things Nelly had to be glad of on that wet Sunday morning as she sat in the Olympic Park studios of Manic. First, that the station's top-tier coffee machine was still functioning after a particularly chaotic Christmas party the night before, and second, that despite the High Court ruling, her Christmas No.1 show was still happening.

The Olympic Park hub, housing East London Hits, Manic Metal UK, and Manic Soul UK, had been a Breeze Media outpost before Manic had swallowed them whole. Now, it was a nerve centre for the most unhinged radio group in Britain, and today, it was mission control for Operation: Ignore the Injunction and Hope for the Best.

Nelly took a slow sip of her coffee, legs crossed in her chair, as she waited for the car that was going to take her and Jamie to Leicester Square, deep in thought. The key thought in her mind was that Dan Kilmare's private prosecution against her had failed, as the Courts had decided it was entirely without merit, a desperate attempt by a bitter man with a new fortune and an axe to grind. It had been a relief, of course—being dragged through a murder trial would have been inconvenient, to say the least—but Nelly wasn't exactly celebrating. The damage had already been done. Global had used Kilmare's case as a weapon in their media war against her, feeding headlines to the tabloids, whispering in the ears of advertisers.

They had failed to ruin her, but they'd given it a bloody good go.

And now, today, she had a chance to remind them why they had wanted to take her down in the first place.

Jamie Wise, who looked like he had aged about ten years in the past week, shuffled into the studio with a grim expression and an oversized Greggs coffee.

"They're onto us," he said, dropping into the chair across from her.

Nelly smirked. "Darling, of course they are."

Jamie pinched the bridge of his nose. "No, I mean they know. The moment our crew started setting up in Leicester Square, some Global exec must have sprinted to their lawyers. James Jenkins has just sent an email directly to Scott, demanding we stand down."

Nelly stretched lazily, feigning a yawn. "And what did our dear leader say?"

"Oh, the Paramount Supreme Leader, General Secretary and Chairman of the People's Manic Party of Great Britain has said that he'll be here in a hour, something to do with putting the au pair on a plane for her Christmas break, but that Scott's already drafting a press statement for when the inevitable 'Global Media storms Manic' headlines drop. He's also instructing the legal team to file another counterclaim." Jamie paused, his lips pressing into a thin line. "Ilya has said that he can get his former colleagues to provide a Novichok-style diplomatic solution if necessary... although instead he's going to get hackers from Moscow's 'finest hacktivists' to flood Global's systems with spam complaints about Capital's playlist."

Nelly let out a sharp laugh. "Oh, I do love when we outsource our chaos. Very on-brand."

Jamie, however, was not in the mood for amusement. He took a long sip of his coffee and sighed. "Look, I get it. You thrive on winding them up. But this time, Nelly, they're genuinely out for blood. If we do this, we're not just ignoring an injunction. We are deliberately pissing off the biggest media company in the country, and they will not stop until they've crushed us."

Nelly tilted her head, giving him a slow, knowing smile. "Oh, Jamie, sweetheart. They've already tried to crush me. They sent their attack dog after me with a bogus prosecution, dragged my name through the press, threatened advertisers, tried to get me sacked… and I'm still here. And now, I get to do what I do best—win."

Jamie exhaled sharply, shaking his head. "You're impossible."

"And yet," she said, finishing her coffee with a flourish, "you still turn up to work every day."

A knock on the door interrupted them, and Laurence Kendal, their Olympic Park technician, poked his head in. "Car's here. You lot ready for war?"

Jamie groaned. "No. But we're doing it anyway."

Nelly grinned. "That's the spirit."

Following Laurence to the side entrance of the studios, where a construction site had set up shop, something about a Barbican style bowl that the London Borough of

Newham had authorised prior to the Manic deal being signed, as Breeze Media had planned to launch a classical music station in East London before the takeover. Nelly had to chuckle at how it was to be under the studios, with three large studios underneath the main complex as well as the bowl, all for the classical music station that Manic were still committing to launching.

The irony, Nelly knew, that the building Breeze Media had in Stratford was 4 stories tall, and had enough room to have been a HQ for the former group, but its Dudley offices, where Midlands Manic was based, had been the group's HQ instead, with London being the technical centre for the small group's RCS setup.

Manic, on the other hand, used the Speke complex for its technical and HQ operations, as it was a Liverpool born and bred company. Technically, Manic didn't need Stratford, as, in Nelly's opinion, the PlayoutONE system Manic used was far superior to the constantly updating RCS Zetta, GSelector, RCS News RCS News, and all the other bells and whistles that Breeze had purchased back when it was an ILR network owned by Woody Bones.

Nelly knew that the former Breeze stations opted out of the Manic network programming whenever they wanted, as they had the RCS system installed, meaning that the Manic network shows were effectively optional for them. The reason? Woody Bones, when he owned the small group, allowed his Programme Directors to opt for their own local and national output, with Breeze continuing the practice, as they trusted their local managers to understand the audience and what worked best for them. It was a policy that Scott Bennett despised, but one he had been forced to tolerate—at least for now—because the Breeze stations still brought in strong revenue. But Nelly knew that Scott's patience had limits.

"No, we're not taking the chart today," Nelly heard the PD for East London Hits, Donald Rigby, say over the phone. "I'm not airing an illegal broadcast and having OFCOM knocking on my door. We're going into a special show with Kelly Johnson, and you can tell Scott that if he doesn't like it, he can bloody well sack me."

Nelly paused for a minute to hear what Donald had to say.

"No, the system allows me to ignore Speke's inputs and create my own playlists for my shows. You want networking, you'd have to get RCS to disable the function on my end. No, I don't care if Scott throws a fit, I'm not losing my licence over this," Donald was saying, his voice tight with frustration.

"Oh, piss off Carmen," Donald then said, and Nelly knew that he was talking to the Deputy CEO of Manic Radio, Carmen Sharpe, a loyalist of Dr Scott Bennett and one of the few people in the company who had enough authority to overrule even the most stubborn Programme Directors. Carmen was known for her no-nonsense approach, her razor-sharp business mind, and the fact that she had once singlehandedly kept Scott from launching a legally dubious Manic-branded cryptocurrency.

Nelly smirked as she listened in. Donald Rigby was a relic of the old radio world, a Programme Director from the days when local radio still meant something, back before networking had turned most commercial stations into glorified Spotify playlists. He'd fought tooth and nail to keep East London Hits semi-independent even after the Manic takeover, and unlike most people at the company, he wasn't afraid to tell Scott Bennett exactly where to shove his legal loopholes.

"He's got a point, you know," Jamie muttered as they walked towards the waiting car. "This is insane, even by Manic standards."

Nelly scoffed, sliding into the back seat of the black BMW that had been sent to ferry them into Central London. "Oh, darling, Donald's just being dramatic. The show is happening. The OB is set up. The crowd is already gathering. And Scott's lawyers are primed and ready to stall any legal challenge until long after the Christmas No.1 is announced. Have you seen the running order?"

Jamie groaned as he slid into the BMW beside her, scrolling through his phone. "Yeah, I've seen it. And I'm trying to pretend I haven't. A song about a fucking sausage roll at number one. A literal novelty charity single about a sausage roll, taking the top spot over every carefully marketed, industry-backed pop star. This is the state of British music in 2019."

"Could be worse. I was a teen when Bob the fucking Builder was the Christmas No.1," Nelly quipped, stretching out in her seat as the car pulled out onto the road. "Well, technically, I was 11, so I wasn't a teen, but who gives a shit about technicalities, right?"

Jamie shook his head, taking another desperate sip of his Greggs coffee. "I do not get why people buy into this novelty Christmas Number One crap. First Mr Blobby, then Bob the Builder, then Rage Against the Machine because people were annoyed at X Factor, now this bloody sausage roll song. I swear, British music fans just collectively decide to have an aneurysm every December. Did you see that Instagram campaign to get Mariah to number one? Yet the running order shows her as being at number 8."

"That's going to piss a lot of people off," Nelly said, grinning. "Mariah's been fighting for the Christmas No.1 for years, and now she's lost to a bloke singing about pastry. Beautiful chaos. Almost poetic."

Jamie groaned, rubbing his temples. "You do realise what this means for us, right? The moment we announce this, Twitter is going to explode. And not in a good way. Mariah fans are going to be coming for our throats. Christmas purists will be rioting in the streets. And Global? Oh, Global are going to have a meltdown, because a friend of mine is the cousin of Will Manning's producer, and she said that they're putting Mariah at #2 as well with Ladbaby at #1, and that Global's executives are already pre-emptively preparing statements about how 'this is a win for novelty charity singles' to avoid looking like they're having a corporate tantrum."

"And the fact we're starting our show at 3 and running it as a 4 hour long show, instead of the usual 3 hour show starting at 4 like Capital's, meaning that both us and Capital will be announcing the same No.1 at roughly the same time? Oh, it's going to be carnage." Nelly smirked, stretching her legs out as the car wove through the drizzle-drenched streets of East London. "You know, Jamie, I live for moments like this."

Jamie sighed, checking the time on his phone. "We're twenty minutes out from Leicester Square, and you do realise Global is probably already on the phone to the police, right? The moment we turn up, it's going to be all-out war."

"Yes, but the best part, darling, is that they won't be able to shut us down before it's too late," Nelly said, tilting her head to look out the rain-streaked window. "You saw the crowd shots on Twitter? It's already packed. If the Met tries to intervene, they'll have a riot on their hands, and the only thing worse than losing to a sausage roll song is looking like you're trying to shut down a Christmas celebration for the people."

Jamie muttered something under his breath that sounded suspiciously like I hate my job but chose not to argue further.

The BMW merged onto the A13, heading west towards the heart of the city, and Nelly checked her notifications. As expected, the online world was on fire.

@ChartFiend: *Leicester Square is RAMMED. Hundreds of people waiting for Nelly Vixen and the Manic Pepsi Chart. Capital FM can PRETEND they're not bothered, but we all know they're FUMING.*

@MediaInsiderUK: *Spotted: Manic's OB team in full force outside Global HQ. Sources say Global execs are 'considering their options' but admit there's little they can do to stop it now.*

@KempLover99: *Roman Kemp is going to have to act like Manic Radio's illegal Christmas No.1 reveal isn't happening outside his office window and I am LIVING for it.*

@drnellyvixen: *On my way, darlings. Save me a mulled wine. 🍷🎄🎤 #ChristmasNumberOne #SeeYouInLeicesterSquare*

Jamie glanced at her phone and groaned. "Why do you do this? Why do you actively antagonise them?"

"Because, Jamie," Nelly said with a smirk, "it's fun."

By the time the BMW pulled up just outside the pedestrian zone near Leicester Square, the chaos was already well underway.

The first thing Nelly noticed as she stepped out of the BMW was the sheer size of the crowd. It wasn't just a couple of hundred people—it was thousands. Leicester Square was heaving, packed shoulder-to-shoulder with fans, curious onlookers, and media vultures desperate to capture the spectacle.

The second thing she noticed? The growing police presence.

A line of uniformed officers was positioned near the entrance to Global HQ, clearly on standby for whatever chaos was about to erupt. The fact that the stage for the Manic event was close to, but not actually, blocking the main doors for Global's headquarters was a legal grey area that Scott's team had exploited brilliantly as the Odeon Luxe next to Global's offices were in support of

Manic's event, due to it potentially driving more visitors to the cinema. A perfect technicality—Global couldn't claim that their HQ was blocked, because technically it wasn't. And yet, the crowd was very much an issue for them.

Jamie climbed out of the car behind her, his face a perfect picture of mild panic. "This is insane," he muttered. "This is actually insane."

Nelly adjusted her coat, smirking. "Oh, darling, you say that like it's a bad thing."

As she made her way towards the stage, she caught sight of Manic's event producer, Tash Crozier, in a headset, furiously gesturing to the tech crew. Tash had the air of a woman who had already been dealing with seventeen different logistical nightmares before breakfast and was now running entirely on stress and caffeine.

"Vixen!" Tash barked, shoving a clipboard into Jamie's hands. "You're right on time. Soundcheck's done, everything's set up, and we've already had two passive-aggressive visits from some Global execs trying to 'assess the health and safety risks'. Scott is currently arguing with Ashley Tabor-King and some legal rottweiler that he's got with him. Thank goodness TGI Fridays are undergoing a refurb and that the Spoons haven't objected to us having the stage extend into their usual outdoor seating area, because otherwise, I think Global would have found a way to get Westminster Council to pull the plug already."

Nelly smirked, taking in the scene. The Manic stage was a full-scale production—LED screens, a sleek set-up with the Pepsi Chart branding, and a massive crowd already hyped up by the warm-up DJ. She could hear the distant hum of Capital's own Christmas show playing inside Global HQ, and the sheer absurdity of it all made her grin wider.

"Where's Scott?" she asked, scanning the scene.

Tash jerked her thumb towards the side of the stage. "Over there, having a very lively conversation with Tabor-King and James Jenkins."

As soon as Tash said that, Nelly looked over towards where the Leicester Square Kitchen was, to see Scott Bennett and James Jenkins arguing, while Ashley Tabor-King had started heading towards the Metropolitan Police officers who were clearly trying to determine whether or not they needed to intervene.

"Two hours to go," Nick Nicholson, one of the people who worked under Tash, said, coming over. "Dressing room is in the staff facilities at the Odeon Luxe."

Nelly adjusted her coat, glancing over at the growing storm near Leicester Square Kitchen, where Scott Bennett and James Jenkins were locked in a heated legal debate. Ashley Tabor-King, the grand overlord of Global Media, was already marching towards the Met Police officers, his face set like he was trying to suppress the world's most public tantrum.

"Oh, this is going to be fun," Nelly murmured, tugging Jamie along with her as they approached the battlefield.

Jamie groaned, nursing what was probably his fourth Greggs coffee of the morning. "We're two hours away from going live, and the CEO of Global is about to try and get us shut down. This is not fun."

Nelly ignored him, turning her attention to Scott, who—despite facing down one of the most powerful men in British media—looked as relaxed as ever, hands in his coat pockets, his usual smirk firmly in place.

"You have exactly two minutes to vacate this site before we escalate this to a full legal injunction with enforcement," James Jenkins was saying, his tone dripping with controlled fury. "You have already been ordered by the High Court to stand down. Your presence here is a blatant act of defiance, and if you persist, you will be held in contempt."

Scott, ever the picture of smug legal confidence, tilted his head. "Funny thing about contempt, James. You have to actually be in court for it to apply. And as you can see, we're rather busy not being in court."

Jenkins' jaw twitched. "This isn't a joke, Scott."

"Oh, I assure you, I take my Christmas programming very seriously," Nelly retorted with a grin. "And right now, my listeners expect me to be on that stage in two hours, revealing the Christmas Number One. So, unless you're planning to personally drag me off in handcuffs, I'd suggest you go back inside and let the grown-ups handle things."

Jenkins turned his glare to her. "Dr Robinson, you seem to think this is some kind of game. Do you seriously want another lawsuit on your hands, especially as you only just escaped a private prosecution for murder?"

Nelly noticed that Tabor-King had gone into the Global offices and left James to deal with the escalating situation outside. The Met officers were still watching, clearly waiting for instructions on whether they should intervene. But Nelly knew what this was—it was a high-stakes game of chicken, and James was hoping Manic would blink first.

Unfortunately for him, Nelly had never been particularly good at backing down.

Scott exhaled dramatically, tilting his head towards Jenkins. "James, mate, I understand that you're just doing your job. I get it. Global doesn't like us. They don't like me. They definitely don't like Nelly—"

Jenkins scoffed. "That much is evident."

"—But the fact is, we have a valid licence for this event, we have permissions from the relevant businesses in Leicester Square, and most importantly," Scott gestured towards the swelling crowd, "we have several thousand people who have turned up specifically to watch us do this show. So, unless you fancy making Global the bad guys who ruined Christmas for a lot of people, I suggest you and your lawyers go back inside and have a nice cup of tea."

"Ah, but the LFB didn't approve it," Jenkins interjected sharply, his tone triumphant. "And without full approval from the London Fire Brigade for an event of this scale, you are in direct violation of the Health and Safety at

Work Act 1974. The Commissioner of the Police of the Metropolis has stated that he was against holding this event on the grounds of public safety, and if the Met decide that this constitutes a significant disruption, they can—and will—order you to shut it down."

Nelly smirked, folding her arms. "So that's your angle, then? Fire safety? You're really clutching at straws, James."

Jenkins didn't so much as blink. "I'm clutching at legal precedents, Nelly. The law is very clear on this—an event of this size without the full clearance of emergency services constitutes a serious risk."

Scott, who had been listening patiently, let out a long, theatrical sigh. "James, mate, I really do admire the effort. But here's the thing—our risk assessment was signed off by an independent fire safety officer. It was submitted to the council. The only reason the LFB didn't rubber-stamp it was because a certain someone"—he gestured vaguely at the Global building—"made a last-minute phone call suggesting it should be 'reviewed' further. And since that 'review' is still pending and hasn't resulted in an official order to shut us down, we're not actually breaking any laws."

Jenkins' jaw tightened. "You are pushing this to the absolute limit, Scott."

"Oh, absolutely," Scott said with a grin. "But that's what makes it fun."

The Met officers were looking between them now, clearly waiting for instructions. Nelly could almost hear the gears turning in Jenkins' head—he knew he had an argument, but he also knew that shutting down a Christmas No.1 event, in front of thousands of people and multiple media outlets, would be a PR disaster of epic proportions.

Then, to Nelly's absolute delight, one of the officers finally spoke up.

"Sir," the senior officer addressed Jenkins, "unless we receive a direct order from the council or an emergency injunction, we don't have the authority to forcibly shut this down."

Jenkins exhaled slowly. "This is going to court again."

Scott beamed. "Oh, I do hope so. Always fun to see Global lose in a legal battle."

Jenkins muttered something under his breath and turned towards the Global building, clearly deciding that this was a fight for another day. The moment he disappeared inside, Nelly let out a victorious laugh.

"Well, that was fun," she said brightly. "Now, let's get ready for showtime."

Jamie, who had been standing stiffly beside her, ran a hand down his face. "You are both actual lunatics."

Scott clapped him on the shoulder. "Welcome to Manic, Jamie. Where legal loopholes are just Christmas decorations with extra steps."

Nelly was already making her way towards the dressing room inside the Odeon Luxe. "Right, Jamie, darling, I need you to check my running order and make sure nothing in there is going to get us pulled off air within the first ten minutes."

****

CHAPTER 17 – The Fuse is Lit
Sunday 22nd December 2019

It was quarter to 3, 15 minutes until the specially extended show was due to commence, and Nelly was getting quite excited as she sat in the staff room of the Odeon Luxe Leicester Square, where the multinational chain had allowed Manic to use as a dressing and presenter rest room until Nelly's Pepsi Christmas Chart show was set to go live.

She stretched her legs out, adjusting the strap of her Christian Louboutin stilettos, and took a slow sip of the peppermint tea that one of the Odeon staff had kindly brought her. The irony of it all—she was about to go to war with Global, to defy a High Court ruling in the most public way possible, and yet here she was, sipping herbal tea in a dimly lit cinema staff room like some zen influencer on Instagram.

"Ready, Nell?" Tash Crozier asked, stepping into the room, her clipboard clutched tightly in one hand, her headset slightly askew as if she'd already had to deal with seventeen different emergencies in the past hour. "We've got a crowd filling the Square, we've got ITV, Sky and BBC News reporting, and we've even got RT, and you'll laugh at this, with coverage ready to stream on their UK channel. Honestly, if I didn't know better, I'd say we've just started an actual revolution."

Nelly had to laugh at the latter network Tash said was going to stream on their UK channel. RT, or Russia Today, one of the Russian state owned broadcasters, was infamous for its ability to spin almost any Western controversy into a gleeful indictment of capitalism and democracy. The idea of her chart show being given the same breathless coverage as a diplomatic scandal was almost flattering.

"Well, if Putin wants to tune in, who am I to stop him?" Nelly smirked, crossing her legs as she finished the last sip of her tea. "But more importantly, do we have everything locked in? Feeds running? Backup streams ready? And, more crucially, is the champagne chilling for when we actually pull this off?"

Tash sighed, rubbing her forehead. "Yes, yes, and I wish you'd take this a little more seriously. The Met are still lingering around, Jenkins is hovering like a vulture, and I'm fairly sure I saw Ashley Tabor-King glaring out of a window on the top floor of Global's HQ like a Bond villain."

"Ah," Nelly exhaled dramatically. "Ashley Tabor-King. A man who built a commercial radio empire by networking it into oblivion and now has to watch his competitors host the biggest OB of the year outside his own front door. A Christmas tragedy."

Tash gave her a look. "Nell. Focus."

Nelly sighed, standing and stretching, adjusting her cream-coloured Burberry trench before checking her reflection in the mirror propped up against the staff lockers. Her blonde waves were immaculate, her red lipstick just the right shade of chaotic yet festive, and her Louboutins gave her that perfect CEO of Radio Anarchy vibe. She was, in a word, unstoppable.

"Alright, let's get this show started," she said, smirking. "I assume Jamie's already stress-drinking somewhere?"

Tash snorted. "Last I saw, he was pacing near the sound desk, clutching his headset like it's the only thing keeping him tethered to this mortal plane."

"Ah, excellent," Nelly grinned. "Let's go ruin some Christmases."

Walking out of the Odeon's staff room, she remembered that she needed to put her earpiece in, one that allowed Jamie, who was sat in the production van on the Leicester Street side of the square, to communicate with her. The production van was parked strategically, just out of immediate Global surveillance but close enough to ensure a smooth live feed. Inside, Jamie Wise was probably on the verge of a nervous breakdown, muttering about how this was, by far, the most legally precarious thing he'd ever been involved in.

As Nelly clipped in her earpiece, the ambient roar of the crowd outside filtered through, a mixture of excitable cheers, drunken December revelry, and the distant hum of Capital FM's own programming—desperately trying to pretend none of this was happening.

She stepped out into the street, where Leicester Square was heaving. A full sea of bodies pressed up against the barriers, neon Christmas lights reflecting off their faces as they chanted her name, snapped pictures, and jostled for the best spots. Manic's Pepsi Christmas Chart Show branding was splashed across the LED screens surrounding the stage, flashing the countdown timer until they went live.

At the foot of the stage, a cluster of Met Police officers stood talking into their radios, looking increasingly stressed as the event swelled beyond what anyone had predicted. Over by the entrance to Global's headquarters, a visibly fuming James Jenkins was speaking in hushed, urgent tones to someone in a sharp suit—almost certainly an external lawyer that had been parachuted in at the last minute to contain the disaster.

And, best of all? Perched up in one of the top-floor windows of the Global building, arms crossed, Ashley Tabor-King himself was watching.

It was glorious.

"Nelly, do NOT acknowledge the Met. Do NOT acknowledge Jenkins. Do NOT say anything that could—" Jamie's exasperated voice crackled into her ear.

"Oh, Jamie, darling," Nelly whispered as she strutted up the steps of the stage, "I'm going to acknowledge ALL of it."

She reached centre stage, where the sleek black mic waited for her. The massive countdown screen ticked down: 00:00:20

The warm-up DJ cut the music. The entire crowd buzzed with anticipation.

00:00:10

From the production van, Jamie let out what sounded like a silent scream.

00:00:03

Nelly's fingers brushed the mic. The stadium-level lighting rig flooded Leicester Square with light.

00:00:01

She inhaled, smiling wickedly.

LIVE.

A massive cheer erupted from the crowd as the Manic Radio station identifier and the Pepsi Chart sweeper aired over the loud speakers and also across the Manic Radio network.

"Hello, my beautiful chaos gremlins! Good afternoon, Britain! And I must add, a very good day to both London's finest, the Metropolitan Police, and also to Ashley Tabor-King, who must be chain smoking like a Victorian chimney sweep up there in his ivory tower at Global HQ! Lovely to have you all with us."

The crowd roared with laughter, cheers erupting so loud that Nelly could feel Jamie's despair through the earpiece.

"Nelly, for fuck's sake—"

"Oh, I forgot to say hello to Producer Jamie, who, if you're listening on the Manic app, on one of the Manic stations, or watching on RT UK, you'll be hearing telling me that I'm being a complete and utter nightmare. But darling, isn't that why we're all here today?"

The crowd erupted into another wave of cheers, camera flashes popping as dozens of smartphones livestreamed the moment. Somewhere in the distance, Nelly could hear the distinct thwack of Jamie likely banging his head against the sound desk inside the production van.

"Now, a few weeks ago, before I went on my holidays, I said that we'd be announcing the number 1 live from outside the Empire in Leicester Square... well, I kind of lied, as we're outside the Odeon Luxe in Leicester Square instead, but details, darlings, details! Now, before we get into the chart, I just want to say what an absolute joy it is to be standing here, bringing you this very special Christmas edition of the Pepsi Chart, powered by Gazprom, where international diplomacy goes hand in hand with the most sanctioned radio show of 2019!"

The crowd exploded in laughter, the ridiculousness of it all sending waves of delighted chaos rippling through Leicester Square. Nelly smirked, flipping her hair back as she leaned into the mic.

"Now, for those of you tuning in on RT, and wondering why there's Global Media signage being covered by Manic Radio branding, let me explain. You see, my darlings, Global Media—owners of Capital FM, Heart, Smooth, and a few other stations your nan listens to— were so deeply concerned about our little Christmas Number One show that they took us to court. Yes, court! Because nothing says 'festive spirit' quite like a High Court injunction!"

The crowd erupted into laughter, with a few chants of "Manic! Manic! Manic!" starting up near the front of the stage. Nelly could practically feel James Jenkins grinding his teeth from across the square.

"Anyway! We're here, we're live, we're not arrested yet, and it's time to count down the biggest tracks in the UK this Christmas! So, grab a drink, grab a mate, and let's find out who's made it to the coveted Christmas Number One spot! How the show works, my little chaos goblins, is simple. We take Spotify's Top 40, add a dash of what we play here on Manic Radio, and rank the charts using a Russian mathematician who Comrade Putin has promoted to Chief Statistical Officer of Questionable Yet Entertaining Data. Because, honestly, do any of us really understand how chart rankings work anymore? No? Good. Then let's dive in!"

"Nelly, don't bring Putin into this, for the love of God," Jamie's voice crackled through her earpiece, practically vibrating with horror.

"Oh, darling," Nelly purred, giving the camera that was on the stage, covering Manic's social media platforms, a mischievous wink, "don't worry. I'm sure the Kremlin has much bigger problems to deal with than my Christmas Number One show. But, speaking of scandals, let's get on with the countdown before Global sends in a legal SWAT team."

The intro to the #40 song kicked in, and Nelly knew it was a Christmas classic, despite the Official Singles Chart, a rival chart, placing it at #42.

Chris Rea's Driving Home for Christmas.

The second the opening piano notes rang out across Leicester Square, the crowd roared in approval. There was something about Driving Home for Christmas that just felt like the start of the season—nostalgic, warm, and, in this case, a beautifully ironic nod to the fact that Global Media were currently watching their Christmas go up in flames.

"Ahhh, Chris Rea," Nelly sighed theatrically into the mic. "A man who understands the pain of just wanting to get home… much like Global Media's legal team, who are probably begging for an early night but are stuck here watching me instead."

The crowd erupted into laughter, and in her earpiece, Jamie let out something that sounded suspiciously like a strangled scream.

"Nelly, you cannot keep winding them up like this—"

"Jamie, sweetheart," she cooed, "I assure you, I absolutely can."

Heading to the podium where a laptop, loaded with Zetta, not PlayoutONE which Nelly used at the Speke studios, was showing the playlist for the show, she tapped a few keys to ensure everything was in order. Even as she did, she caught sight of the security detail at the periphery of the crowd, Metropolitan Police officers standing stiffly, clearly waiting for the moment when Global would make another move to shut this down.

She then noticed James Jenkins, who was stood stage left, right by the doors to Global's offices, talking to some of the Metropolitan Police officers, gesturing animatedly in her direction. Oh, this was getting good.

As the track ended, Nelly dragged Jamie up on to the stage, grinning at him while she did.

"That was Chris Rae's Driving Home for Christmas, and look what dirty stop out has finally made it to the stage... it's Producer Jamie everyone!"

The crowd cheered as Jamie stumbled onto the stage, looking like a man who had been dragged through the trenches of radio chaos and lived to tell the tale. His headset was still perched on his head, his Manic-branded hoodie slightly askew, and his Greggs coffee—which he was still clutching for dear life—was now likely more milk than caffeine at this point.

"Jamie, darling, you look absolutely thrilled to be here," Nelly teased, handing him a microphone.

Jamie took a long, suffering sip of his coffee before sighing heavily into the mic. "I hate you so much right now."

The crowd burst into laughter, while Nelly grinned, slinging an arm around his shoulders.

"And that, my dear listeners, is the sound of a producer who has spent the last week dealing with lawyers, police officers, and several high-ranking executives who would rather chew glass than let this show happen. And yet— here we are!"

More cheers.

"In all seriousness," Jamie muttered, rubbing his temples, "I would just like to remind everyone here not to storm the Global Media offices, not to incite a riot, and for the love of God, please don't give the police any excuse to shut this down."

Nelly gave him a knowing smirk. "Jamie, darling, it's almost like you don't trust me."

Jamie turned to face her, deadpan. "I don't."

The crowd erupted into laughter again, while Nelly gasped in mock offence.

"Well, in that case, let's prove I can be responsible by getting on with the show! Coming up next in the Christmas Chart, at number 39, its… a new entry!"

The sweeper for the new entry blared through the speakers, and the crowd cheered as the track loaded up on Zetta. Nelly glanced at the screen and smirked.

"Well, this is a fun one," she purred into the mic. "Coming in at number 39, it's Harry Styles with his new track, Falling. Of course, when he was with Wand Erection—"

"Nelly, its One Direction," Jamie cut in quickly, glaring at her. "For the love of all things holy, Nelly, can we not get sued today?"

The crowd roared with laughter, clearly enjoying the show more than Global's legal team would. Nelly merely flashed an innocent smile, twirling a loose strand of hair between her fingers.

"Oh, Jamie, sweetheart," she purred, "I'm simply reminiscing about the good old days of boy bands and fangirl wars. Now, let's enjoy this new one from Harry Styles before the Met decide we've exceeded the legal limit for fun."

As Falling by Harry Styles filled Leicester Square with its melancholic melody, Nelly glanced toward the left side of the stage, where James Jenkins was still locked in deep discussion with the Metropolitan Police officers. He was gesturing toward her, toward the stage, toward the entire event, his expression growing increasingly animated.

Jamie, noticing her gaze, let out a weary sigh. "For once, could you not poke the bear?"

Nelly feigned innocence, placing a delicate hand on her chest. "Jamie, darling, I would never."

Jamie gave her a deadpan look. "Nelly, every time you say that, something explosively illegal happens within five minutes."

She smirked, but before she could respond, Tash's voice crackled into both their earpieces. "Heads up. The Met are asking for a word. And by 'asking,' I mean 'politely but firmly making it known that they will shut us down if we don't cooperate.'"

Jamie groaned, rubbing his temple. "Oh, great. Here we go."

Nelly took another sip from her water bottle, her mind already calculating exactly how much she could push this before it turned into a genuine disaster.

She made her way down the steps of the stage, strolling confidently towards the small cluster of officers, where Jenkins was mid-rant, flanked by a suited man who screamed corporate lawyer.

"Gentlemen! To what do I owe this utterly delightful honour?" she greeted them cheerfully.

Jenkins shot her a glare so cold it could have frozen over the Thames. "Dr Robinson," he said, his voice tight. "You are in direct violation of a High Court order. I suggest you shut this down before the police have to forcefully intervene."

"Oh, James, darling, you make it sound so dramatic," Nelly purred, folding her arms. "We're simply counting down the Christmas No.1. It's a public service, really."

Jenkins' lawyer, an older, silver-haired man with a permanently unimpressed expression, cleared his throat. "Ms Robinson, Global Media obtained an injunction explicitly prohibiting this broadcast from occurring outside our headquarters. You are currently in wilful breach of that order."

The Met officer, a stocky man in his late forties, spoke up. "Miss—sorry, Doctor—Robinson, we're asking you to comply voluntarily before we have to escalate this."

Nelly feigned a pout. "Oh, escalate—such a strong word. Officer, we do have all necessary permissions to conduct an outdoor event here, as provided by Westminster Council. And as for the injunction, well… our legal team are working on it, as we speak. It's a little bureaucratic limbo at the moment."

Jenkins let out a sharp breath. "You cannot just ignore a court order, Nelly."

She tilted her head. "And yet… here we are."

Jamie, who had joined the discussion, pinched the bridge of his nose. "I hate this. I hate everything about this."

Jenkins took a step forward, his patience clearly eroding. "If you do not immediately cease broadcasting, we will be forced to take further legal action."

Nelly smirked. "James, sweetheart, what more can you possibly throw at me? You already dragged me through a private prosecution for murder." She turned toward the officers, gesturing around theatrically. "And look at this crowd! Would you really like to be the ones who ruin Christmas for all these lovely people? Imagine the headlines!" She gasped dramatically. "Grinch Stole Christmas No.1! Global Media Cancels Festivities! I mean, it's practically a PR disaster waiting to happen."

"I think you'll find, madam, that the private prosecution was not a Global action but by an employee who is free to, on their own volition, take legal recourse as they see fit," the mid-30s lawyer stated with the conviction of someone who, Nelly noticed, would rather be with family and not stuck in Leicester Square on a wet Sunday evening arguing over a radio show.

The Met officer sighed, rubbing his temple in exasperation. "Look, Dr Robinson, I'm not here to get involved in media wars. My job is to make sure public order is maintained. And right now, this is looking increasingly like a situation that could spiral."

Nelly placed a hand on her hip, glancing over at the sea of people gathered in the square, all buzzing with excitement, completely unaware of the legal wrangling happening just off-stage. The cameras were still rolling, the livestream was still broadcasting, and every second that ticked by meant the show was going ahead exactly as planned.

"Officer," she said sweetly, "I completely understand your position. But if you think for one second that I'm about to pull the plug on the biggest Christmas Chart show this country has seen in years… well, I hate to disappoint you."

Jenkins looked like he was about to explode. "Nelly—"

"James," she cut him off smoothly, "it's happening. The show is live. The crowd is loving it. And by the time you lot figure out a way to legally stop us, we'll be packing up and heading to the afterparty."

****

CHAPTER 18 – Explosion of the Fuse
Sunday 22nd December 2019

"And now, it's your Christmas Top 10," Nelly announced at 6 o'clock, as the lights on the Leicester Square stage pulsed in sync with the anticipation in the air. The crowd, packed shoulder to shoulder, erupted in cheers. Even from her vantage point, Nelly could see people hoisting their mates onto their shoulders, waving homemade signs, and streaming the event live to thousands more online.

"Alright, Nell, let's get through this without taunting Global, the Met, or any major world powers, okay?" Jamie said, standing next to her, a pained expression on his face, which Nelly knew he was putting on to make it as if he were already exhausted from the sheer chaos of the day. His Greggs coffee—God knows how many he'd gone through—was clutched in one hand like a lifeline, and his headset dangled around his neck. He had the air of a man who had fully given up trying to stop the inevitable and was now just hoping to survive it.

Nelly, of course, had no such concerns.

"Oh, Jamie, darling," she purred into the mic, flashing the crowd a wicked grin. "I make no such promises."

The audience roared their approval as Jamie exhaled sharply, shaking his head. "I should've taken that job at Bauer when I had the chance."

Nelly ignored him, turning her attention back to the stage's massive LED screen as the numbers flashed up.

"At number 10, the first of our top ten Christmas tracks this year, it's… a load of golfing geriatrics and a mentally retarded Australian... it's...."

The sound of Tones and I – Dance Monkey blasted through the speakers, sending a ripple of cheers, groans, and a few exaggerated sighs through the crowd.

"Oh, come on," Nelly scoffed into the mic, shaking her head. "Dance Monkey? Still? Who's still buying this? Who's streaming this on loop like some kind of psychological warfare experiment?"

Jamie covered his face with his hand, already regretting every life decision that had led him to this moment. "Nelly, you cannot just insult the Christmas Top Ten."

"Jamie, darling, I absolutely can," she shot back, flipping her hair. "Listen, respect to Tones & I, but this song has been around for ages. If you're still listening to Dance Monkey in December 2019, I need you to take a long, hard look at your Spotify habits and ask yourself—why? Who hurt you? Do you need new music recommendations? Anyway, here it is."

Nelly knew that she had 3 minutes until she needed to do her next link, announcing the 9th placed track, when she saw a man in a suit approach James Jenkins and the Metropolitan Police officers who were stood near the stage-left barricades. Even in the neon glow of the Christmas lights and the glare of the stage floodlights, she could see Jenkins' expression tighten. The suited man—a barrister, no doubt—was flipping through a legal folder, gesturing sharply at the stage, his movements rigid with frustration.

Looking at the man's briefcase, however, Nelly noticed the crest of the City of Westminster Council, and she knew, from Scott Bennett's saying that an emergency enforcement order could be obtained, which would mean that the police could—

"Nell," Nick Nicholson said over her earpiece, and she knew that the events assistant was starting to panic by the way he had sounded slightly breathless in her ear. "You've got a new problem. I'm in Burger King on Bear Street and I can see 5 Police vans pulling in from Charing Cross Road. Looks like they're gearing up to intervene."

Nelly exhaled slowly, pressing her tongue against her cheek as she considered her options. Five police vans? That wasn't a casual observation team—that was an operational response. If Westminster Council had issued an emergency enforcement order, then the Met had legal grounds to physically intervene and shut them down.

"Jamie, darling," she murmured into her mic, shifting her weight onto one hip as the beat of Dance Monkey carried on behind her. "You might want to brace yourself."

Jamie, who was still rubbing his temples like a man deep in existential crisis, blinked at her. "Oh, what now?"

"Nick says the Met's tactical team just rocked up. Five vans. Looks like Jenkins got his wish."

Jamie swore under his breath, stepping slightly away from the mic to mutter into his earpiece. "Tash, do we have a back-up plan if they pull the plug?"

In her ear, Nelly heard Tash Crozier's voice, tight with tension. "If they pull the plug, playout won't be affected as it's still going through Stratford, as we're using their setup as the host station for the broadcast, so it'll keep running regardless of what happens here. But if they physically remove you from the stage? Well, that's a whole different mess."

Nelly smirked, shifting her weight onto one foot as she glanced back at the police vans now pulling up on the edge of Leicester Square. The crowd, oblivious to the legal drama playing out behind the scenes, continued singing along to Dance Monkey, swaying and laughing, wrapped in the kind of festive chaos that only a rogue radio broadcast could bring.

"Well," she murmured, her voice dripping with amusement, "it would be terribly rude of me to leave before we get to Number One, wouldn't it?"

"Nelly, please, for once in your life, just—" Jamie started, but before he could finish, Dance Monkey came to an end, and the sweeper for Number Nine blared through the speakers.

"Alright, my darlings, we move on!" Nelly purred into the mic, her voice smooth and unbothered. "Coming in at Number Nine—oh, this is a tune, as it's a new entry!"

The sweeper that signified that a new entry flashed across the LED screen, the crowd erupting in anticipation as the track loaded up in Zetta. Nelly flicked a glance towards the approaching police officers, who were now in quiet discussion with the suited Westminster Council barrister. James Jenkins was watching her like a hawk, his arms crossed, his jaw set, waiting for her to break.

She wasn't going to give him the satisfaction.

"Coming in at number nine, it's a new entry from Croydon's very own Stormzy!" Nelly announced, "It's... Lessons"

Nelly knew that Lessons, a single that the English-Ghanaian rapper, singer, and songwriter born in the London suburb of Thornton Heath, would be a crowd pleaser, having listened to it the previous night while in her Premier Inn near the Olympic Park, and that it would resonate deeply with the audience in Leicester Square, especially given Stormzy's recent dominance in the UK music scene.

"But first," Nelly said, dragging the opening backing music to the Blues Brother's Everybody Needs Somebody, the instrumental version with no backing vocals, into Zetta, interrupting the track's intro as she leaned into the mic with a knowing smirk.

"But first, my darlings," she purred, "I'm so glad to see so many of you lovely people here tonight and we would especially like to welcome all the representatives of London's law enforcement community who have chosen to join us here in Leicester Square at this time. We do sincerely hope you'll all enjoy the show and please remember people, that no matter who you are and what you do to live, thrive and survive, there're still some things that make us all the same. You, me, them, everybody, everybody..."

The moment the Blues Brothers instrumental kicked in, the crowd erupted with laughter and cheers. The sheer audacity of it—taunting the Met Police with a cheeky monologue as they prepared to shut her down—was peak Nelly Vixen. Jamie, standing beside her, let out the kind of exhausted groan that suggested he was ready to resign on the spot.

"Nelly," he muttered, his voice just loud enough to be caught on her mic. "You are actually insane."

Nelly, without missing a beat, grinned at him before turning back to the crowd. "Ah, Jamie, darling, you wound me. I'm merely extending the spirit of Christmas to our lovely law enforcement guests!"

The crowd, catching on to exactly what she was doing, started chanting along with her.

"You! Me! Them! Everybody! Everybody!"

Somewhere near the stage-left barricades, Jenkins looked like he was about to spontaneously combust. The suited barrister from Westminster Council was gesturing furiously at the police officers, while the senior Met officer—who had clearly been dreading this moment—rubbed his temples like a man reconsidering all of his life choices.

Jamie, now openly facepalming, hissed into his mic, "Nelly, for the love of God, just get to Stormzy before they drag you off stage."

Nelly, still smirking, let the Blues Brothers instrumental fade out, transitioning seamlessly into Lessons by Stormzy. The moment the beat dropped, the crowd lost their minds, jumping and waving their arms, the energy shifting from cheeky rebellion to full-blown party mode.

But even as the track played, she knew this was far from over.

"Lovely intro Nell," Dr Scott Bennett said through her earpiece. "I'm about to have a chat with the Old Bill and our… friend… from Westminster Council. Stay put, keep the show running, and do not—I repeat—do not punch a police officer if they try to move you."

"Oh, Scott, darling," Nelly murmured, watching as the suited barrister and the senior Met officer moved towards the stage steps, "you really think so little of me."

"I think exactly enough of you," Scott shot back, his voice sharp with amusement. "Now, hold the fort—I need to make sure Jenkins doesn't get his Christmas wish of having you dragged off-stage live on RT."

Jamie, still standing beside her, took a deep breath, gripping his coffee like it was a life raft in a storm. "This is it, isn't it? This is the moment I have to start updating my CV."

"Jamie, darling," Nelly cooed, slinging an arm around his shoulder, "you'll be legendary after this."

"Or unemployed," Jamie muttered.

Nelly turned her attention back to the crowd as Stormzy's Lessons reached its closing notes, the bass vibrating through the stage. She shot a quick glance at the clock in the corner of her playout screen—6:08 pm. Less than an hour to go. If Scott could stall long enough, if she could keep the momentum of the show rolling, they might just get away with this.

Might.

"Alright, my little Christmas elves," she purred into the mic as the crowd settled, still buzzing from Lessons. "We move swiftly on to number eight, and oh, this one's a festive classic, and, if you listened to DJ Manic all month, you'll know that on his throwback show, if the word Christmas was muttered by him or his producer, he'd play this song..."

"Iiiiiiiiiiiiiiiiiiii... don't want a lot for Christmas...." the sweeper for the number 8 positioned track went, and Nelly knew, from the running order, that Mariah's track was the slated song for this spot.

A collective mix of jeering, cheering and chanting erupted from the crowd as the unmistakable opening notes of "All I Want for Christmas Is You" blasted through the speakers.

Nelly couldn't help but chuckle. "Ah, Mariah. The undisputed queen of Christmas... except, apparently, not the queen of the Christmas Number One!"

The crowd lost their minds. Some were booing playfully, others cheering wildly, and a few had started a chant of "Justice for Mariah!"

Jamie, who looked like he had emotionally checked out of this entire experience, rubbed his temple. "I cannot believe you just did that."

Nelly smirked, leaning into the mic. "Look, I don't make the rules, Jamie—I just announce them. And according to our data, Miss Carey has landed at number eight this year. A respectable spot, but let's be real—she's going to be fuming."

A ripple of laughter rolled through Leicester Square.

"Now, now," she continued, raising a manicured hand. "Mariah, if you're listening—and I'm sure you are—I'd just like to say… please don't sue me. I had nothing to do with this."

Jamie groaned into his mic. "You have literally everything to do with this."

Meanwhile, near the stage barricades, Nelly noticed James Jenkins' face turn the colour of an overcooked turkey. He was deep in conversation with the senior Met Police officer, who had his arms folded, listening with a neutral expression that suggested he'd rather be anywhere else.

Scott Bennett, standing nearby with his usual air of chaos and legal invincibility, had his hands in his pockets, his expression unreadable as he listened to the increasingly irate Westminster Council lawyer.

Over her earpiece, Tash Crozier's voice came through, tight with barely contained amusement.

"Nelly, Global just tweeted."

Nelly's grin widened. "Oh, go on then, darling. Read it out."

Tash cleared her throat dramatically.

"Global Media wishes to clarify that our programming remains unaffected by unauthorised activity taking place in Leicester Square. We will continue to bring audiences the best in Christmas entertainment via Capital, Heart, and Smooth Radio. We will not be commenting further."

Nelly snorted. "Translation: They're losing their minds, but don't want to admit it."

Jamie, exhaling sharply, checked his phone. "Oh brilliant—Digital Spy is imploding. The Mariah fans are absolutely raging."

"Fantastic," Nelly grinned, tossing her hair. "I do love being a part of a cultural breakdown."

****

By time the next two tracks, Arizona Zervas' Roxanne, and Stomrzy's collaboration with Headie One, Audacity, played out, Nelly knew she had 35 minutes to drag the final 5 tracks of the chart out as long as possible before the show ended, as she caught sight of Scott Bennett making his way towards the stage, his movements controlled and deliberate, but his expression laced with amusement. The Met officers, still deep in discussion with

James Jenkins and the Westminster Council barrister, had yet to make a move, and that told Nelly everything she needed to know—Scott was stalling them.

Good.

If he was stalling, it meant they didn't have a clear-cut order to shut the event down yet. And if they didn't have that, she still had time to drag this out just enough to make sure the show hit the finish line before they pulled the plug.

"Alright, darlings," she purred into the mic, adjusting the earpiece as Jamie looked at her with the weary resignation of a man who had long since given up on maintaining any sense of control. "We're down to our final five, and this is where things really get exciting."

The crowd erupted in anticipation, the sheer weight of thousands of people buzzing with energy.

"But first," she smirked, glancing down at her screen, "before we continue—quick question. Is anyone here slightly surprised that Mariah didn't make the Top Five?"

A mix of cheers, boos, and exaggerated groans rippled through Leicester Square. The Justice for Mariah brigade was still holding strong, while others were fully embracing the festive chaos.

Jamie, muttering into his mic, tried to cut in. "Nelly, I swear to—"

"Now, now, Jamie," she interrupted smoothly, turning to face him with an exaggeratedly innocent smile. "Let the people speak."

"The people are about to witness a police intervention live on air, and you're winding them up over Mariah Carey."

Nelly shrugged. "I like to keep things interesting."

Before Jamie could fire back, the number five sweeper blared across the speakers, and the entire crowd tensed in anticipation.

"Alright, coming in at Number Five, it's—oh, my, what do we have here?" Nelly drawled, tilting her head as the title flashed across the massive LED screen. "Oh, now this is controversial, very controversial…"

Wham.

Last Christmas.

"Now, I don't give a fuck… shit, I just 'accidentally' swore on radio, live here in Leicester Square—"

A series of cheers from the crowd followed by groans from Jamie, who immediately clamped his hand over his mic, as if he could physically prevent an OFCOM complaint from materialising out of thin air.

"Nelly, for the love of everything holy, you cannot just swear live on a networked broadcast!" he hissed, his voice crackling in her earpiece.

"Oh, darling," Nelly purred, unfazed. "It's Christmas. I'll put a fiver in the swear jar, and we'll all move on."

The crowd, however, was loving it, their cheers rolling across Leicester Square like an avalanche.

"As I was saying before I was so rudely interrupted," she continued smoothly, flashing Jamie a grin, "coming in at Number Five on the Pepsi Christmas Chart, I don't give a flying fizzlewog if you're lucky to avoid this, but... Last Christmas, you had a big fart!"

"But the very next day, you gave it away!" the crowd chanted back at her, their voices booming across Leicester Square in perfect unison.

Nelly threw her head back and laughed. "See, Jamie? This is culture! This is tradition! This is the spirit of Christmas—a legally dubious outdoor broadcast, a high court injunction, and a crowd of slightly drunk Londoners singing Wham! at full volume!"

Jamie pinched the bridge of his nose. "I am *begging* you to stop antagonising the police before they shut this down."

Before Nelly could retort, she caught sight of Scott Bennett standing at the foot of the stage, a knowing smirk playing at the edges of his lips. His hands were in his pockets, his posture as relaxed as ever, but his eyes flicked toward the senior Met officer, who was now holding a radio to his mouth.

Nelly knew that that wasn't a good sign.

Jamie must have caught onto it too, because his voice was suddenly a lot sharper in her earpiece. "Nell, you need to start moving this show along now. Scott's buying time, but if the police escalate this to an emergency public order issue, we will be shut down."

Nelly sighed dramatically into the mic, pouting as if she'd just been told Christmas itself was cancelled. "Oh, alright, since we are apparently on borrowed time, let's keep things rolling. Here's Wham with Last Christmas!"

As the unmistakable opening synths of Last Christmas rang through Leicester Square, the crowd erupted into a full-blown singalong, swaying with arms around each other, phone flashlights held high like a Christmas-time festival.

Nelly, smiling smugly, turned to Jamie, who was rubbing his temples so aggressively she half-expected him to give himself a migraine on the spot.

"You see, Jamie," she cooed into the mic, "this is why we do what we do."

Jamie exhaled sharply. "We do radio, Nelly. Not incite public disturbances while actively being pursued by the legal team of Britain's largest media company."

"Oh, semantics." She waved him off.

But even as she revelled in the sheer madness of the moment, her eyes flicked towards the group of police officers near the barricades. The senior Met officer—whose patience was visibly wearing thin—was now deep in conversation with Scott Bennett, who was still wearing his signature I-know-exactly-how-far-I-can-push-this smirk.

James Jenkins, however, was looking more furious by the second, his arms crossed so tightly it was a wonder his suit didn't rip at the seams. The Westminster Council barrister, clearly sensing that time was running out, was making yet another frustrated appeal to the officers.

They were running out of road.

Nelly sighed, rolling her shoulders as she glanced down at the running order. Alright, we can do this. Just three more songs, then we're home free.

As Last Christmas faded out, she flicked the mic back on.

"Right, my festive little gremlins, we're into the final stretch! Coming in at Number Four… oh, I know this one's going to cause a few arguments—"

A tense beat.

"But we'll find out, after the break, here on Manic Radio, with the Pepsi Chart, powered by Gazprom, live from Leicester Square!"

As the ads for Pepsi, Spotify Premium, and a curiously placed Injury Lawyers 4 U commercial rolled out across the speakers, Nelly took a moment to step back from the mic, stretching her arms dramatically. The crowd was still buzzing, but she could feel the tension shifting now—the police weren't just observing anymore. They were preparing.

And, as if someone blew a whistle, riot uniformed officers of the Metropolitan Police started making their way towards the barriers.

Not to keep the broadcast going.

Not to negotiate.

To shut it down.

Nelly knew that moment had arrived. The moment Global had been salivating over. The moment James Jenkins had been waiting for. The moment Westminster Council's barrister had probably already drafted a smugly-worded press release about.

And, naturally, she wasn't going to let them have it that easily.

"Jamie, darling," she murmured into her earpiece, adjusting the strap of her Louboutins with infuriating nonchalance as she watched the line of riot-uniformed Met officers push their way through the crowd. "What are the odds they actually let me finish this show?"

Jamie's response was immediate. "Zero. Absolutely zero. Nelly, they're about to kill the power."

Over her other earpiece, Tash Crozier's voice came through, tight with tension. "Scott's trying to stall, but they're insisting on immediate enforcement. We're about to go off-air, and I mean *any second now*."

Nelly exhaled, stepping back up to the mic just as the last ad wrapped up. She had mere moments before this became a full-blown Christmas riot, and if she was going out, she was going out with a bang.

She flicked the mic back on.

"Alright, my darlings," she purred, her voice smooth as silk, "it seems we might be experiencing a *tiny* bit of a technical inconvenience in the very near future—"

The crowd booed loudly as some started noticing the approaching police officers.

"—but don't you worry," she continued, raising a hand to silence them. "Because before they try anything ridiculous, I'd just like to say…"

She turned, looking directly at James Jenkins, standing near the stage barricades, looking like a man who had finally won.

"…James, sweetheart, we'll always have next Christmas."

But she couldn't hear that on the feedback in her other earpiece, and she knew what had happened.

Someone had killed her mic.

Someone had stopped her transmissions at the production van, meaning that everything had just gone off air.

For the first time in her career, Dr Nelly Vixen was silenced.

The crowd, confused at first, started murmuring as the music abruptly cut out, the LED screens around the stage freezing mid-animation. The massive "Pepsi Chart LIVE" banner flickered, then cut to black.

The realisation hit like a shockwave.

A deafening chorus of boos erupted through Leicester Square.

Jamie, standing beside her, exhaled like a man whose soul had just left his body. "Oh, fuck."

Nelly, unfazed, simply arched an eyebrow. "Well, well, well. Looks like someone really wanted to win Christmas."

She knew exactly what had happened. The Met had ordered the power cut. Either Scott hadn't been able to stall them any longer, or Westminster Council had found a way to bypass his legal tricks. Either way, Manic's rogue Christmas broadcast had been shut down.

James Jenkins, standing just beyond the stage barriers, was already smirking, his arms folded in smug satisfaction. The Westminster Council barrister next to him was furiously scribbling notes, likely drafting an official statement even as the chaos unfolded. The police, now positioned in a semi-circle near the stage, were clearly ready to intervene if things escalated.

And judging by the mood of the crowd, escalation was about to happen.

The chant started near the front, rippling out like wildfire.

"TURN IT BACK ON! TURN IT BACK ON!"

Jamie turned to her, looking genuinely panicked. "Nell, this is getting out of control."

"Oh, darling," she whispered, stepping forward, arms spread wide, "it's already out of control."

Without the sound system, she had no mic, no speakers, no way of addressing the entire square at once. But she didn't need them.

She climbed onto the DJ booth, raising both hands dramatically, her Burberry coat billowing slightly in the cold December wind.

The crowd—confused, angry, on the verge of something explosive—turned their attention back to her.

She grinned.

"WHO WANTS TO FINISH THIS SHOW?!"

A roar of approval answered her.

She didn't have the playout system. She didn't have the broadcast feed. But she did have a crowd of thousands, their energy still electric, still desperate for a finale.

"SCOTT!" Jamie hissed into his headset, still hoping for some miracle fix from the production van. "IS THERE ANY WAY TO GET BACK ON AIR?"

Scott Bennett's voice crackled back over the comms, exasperated but still very much enjoying the madness. "Not unless you want to take a crowbar to a police junction box, Jamie."

And for the first time, Nelly Vixen was defeated.

****

CHAPTER 19 – Capital Punishment
Monday 30th December 2019

A week had passed since the Pepsi Chart Massacre of Leicester Square, as the press had gleefully dubbed it. Seven days since Nelly Vixen had stood victorious on stage, counting down the UK's Christmas No.1, only to be silenced by the Metropolitan Police under the orders of Westminster Council, acting on behalf of Global Media.

Seven days since she'd been publicly defeated.

Well.

That would have been the case—had she actually acknowledged it as a defeat.

Instead, Nelly had spent the week doing what she did best—leaning into the chaos. She'd let the media run riot, let the headlines scream about legal loopholes, defiance, and the "most controversial radio shutdown in British history." She'd let Twitter spiral into meltdowns, with #JusticeForNelly trending for three days straight, while conspiracy theorists debated whether the shutdown had been a planned censorship campaign against independent broadcasters.

But most importantly? She'd not apologised.

And now, as she stepped into the offices of Manic's Liverpool HQ, she knew that the war was only just beginning.

The glass-walled meeting room—affectionately called The War Room—was already occupied when she strode in, draping her Burberry trench over the back of a chair before helping herself to a cappuccino from the Nespresso machine.

Scott Bennett, Manic's CEO, stood by the window, hands in his pockets, his gaze fixed on the drizzly Merseyside skyline. He looked irritatingly calm, given that his company had just suffered a highly public legal loss.

Jamie Wise, on the other hand, looked like he hadn't slept since Leicester Square. He was slumped in a chair, his usual Greggs coffee in one hand, dark circles under his eyes, and the haunted expression of a man who had witnessed far too much.

And then there was Carmen Sharpe, Manic's Deputy CEO and the woman tasked with keeping Scott Bennett's worst impulses in check. She sat at the far end of the table, arms folded, a fresh pile of legal documents in front of her, her expression unreadable.

"Well," Nelly said breezily, stirring a sugar cube into her coffee. "That was fun."

Carmen didn't even blink. "Nelly, you cost us three advertisers, got us hit with an official OFCOM review, and nearly started a riot."

Nelly took a delicate sip. "I did say 'fun', didn't I?"

Scott finally turned from the window, a slow smirk pulling at the corner of his mouth. "Oh, let's not be too hard on her, Carmen. After all—it was worth it."

Jamie let out a strangled noise. "Scott, for fuck's sake—"

"Oh, relax, Jamie," Scott waved a hand dismissively, taking a seat at the head of the table. "No one actually cares about OFCOM. They'll slap us with a warning and move on. And as for the advertisers?" He leaned back, utterly unconcerned. "Coca-Cola's already sniffing around to replace Pepsi as sponsor next year."

Nelly arched a brow. "You want to do it again?"

Scott grinned. "Why wouldn't I? We've never had these numbers before. RAJAR overnight data shows our listenership doubled during the broadcast. Social media engagement hit an all-time high. And as for the PR fallout?" He let out a chuckle. "Global wanted us silenced, but all they've done is prove that we're dangerous. That we're bigger than they thought. And that—" he pointed at Nelly "—you're the most notorious radio presenter in Britain right now."

Jamie groaned, rubbing his temples. "Oh, fantastic. Another unhinged publicity stunt incoming."

Carmen, however, wasn't smiling. "Scott, be serious. You might not care about OFCOM, but Global does. They're taking this very seriously. James Jenkins is already preparing a full legal case against us. If they successfully argue that we deliberately defied an injunction, Manic could face a network-wide broadcasting penalty. We could lose licences over this."

Nelly hummed. "Ah, yes. And how exactly are Global spinning this?"

Carmen pulled out her phone, tapping the screen before tossing it onto the table. The latest article from The Guardian was open.

"GLOBAL MEDIA: "MANIC RADIO IS A DANGER TO RESPONSIBLE BROADCASTING"

Global Media has accused rival broadcaster Manic Radio of "reckless, unlawful, and irresponsible behaviour" following the shutdown of their Christmas No.1 event in Leicester Square last week.

Speaking to The Guardian, Global's Deputy Head of Legal, James Jenkins, confirmed that the company is now seeking "full accountability for Manic's blatant disregard of UK broadcasting regulations."

Jenkins stated: "Manic Radio's actions were not just a breach of a High Court order—they were a deliberate attempt to provoke legal conflict and undermine the integrity of British broadcasting. They have demonstrated a pattern of behaviour that is hostile to regulation, and we will be pursuing all available legal options to ensure they are held accountable.

Attempts to contact Manic Radio Group's CEO, Dr Scott Bennett, a Doctor of Law, were unsuccessful, however a spokesman for Manic Radio stated: 'We stand by our presenters, our programming, and our audience. This was not about defying the law—it was about delivering the biggest, most exciting Christmas Chart event in British history. We make no apologies for putting radio back in the hands of the listeners.'

Westminster City Council, who had granted an emergency enforcement order during the event, said in a statement that 'public safety was our primary concern. With the crowd size escalating beyond initial projections, we had to act to ensure that emergency services could operate effectively. The shutdown was necessary and proportionate.'"

Nelly laughed at that last line, shaking her head. "Necessary and proportionate? Oh, come on. They sent riot police to shut down a chart show. They acted like I was declaring an independent state in Leicester Square."

Jamie groaned, swiping Carmen's phone to read more. "Jesus. Jenkins is throwing everything at us. This bit here—'hostile to regulation'? That's code for 'we're trying to get OFCOM to pull their licence.' They're not just pissed off, they want us gone."

Scott, however, looked amused. "Let them try."

Carmen shot him a warning look. "Scott, this isn't a joke. They're coming for blood."

Scott leaned forward, drumming his fingers on the table. "And we give them blood."

Jamie visibly recoiled. "Oh God. No. Absolutely not. Whatever unhinged idea you have, no."

Nelly, intrigued, leaned in. "Scott, darling, what exactly are you thinking?"

Scott smirked. "They want to go nuclear? Fine. We beat them to it. If Jenkins wants a war, we escalate."

Carmen looked like she was ready to throttle him. "Scott, no. You are not taking this further. We are already under scrutiny."

Scott ignored her. "Think about it. They're framing us as rogue broadcasters, right? Well, we lean in. We double down. We make them look like the uptight corporate villains while we—" he gestured between himself and Nelly "—become the rebels. The people's radio."

Nelly grinned. "Ah. You want to weaponize our cancellation."

Scott pointed at her. "Exactly. We own this narrative. We hit back, hard."

Jamie groaned. "I am begging you both to be normal."

Scott grinned. "Come on, Jamie. Where's your sense of adventure?"

Carmen, meanwhile, looked ready to throw her coffee at Scott. "Scott, I swear to God, if you try anything that gives Global actual grounds to have our licences revoked, I will personally bury you in regulatory paperwork."

Scott waved a hand dismissively. "Relax, Carmen. I have a plan."

Jamie muttered, "You always have a plan and it's always horrific."

Scott ignored him, leaning forward. "First, we go big with a statement. Not some half-arsed corporate PR nonsense—we go direct. Video, social, full-page newspaper ads, the works. We frame Global as the establishment bullies shutting down free speech."

Carmen pinched the bridge of her nose. "Scott, for the last time, this isn't about free speech—"

Scott cut her off. "It doesn't matter what it's about. Perception matters. If we can make this look like a fight between corporate censorship and the last independent voice in UK radio, we win the public battle."

Nelly leaned back in her chair, sipping her cappuccino. "And how, exactly, do we sell that narrative?"

Scott smirked. "Simple. We turn this into something bigger than just Leicester Square. We challenge Global directly. A live, unfiltered, head-to-head showdown. And we dare them to take us on."

Jamie made a strangled noise. "Oh my God. You want to debate Global live on air? Have you lost your entire mind?"

Carmen looked murderous. "Scott, if you even think about publicly challenging Global's legal team, I will have Jenkins personally serve us an injunction before breakfast."

Scott waved her off. "They won't accept, Carmen. That's the point. They'll ignore us, which makes them look weak. And if they do engage, they lose—because the moment they come at us, we spin it into Global vs. The People."

Jamie let out a slow, despairing breath. "Jesus Christ. You're serious."

Scott nodded. "Completely."

Nelly, intrigued, tapped a manicured nail against the table. "And what's my role in this?"

Scott grinned. "You? You become the face of this fight. The uncensored voice. You keep pushing, keep poking at them. You make Global flinch."

Nelly smirked. "You want me to make them bleed."

Scott raised his coffee cup in a mock toast. "Exactly."

Jamie turned to Carmen, looking utterly defeated. "Please tell me one of us is going to stop this madness."

Carmen looked at Jamie and sighed. "I will. Scott, if you continue with this, I'm going to go to the Board, and have you removed as CEO before you bring this entire company down with you."

Scott chuckled, entirely unbothered. "Oh, Carmen, you wound me. But come on, you know this is the play. We don't just survive this—we make it our biggest win yet."

Carmen shook her head. "No, Scott. You're playing with fire, and Global will not hesitate to burn you to the ground."

"Let them try," Scott shot back. "Because the difference between us and them? We thrive in chaos."

Jamie groaned, rubbing his temples again. "You two might thrive. I, on the other hand, would like to live to see 2020 without being named in an OFCOM investigation."

Nelly took another slow sip of her cappuccino, watching Scott with an expression of pure amusement. "Alright, let's say I'm interested. What's the next move?"

Scott leaned forward, eyes gleaming. "We do what we do best—we disrupt. We take the fight directly to Global's doorstep."

Carmen's eyes narrowed. "Scott."

"No, no, hear me out," he said, grinning now. "Global thinks they've won. They're sitting in their ivory tower, patting themselves on the back for getting us pulled off air. But what if, instead of hiding, we show up right outside their offices again—"

"Absolutely not," Carmen snapped.

"—and this time, we don't just broadcast. We challenge them."

Jamie let out a strangled noise. "For the love of God, Scott."

But Nelly was already smirking. "You want to park the Manic Battle Bus outside Global HQ and goad them into a response."

Scott pointed at her like she'd just solved a complex riddle. "Exactly! We turn Leicester Square into round two of the fight. We take the Manic brand and physically place it where Global can't ignore us. We challenge them to a live debate, we taunt them on-air, we make it impossible for them to pretend we don't exist."

Carmen was visibly trying to control her breathing. "Scott. You cannot just park a fully branded Manic bus outside Global's headquarters and demand a fight."

Scott grinned. "Why not?"

"Because that's literally harassment."

Nelly, however, was clearly considering it. "Technically, if it's public property, there's nothing illegal about it."

Jamie threw up his hands. "Oh my God, I work with lunatics."

Scott ignored him. "Think about it. If we park outside their offices, the press will swarm. And if Global tries to move us? Boom—corporate censorship, round two. Jenkins and Tabor-King will be scrambling for a response."

Carmen exhaled sharply, pinching the bridge of her nose. "Scott, I swear to everything holy, if you go through with this and Global sues us, I will personally make sure you spend the next five years buried in legal proceedings."

Scott simply grinned. "Worth it."

Jamie slumped back in his chair, looking like a man who had entirely lost control of his life. "Fine. Screw it. We're all going to die on this ridiculous hill anyway. When's the bus arriving?"

Scott checked his phone, then flashed them a gleeful smile. "First thing New Year's Day."

Jamie groaned. Carmen looked ready to murder someone. And Nelly?

Nelly Vixen leaned back in her chair, her smirk widening.

"Excellent."

****

Books by Thomas Brant

Broadcasting Boundaries Series
BROADCASTING BOUNDARIES
BROADCASTING CHAOS
BROADCASTING DISRUPTION

The Wirral Gal Series
THE WIRRAL GAL... IN SPEKE
THE WIRRAL GAL... NOW A MAM

Other Stories in the Manic Radio Universe
THE BROOKES BABES
THE DAY THE QUEEN DIED
VIXEN

www.ingramcontent.com/pod-product-compliance
Lightning Source LLC
Chambersburg PA
CBHW031057130726
47906CB00008B/637